COP DADDY NEXT DOOR

A SMALL TOWN COP ROMANCE

CRESCENT COVE
BOOK 13

TARYN QUINN

RAINBOW
rage
PUBLISHING

Cop Daddy Next Door
© 2022 Taryn Quinn
Rainbow Rage Publishing

Cover by LateNite Designs
Photograph by Eric Battershell Photography
Model: Assad Shalhoub

First print edition: September 2022
ISBN Print edition: 978-1-940346-79-3

Creatives are a whole different beast.
This is to all the romance authors who write from the heart, no matter the
subject matter.
We admire you so much.

ONE

LATE SUMMER MORNINGS WERE MEANT FOR LAZY, LEISURELY DOG WALKS. At least until my dog dropped the biggest specimen I'd seen since I'd changed her dog food.

She was tiny. What she'd left behind decidedly was not.

"Okay, kid, we're going back to the old food once we use up the last of the new. Got it?" I bent to pick up what she'd left behind, though she'd dropped it on the edge of my own lawn. But it was odiferous enough that there was no way I was leaving it behind.

Francie ignored me and kept sniffing her way down the street, as far as her retractable leash would take her. Which wasn't far. She was too small to be given any sort of free rein since most normal-sized dogs could trample her.

With a sigh, I tied off the poop sack and tossed it in the handy receptacle provided nearby by the town then narrowed my eyes at the adjoining property. It had been for sale for six months.

Long enough that I'd gone back and forth about buying it about a dozen times.

Could I afford another prime property? No, I could not. Buying the first one had stretched me almost to the breaking point. I was a

1

humble public servant, the newest cop on the Crescent Cove Police Department.

Homes here were, by and large, out of reach for people at my pay scale. Luckily, I'd always been a saver—okay, just for the last four years when I'd decided I couldn't toss away money on an apartment forever. There was no way in Hades I'd ever move home again, even if my little sister begged me to get the "heat" off her.

I didn't mind having a simple lifestyle so I could live in the location I loved. Plus, I was duty bound to reside in town, so I made do. But making do was a far cry from snapping up a second property so that I had enough lawn to warrant that fancy ass riding lawn mower that twenty-year-old Mav would've scoffed at.

Hey, a man's tastes changed as he got a little older. Some, anyway.

When it came to one particular taste...

I licked my lips, taking in the view. A curvy redhead sauntered down the narrow dock attached to my modest boat launch, conveniently located just across the street from my property. The grassy knoll in front of it was perfect for a summer picnic by the water, if I was a picnicking sort of guy.

I was not.

But that sexy redhead in a thin white eyelet blouse—having a sister obsessed with clothes had filled my head with nonsense—and obscenely short jean shorts made me reconsider.

She was wandering barefoot on my property, but I wasn't about to arrest her for trespassing. Not with those curls drifting on the wind and that cute heart-shaped backside swaying provocatively. She plopped down on the edge to dip her feet, which was basically a joke because she was short as hell and probably couldn't *reach* the water.

Compact. Built for—

Oh *hell* no.

"What are you doing here?" I demanded, pulling on Francie's leash a bit too hard. She yelped and I cursed under my breath. "Sorry, baby, Daddy didn't mean to—"

I shut my eyes and prayed the trespasser would be gone when I opened them, heart-shaped ass be damned.

"Daddy?" She let out a loud laugh that proved my eyes had not deceived me. I should've recognized the sex hair. It wasn't as if I hadn't noticed it before.

How a woman could have sex hair and the spirit of a demon seemed to be one of life's cruelest mysteries.

I pulled myself up to my full height—a full foot over hers, I might add—and exhaled slowly as I tugged on Francie's leash. She trotted closer without complaint, the tiny pink bow in her brown fur tilting precariously.

Oh, shit, the bow. I had to ditch it. It wasn't as if I was a bow man. She'd been wearing one when I found her, so I'd wanted her to have something familiar even if her old owners were assholes who'd left her behind when they moved away.

I'd have to slip Francie's bow in my pocket before Vanessa saw it and crowed about my dog's stylistic choices at every family dinner until the end of time.

"May I help you?" Discreetly, I nudged my Yorkie behind my leg. I'd have to swing her up and pluck off the bow in one smooth, synchronized movement.

My palms sweating from the unnaturally hot September day should help. *Not.* And no, I was not sweating because my sister-in-law's nipples were outlined in frigging white eyelet.

Fuck me.

She cocked her head. "Did I call for you without realizing it? GQ, can you help me dip my toes?"

I ignored her, as I'd done for most of the last seven months my older brother had been dating—and now engaged to—her twin sister. Sometimes I poked fun at her. Sometimes I rolled my eyes at her.

But ignoring her was usually best for my sanity.

It wasn't fair that she was just as annoying as she was hot. Though no one said I had to talk to her to have sex with her…

Nope. That was officially off-limits. Family boundaries and all. But fantasies didn't hurt anyone. It was better than getting irritated at her, considering that was exactly the response she wanted.

Even her calling me GQ was designed to piss me off. Sure, I tended

3

to dress up rather than down most of the time I was off-duty. But I enjoyed getting my hands dirty. I was a cop, for Pete's sake. I had a dog—something I had not planned. And I worked with wood and ice and fire and enjoyed it immensely. I wasn't some model type who strutted around sucking in my abs.

But silence was golden when dealing with Vanessa Monaghan's smart mouth.

"Not sure if you're aware, but this is my dock."

She managed to splash her feet. "Oh, yeah?"

"Yeah. So, if you need something, let me know."

She shifted to sit cross-legged facing me, her hair blowing around her shoulders from the breeze. "I was told this dock was a shared access space."

"Shared between residents," I said carefully.

She'd found a new focus, however.

"Aw, well, look at you, sweetheart. Come here." She held out a hand and my disobedient dog ignored my requests to stay put and trotted right over to her, rubbing her face into her palm with adoration. "I heard you had a dog." Her lips twitched. "Didn't know it was a cockapoo."

"Francie's a Yorkie." I angled my chin. "Who told you I had a dog?"

"Little birdie."

"Named Tabitha?"

Shrugging, Vanessa let out a delighted laugh as Francie tugged me forward and scampered into her lap. She circled a couple times to get the right spot then plopped down and laid her head on Vanessa's bare thigh just beneath the frayed hem of her jean shorts. "She's so sweet. Sure she's your dog?"

"Last I checked. You don't have any pets."

"No."

"Why not?"

"I'm not big on putting down roots. Hard to fly if you're always tethered to the ground."

With a frown, I gave up trying to urge my dog to return to me. She obviously had found a place to rest she liked better.

4

I also would not mind being stationed in Vanessa's lap. My mouth, at least, if not the rest of me.

"Yeah, well, you seem pretty stationary to me."

"I am now. But you never know when the open road will call." She gestured wildly. "Sometimes you just gotta split to check out some new surroundings. See new people, think new thoughts." She grinned. "Lay your head in new beds."

I clenched my jaw. "Didn't you promise your sister to be her birthing coach?"

"That's not for six weeks and you know your brother won't settle for being the backup."

I snorted. "Don't be so sure. He fainted when Tabitha cut herself in the kitchen."

"And he's a cop?"

"We all have flaws, Pocket Plus." I tugged on the leash and Francie finally dragged herself away from her new love with a look of longing that did not fit an acquaintance of less than five minutes.

Though with all the family shit going down over the next few months—the Jack and Jill wedding shower so "the guys got to be included", the impending birth of my first niece, the wedding shindig between our siblings, then assorted joint family dinners and holidays —Francie would have plenty of time to get to know my new sister-in-law.

As would I.

I was tempted to make the sign of the cross, and I was not even slightly religious.

"Your brother's a good guy," she mused, brushing dog hair off her shorts.

"Must you sound so shocked?"

"I must. Your kind doesn't have the best track record with unplanned pregnancies, gotta say. Usually, there's some variation of "it ain't mine," or "how could it happen, I wore a rubber," or even "I'm not ready," as if women are born ready." She kept on brushing off her lap as if golden-brown hair clung to every inch of her.

I frowned as the silence extended. She cleared her throat and

5

looked up with a weighty enough glance to throttle me. "Anyway, I was there. Brady didn't do that. He stood up from the first. And kept right on standing up."

My voice deserted me. I wasn't even sure why. Just words unspoken passed between us in that moment while the birds chirped merrily in the trees and the hot sun scorched the back of my neck, freshly exposed after my haircut that morning.

And none of that mattered at all, except in this moment, everything seemed to. I couldn't quite catch my breath.

"My brother's one of the good ones," I said when my lungs finally figured out how to work again.

"What about you?" Slowly, she rose, still brushing off her shorts although there was no way Francie could've lost that much hair from her tiny body.

"What about me what?"

"Are you good?"

Now my breath caught for an altogether different reason. I hadn't imagined that flirty pause before she finished her question. But I was used to paying attention to tone and body language when questioning a suspect or trying to determine guilt. She didn't want me to get too close or to pick up more clues than she was willing to give.

"What I am is smart."

A cocked brow was her only response.

"Why are you on my dock?" I asked as Francie parked her furry behind on my shoe.

"You're like a dog with a bone." I didn't miss how her gaze dropped below my waist and lingered for a second before she grinned. "But I like a man who's persistent. Remember what I said about joint access?"

"Huh?"

"Says he's smart, though he can't recall basic details. *Tsk, tsk.* Good thing you're cute, GQ." She flicked her fingers through the ends of her hair and did a little pirouette complete with heel kick. "Haven't you wondered who would move in next door?"

My stomach twisted itself around the bacon and egg sandwich I'd had for a late lunch at The Rusty Spoon. After taking my mom to the dentist, I'd stopped off on Main Street for lunch that didn't come out of a box or a can.

The life of a single dude wasn't always roses, but the joy of limited female chatter could not be overstated. Even now, I was starting to get the itch from too much talking.

I had to admit she was easy on the eyes. Easy on the tightness in my groin too, which served her right if she'd seen anything she shouldn't have—since she'd so obviously checked me out.

But hotness was one thing. *Next door* was quite another.

"I've actually thought of buying the land myself," I said quickly, hoping the possibility Van had sneaked into the neighborhood wasn't a done deal.

I could call my real estate agent and tell her I wanted the property, draw up the papers, and see if I could secure a mortgage. Vanessa only worked at her sister's bakery on a sporadic basis. Some days she worked twelve hours, some days three. It wasn't as if her funding situation could be better than mine.

It couldn't be too late.

"Too late," she said cheerfully, patting my chest as she walked past me into the street without checking for passing cars.

I had a feeling that was how Vanessa Monaghan lived her entire life.

"See that cute little vehicle over there?" She pointed across the street. An ancient hunk of metal was parked on the rundown path that bisected the property. Normally, the only thing on that path were weeds working their way up through the cracks in the narrow strip of blacktop.

Now a rusty mint-green school bus sat in the space with a makeshift awning open on the side. A single green-striped lawn chair circa 1981 was stationed beneath it next to a cooler of the same decade. I was pretty sure I had a stack of drawings in my mom's memories trunk with the same Igloo pattern embossed on it.

Francie tugged on the leash, dragging me out of my shocked stupor. When people pointed, she thought that meant fetch. And while I wished my dog could cart that eyesore off the property, that would be an impossible feat.

"I can pay you instead," I said in a fervent undertone, ready to offer her just about anything so I didn't have to look out my window and see that thing every day.

I didn't appreciate being called GQ, fine, but I did have *some* standards for how things looked. Especially since I'd busted my hump to even get in this neighborhood in the first place.

Not to mention our neighbors would not look kindly upon her if she didn't get that out of here. Property values would plummet. She would likely be driven out of the neighborhood, something I couldn't let happen because we soon would be family by marriage.

As an officer of the law, I was duty-bound to handle this problem before it became one.

Bad enough I had to listen to Christian, my fellow cop, rant and rave about her inappropriate parking fetish. Never mind her inability to parallel park that behemoth and the van she'd driven before it without leaving two wheels on the curb.

This was just taking it to the next level.

"Pay me?" She bent to stroke Francie's wiggling ears before straightening and crossing her arms. "Whatever for?"

"I really want that land. And the property doesn't even have a house yet. So, you'd have to build, and clearly, you prefer to keep rolling on. So, you know, don't quell your impulses."

"Oh, honey, I never quell. I'm basically *unquell*-able."

Her lips were twitching with barely suppressed laughter. At me, I was quite certain.

"Tell me what you want. No limitations. I'll buy you out. I'll offer you anything you want. I should've bought the damn land. Just dragged my feet too long. I'm staying put. Probably fucking forever." I tugged Francie toward me again as she went up on her hind legs to dance in front of Vanessa.

True love must never part, I supposed.

My new neighbor put her hands on her hips, her lower lip jutting out in the faintest pout. I went stone hard in an instant.

Yet another reason she could not live mere inches from my bed. That was a recipe for disaster. For all I knew, she'd wander over barefoot and braless to borrow sugar and the use of my dick when she ran out of batteries for her vibrator.

I was weak. I'd say yes. And I'd probably live to regret it for years, if not generations. She was the sort of woman who would carve her name into my leather seats ala Carrie Underwood if she thought I'd messed up.

I had an impressionable dog to think about. I couldn't screw Van indiscriminately without considering the implications. My brother had parented a dog with Tabitha before they were committed to each other and look what happened.

Now they were having an actual human child.

And oh, yeah, there was also my brother's impending marriage to consider. Vanessa and I hating each other would not be good for family get-togethers, and there wasn't a chance in hell we could stay on polite terms if we rolled into bed.

Or onto the kitchen counter. I wasn't choosy and I was willing to bet neither was she.

Then again, maybe I shouldn't send her packing—

No. Doing this now, whatever her terms, was protecting my family from the kind of drama probably worthy of a future episode of *Jerry Springer.*

Brady could thank me later.

"Let me get this straight," she said slowly. "You're trying to buy me out so you don't have to live next door to me?"

I nodded. "Yes. If you think about it, you'll realize it wouldn't be a good idea."

"Why not?"

Because my salacious thoughts toward you would get me arrested in about twelve states if I actually acted on them. And I'm an honorable man.

At least I was pretty sure.

I was sweating heavily and not just because the sun was beaming straight into my brain. "Trust me, it's not wise."

"Why?"

"It's just not. Francie, stop wiggling and plant your behind this instant."

A sudden wetness soaked my sock.

I looked down, unable to believe what I was seeing.

My dog was peeing on my shoes. Not only that, she'd lifted her leg and aimed like a male dog, because she'd hung out with a bad crowd at doggie daycare last week and apparently wanted to thumb her nose at my rules.

Or her leg.

Vanessa swallowed a laugh as I stood there motionlessly in my dripping shoes. "Why?" she repeated. "Why is my living next door such a bad thing?"

"Do you really need me to spell it out?"

"Yes, I do. We haven't exactly been besties thus far, but I didn't think you'd want to take out a restraining order against me. Now your fellow cop with the stick up his ass is a different story. I'm toxic waste, according to that prick Masterson. But he probably hasn't gotten any since college—"

I stepped very close to her and used my height to loom over her so she had to crane her neck to meet my gaze. Finally, she closed her mouth.

Momentarily.

"I want to do the kind of things to you that don't fit a nice family dinner, Pocket Plus."

"Murder?"

I almost laughed. Almost. But my pants were too tight and my head hurt and she'd caused both. As usual.

I shook my head.

"Sexually?" She gasped it loudly enough both of my heads pulsed. "Why, you dirty bastard." Then she grinned. "I'm available anytime after seven."

"No." I pointed at her, and Francie jerked to high alert, ready to scrabble off after her nonexistent stick. "Not you, dog. And no, forget it. Not happening. You are not going to wander over without a bra and lure me into bed."

COP DADDY NEXT DOOR

She peeked into her shirt. "I have a bra on. But that's easily rectified." She started to wrestle with her clothes, probably so that she could do that remove her bra under her shirt trick that all women seemed to know.

"I will arrest you for public nudity if you don't stop right now." I didn't point this time.

Her bluer than blue eyes fired with interest. "Cuffs are interesting."

"You are an actual menace."

"Valid." She tucked her tongue into her cheek. "Can you even walk right now?"

"I hate you."

"So...no."

She was studying me below the waist again. My dick didn't seem to mind, if the whole stretching and preening thing he was currently doing was any indication.

Usually, I didn't personify my cock as separate from me. But at this moment, I no longer felt in control of it—or this situation.

Definitely not this woman.

"Okay, I'm intrigued. What are you prepared to offer me beyond the price I paid for this property?" She licked her lips and held up a hand. "Not more money. I have enough of that."

"How? You work in a bakery."

"Never mind that. What else is on the table?" She tucked her thumbs in the belt loops of her shorts. "How about a free lifetime park anywhere I want pass?"

"I can't break the law for personal gain."

"Dammit. Then what else do you have?"

"I can make you an ice statue of your choosing. In the winter," I added, in case she failed to grasp that was a cold weather activity.

Or I could make her something out of wood, but I'd save that for a Hail Mary option. Wood was insanely expensive right now.

"Nah, you make them gratis for my sister. I can just steal one of hers." She smiled. "Keep going."

"I can convince Christian to toss one of your outstanding tickets.

11

One," I enunciated carefully, despite the fact I had no idea how I would pull that off.

Christian wouldn't let his own mother out of an overdue parking ticket, forget a woman with a stack a mile long.

"Try twenty and you're getting warmer."

"You have twenty outstanding tickets?"

"Actually, I think I'm forgetting some." Her tone was far too perky. "One of these days, I'll probably get arrested. Never been arrested. *Yet.*"

She made it sound like a bucket list item she wanted to check off.

I rubbed my forehead. She was obviously crazy, which everyone knew meant she'd be off-the-charts hot in bed.

Hmm, maybe I was thinking about this all wrong. Maybe hair of the dog that bit me would be the quickest way to get through this sticky situation.

Buddy, you're in big trouble.

But there was one thing I knew I had in spades. An ability that had served me well since high school. I might get harder than a steel pike in seconds flat with the proper inspiration, but I knew she wouldn't take me down before I sank her battleship first.

"I'll make you a deal."

One slim red eyebrow arched as she waited.

"If I can make you come before I do, you'll sell the land to me."

She stared at me for so long I was sure she'd never go for it. Then she started to laugh, long and low. "You're afraid to have sex with me, so your idea to solve this situation is to…have sex with me?"

"I did not say sex. Coming does not require penetration."

"Thank you for the sex ed class." She shook her head. "You like pushing your luck, hmm? I called it earlier. Cute but not bright. Though you are male, so one can only ask for so much."

I gritted my teeth. "There are plenty of other equally desirable properties available in town or nearby. You'll walk away ahead any way you cut it."

"I'll walk away with the money I paid and one measly orgasm? Pal, I had two before breakfast." She propped her hands on her hips. "Do better or I'm headed back to my bus. Hey, do you keep your bedroom blinds open, by any chance?"

I sucked in a deep breath. "Two waived parking tickets, a pass for free parking on Sundays, the full price of the land plus five percent and one not at all measly orgasm for you to move far away. And take that traveling tin can with you."

She tapped a blood-red nail on her crossed arm. "Sundays already have free parking. Try again."

"If I get fired, I can't pay my mortgage."

"Okay, forget the parking pass. Two waived parking tickets and best two of three on the orgasms. Whoever gets to two first."

"Honey, I'm not even going to get to one, so you have yourself a deal." I flashed a cocky grin that stayed firmly in place until she extended her hand to shake.

I was supposed to touch her now? I hadn't fully considered that.

Fuck.

Stiffening my spine, I reached toward her and grabbed her hand for a quick shake. Then I wrapped my dog's leash around my hand and crossed the street.

That I managed not to speed-walk was a minor victory.

"When is this happening, GQ?" Her voice was thick with laughter.

I'd worry about that after I took an ice cold shower. "I'll be in touch."

TWO

VANESSA

DAMN MY IMPULSIVE MOUTH.

As I crossed the grass to my beloved bus, I left the swing in my step to prove I'd meant what I said.

I didn't. I was an idiot.

He wasn't looking in my direction, anyway. He was escaping for his cute little house.

Cute houses were my downfall. And hot guys in uniform.

Or out of it.

He was going to be my brother-in-law in a few weeks. Okay, a month. *Ish.* My sister was dragging her heels on the actual date.

Normally, I'd be following her lead. I typically wanted to sprint to the county line when someone mentioned settling down, but my sister wasn't built like me. She liked order and knowing what was coming. For God's sake, she actually used her spreadsheet apps daily.

I wasn't sure how we'd come out of the same womb.

My idea of collecting receipts was a shoebox and a prayer during tax time. The fact that my receipts were overflowing this year was also a new thing.

As was my new acquisition.

I patted the rusty skoolie I'd bought on a whim. Well, it would be a skoolie when I was done with it. Right now it was a gutted vintage school bus held together with a bunch of plywood and stapled fabric.

I plopped my butt on my chair on my actual property.

Mine. Signed on the dotted line and all.

Also a wild new part of my life. But I wasn't too worried about it. I could rent it out as a camper space if I wanted to get back out on the road.

Even with the new—actually, quite old—school bus waiting for a wild excursion, I didn't have my usual urge to hop in the driver seat and head on to the next adventure.

I liked the quirky town my sister called home with her Hot Cop.

I wasn't sure about his brother.

Said brother was walking across his football field-sized front lawn very fast with the cutest dog on the planet under his arm like a football. I'd caught Officer Studly trying to hide the cute little bow on her head, and somehow that made it all the sweeter.

Nope.

He wasn't sweet.

He had a smart mouth wrapped in a super hot package. Including one other package that made my stupid and very impulsive tongue agree to the orgasm bet.

It had been a damn long time since I'd had anything that size near me that wasn't silicone-wrapped. In this town, it was the safest form of sexual activity. The Cove was almost its own episode of the *Twilight Zone*. It didn't seem to matter what kind of contraceptive methods both parties used, the babies kept manifesting.

Hmm.

Maybe that would be a way to get around things.

Would Officer Delicious prefer to fuck me blind with Mr. Blue Bonanza? That way neither of us could worry about the little blue lines on an EPT.

I tapped my finger on the arm of the rickety chair, trying to ignore the fact that my butt was slowly sinking toward the patchy grass beneath it. I would not give him the satisfaction of getting up.

Especially since he turned back to look at me before he disappeared around the side of his house.

I resisted the urge to wave at him even as grass tickled the edge of my shorts.

Once he was out of view, I popped out of the chair and clambered up into Skully the Skoolie. Named mostly for one of my all-time favorite characters on this spinning rock we called home. Dana Scully from X-Files didn't sound like she should be my favorite since she was very studious and analytical, but I just loved watching her try to block Mulder's wild and impulsive mind.

I was more of a Fox Mulder myself.

But I appreciated Scully's bright and beautiful brain. And she was a kickass redhead like me.

Most people were watching teen dramas, but my sister and I had lived for older tv shows and 80s movies. Mostly so we'd have something to talk to our parents about. We didn't have much in common with the very studious Dr. and Dr. Monaghan.

Some of my best memories with my mother were when I was sick and we'd watch TV Land with fat bowls of cheap ramen noodles.

I tapped the trio of crystals dangling above my...bed. Ish? My newest friend Luna had put together the crystal arrangement for me. I needed all the good mojo and luck to get this rolling rust heap into shape. I'd managed to create a makeshift bed with some foam for padding and my favorite sleeping bag. RIP to the former seams that were now joined with some flannel I'd found at a craft store. It was surprisingly comfortable.

I'd slept on far worse.

My bed was a problem for another day. For now, I needed to work on my next order to be able to pay for upgrades.

I'd showered and gotten myself together at my sister's place. I really needed to figure out the whole running water and electricity thing, but that was for another, *another* day.

Or until I got hungry later.

Tabitha Monaghan—soon to be McNeill—was usually sleeping at

her man's house. And until she gave up her lease, I would be using and abusing her apartment.

Not that she noticed.

I could see why. Her Hot Cop manslice was very distracting. As were the dogs and the big old baby belly making her act a bit more like me with all my scatteredness. She was getting pretty huge and an interesting mix of terror and chaos churned around her most days.

Terror I understood.

The baby thing made me antsy, but I would be here for my sister, no matter what. I'd been out of her life for far too long. How itchy the baby made me was *my* problem, not hers.

Not to mention the joy she radiated that was still foreign to me. Being tied down sounded scary as hell.

And so did the stretch marks. I had enough of those on my boobs, thanks.

Okay, so they weren't much to speak of, but they'd arrived practically fully formed the summer I turned fourteen—even itty bitty titties had stretch marks.

I dropped on the makeshift bed. I wiggled around until I found a less lumpy spot to cushion my butt. I really needed to get on finding a mattress that fit in here.

I pulled my iPad out of the charging station I'd built into the wall. I didn't have as many bills as the average bear, but I still needed to work for a living. Even if that included drawing monster peen.

Hidden in a brightly embroidered bag hanging on a hook was my drawing glove. Digital artwork was definitely not where I'd seen myself going when I left Syracuse after high school. And yet here I was.

I'd always loved to draw weird anime characters through high school and that had morphed into my own style over the years. I'd been an early adopter of the online marketplaces, and I'd sold a lot of commissioned sketches to put food on the table.

An inordinate number of Castiel and Dean Winchester fan drawings had been the bulk of my orders for a long time. I could see the appeal in Dean for sure. He had that rugged and yet pretty aspect that was catnip for most women, including me.

I also found it hilarious that cis-het women loved the idea of him boning an angel. Who was I to keep them from their fantasies? Those drawings had become a lucrative corner of my portfolio.

And that had transitioned into my current portfolio. Monster porn —err, romance.

I loved my damn job.

A few sketched lines for a warmup turned into a strong jawline and full lips. A slightly crooked nose led up to a strong brow line.

Smirky lips with just a hint of fang decided to make themselves known. Happy accidents always ramped up my excitement. A few taps later, I sharpened the lines a little and made the eyebrows far more arched than a regular man.

Than...

Crap.

I zoomed out.

He looked like Officer Studly.

Maverick McNeill.

My Apple pencil hovered over my iPad. My other fingers were automatically on my miniature keyboard I used for edits. I could easily delete the sketch. Just a few taps and bye!

Instead, I exaggerated a few of the strokes, making his eyebrows even more arched. Quickly I elongated his already elegant, artistic fingers, adding drips of blood. The quick adrenaline rush made me bolder. I grinned down at the drawing and added a few more droplets at the fang.

The drawing took over and my imagination raced along with it. Somewhere in the back of my mind I noticed the sunlight over my shoulder changed from bright to a tiny flicker, but I was too engrossed in creating to move.

Finally, my eyes begged for mercy. The days were getting shorter and my shoulders ached from being crouched over my iPad. I'd have to figure out a better lighting situation too.

I didn't even know how long I'd been at it.

Sometimes my artwork was like that. A fugue state took over and I came out the other side, dehydrated and starving.

The growl of my belly told me I'd been down the rabbit hole for far too many hours. And the fifteen percent mark in the corner of my screen made me wince.

But the piece was hella sexy and sinful.

It still had traces of my new neighbor, but I'd created an otherworldly Jack the Ripper aspect to it. Blue highlights gleamed off the top and brim of a jet-colored top hat and along the wide shoulders of the deep dark coat. Lacy sleeves peeked from his cuffs. A splash of blood dripped there too and from his long, wicked fingers.

The tips were almost claw-like and made me shiver. The sketch was hot and dangerous.

Threatening in an erotic way.

A hank of ebony hair hid part of his face and by the end, the character had taken on a life of its own. I tipped up the face to stare dead on at the viewer.

And in that, I saw Mav.

The devil with a bold stroke of lust gleaming in his black eyes.

Instinctively, I sent a screenshot over to one of my favorite romance authors. She used me often for fan art for her website and special covers for her die-hard fans. Something about the character made me think of her.

The author was very much like me and either would reply instantaneously or hit me back in two days when she came out of a writing binge. When I didn't hear the immediate chime from a reply, I hooked my iPad back into the charger and called it a day.

I needed food, anyway.

I wiggled my way to the end of the pallet and stuffed my feet into my flip-flops. I was digging the warm stretch of days we were enjoying in September.

Especially since I needed to find a way to heat Skully.

Being impulsive was much easier in the summer. Why I usually stayed in the warmer climates.

And yet, here I was. What was it about this town? Some wild magnetic pull? Were all the babies more like pins?

Stay! We will make you love it.

Maybe I'd have to tell my author friend about the Cove too. Seemed right up her paranormal alley.

I grabbed my favorite hoodie and opened the door. The scent of grilled burgers about knocked me down. Music and the yippy howls of a dog lured me into the enemy camp next door.

Francie was howling in time to Alice in Chains. Pretty impressive. I pulled the hoodie over my head and followed the well-tended path around the side of the house to a detached garage. Or maybe it was more of a barn.

Whatever it was, the huge doors were wide open. Inside was a feast of tools, and speakers the size of my tires flanked each side facing into the shop. I was pretty sure I saw a motorcycle under a tarp in the back. More importantly was the grill and the streaming scent of hot dogs and burgers along with something spicy.

I let out an audible groan. He was making street corn.

"No way."

Francie stopped howling and ran over to me, bouncing around my ankles. Her tiny pink bow had been righted and gave her a puppy vibe I couldn't resist.

I scooped her up and she immediately burrowed into the large pocket in the front of my sweatshirt. She did it so fast that I had a feeling she did it often.

Daddy came out of the garage-slash-workshop-slash-barn and stopped, crossing his arms over his own hoodie.

Yep. Bingo.

Francie peeked her head out and yipped, then she licked my fingers as I immediately soothed her with a scratch under her chin.

"Can I help you?"

I peeked around the grill, trying on a bright smile. "Maybe. If you're feeling neighborly."

"And if I'm not?"

"I'll steal your dog."

"You do realize you're talking to an officer of the law, right?"

I shrugged. "I'm sure she'd come back eventually."

He rolled his eyes. "Probably for the same reason you're here."

"Sex?" I widened my eyes. "Why, Officer GQ, that's very disturbing."

I hadn't meant to say the s-word already. I mean, it had been a while and I was always looking for a new technique for some fun, but I wasn't actually looking for an orgasm.

Maybe a burger and then an orgasm though.

Sex wasn't on the table yet. But a neighborly orgasm wasn't a bad deal. Or some edging. I didn't want to let him win that easily. Or at all.

Not at all was the correct answer, Vanessa Vail.

I was too hungry for linear thought, obviously.

"Take pity on a girl."

"After you accused me of beastiality?"

"You know the term?" I narrowed my eyes. "Should I worry?"

"You're too ridiculous for words."

I got that a lot. I was well aware I was too much for most people. A fact that usually made me even more outrageous.

I spotted the camping chair just outside the huge barn doors and plopped myself down. Francie peeked out of my pouch and wiggled her adorable little nose before returning to burrow next to my belly.

"She does this a lot?"

He gave a careless shrug and picked up a pair of tongs hanging from the side of the bright red grill. It was a weird egg shape, but man, everything inside smelled like heaven.

"If I feed you, will you scram?"

"Probably." I reached into my pocket and stroked Francie's soft fur. "Your dog is pretty cute. Enough to deal with your company."

"You're the party crasher here."

I craned my neck. "No party. Or is it a party of one?" I comically widened my eyes. "Or are you having a party yourself? Do you need to wash your hands?"

"You're exasperating."

"Doesn't answer the question."

"I do need to wash my hands, but that's because I was working in my shop."

"Not on your own tool?"

He shook his head, but his lips twitched.

I slid out of my flips and tucked my feet under me cross-legged. I liked this camp chair. It was bigger than mine and didn't sag. Maybe I'd steal it *and* the dog before I went home.

"So is that where the magic happens?" I nodded to the shop.

"Usually my king-sized bed."

"King? Fancy." I actively ignored the tingles buzzing along my skin. "I meant the ice sculpting stuff."

"Oh." He turned over the corn and my mouth watered. Then my eyes drifted to the chef. Not a bad view either. I did enjoy a tight bum.

"Yeah, I do that mostly in the winter. Too hot to make ice last. I do some wood sculpting the rest of the year."

My gaze shot up from the two-handed perfect curve of his behind to his face. He was arching a brow at me, but whatever. He'd been ogling me earlier, though I was almost sure he thought I hadn't noticed. "No shit?"

"No shit."

"Like whittling? Grandpa and his wee knife?"

His nostrils flared. "Chainsaw and chisel."

"Chainsaw? Okay, I need to see this." I tried to get up and he waved me back down.

"Food."

"Okay. You convinced me." I sat back and let him bring it to me.

He held two plates full of delicious goodness. "C'mon, we can eat inside like civilized people."

"Boring."

"Unless you like naked hot dogs."

"Depends on the size of the brats."

"There's a brat here, but it ain't on the grill." He left me and walked inside, the screen door slapping behind him.

Francie stuck her head out of my pocket. "Evidently, we're going inside."

She yipped at me and wiggled out, then she hopped out of my pocket to follow her dad. Instead of waiting for me, she nosed her way into a tiny dog flap beside the screen door.

"Okay then."

"I only let her go in and out the dog door when I'm home," he called back as if he suspected I was judging his doggie parenting choices. Maybe I sort of had been.

Now I was judging my own choices.

I wasn't sure going inside his house was a good idea, but I couldn't deny I was curious to see what kind of digs a bachelor cop had. Especially when he had a surprising art background in there to make him just a bit too fascinating.

After I opened the door, I swallowed a gasp.

Not at all what I was expecting. And yet it matched him. The door lead into the kitchen. Butcher block countertops gleamed in soft honey and walnut shades. The cabinets were deep green and obviously custom made for a man of his height.

Even the countertops were a little tall, coming well above my waist. Not that it was a stretch. Most things were too tall for me. Instead of painted, the green was a stain that urged me to touch.

I didn't have much impulse control and found myself dragging a fingertip along carvings in the kitchen island's doors. A tiny bird was tucked in one corner and a larger cardinal peeked from another. Instead of green, he'd added a touch of red stain to make the carvings stand out.

"This is...*wow*."

He glanced at me through a thick hank of hair that had fallen forward. "Thanks."

I shivered a little, reminded of my vampire drawing that had held me obsessively all day.

Seeing him in the flesh after I'd drawn his likeness was jarring. Enough that I was very glad I had a hoodie on. No need to give him a heads up on just how attentive my headlights were to that penetrating glance.

Very annoying, as well.

Especially when tingles followed the tightening of my nipples on a more southernly track. Instead of staring at the tall, dark, and delicious male a few feet away, I let my gaze trip over the other touches he'd added to the room. The crimson bar stools under the kitchen island, the banquet-style built-in that made use of the small kitchen and showcased more of his carving talents.

I could spend all day finding the little bits of himself he'd added to the room.

But my stomach overrode my curiosity. I quickly washed my hands and followed him to the back of the kitchen.

"Stool or bench?"

"Since I'd probably need you to boost me onto the seat, we'll go with the bench."

His jaw flexed in a most distracting manner.

I really shouldn't have made that bet. It had been much easier to spar with him at my sister's bakery than to think about him naked.

The old jeans he was wearing left little to the imagination in that regard. Denim had a habit of making outlines around the most *interesting* things.

Did I mention it had been a damn long time since anything but silicone had been in my hands?

But street corn won over orgasms.

At least for now.

THREE

 Maverick

I SPENT THE NIGHT TOSSING AND TURNING. AND IT WASN'T BECAUSE THE meal I'd made us hadn't hit the spot.

As a rule, I didn't lack female companionship. I wasn't exactly a player to the extent my older brother had been before he'd been changed by the love of a good woman, but I'd had my share of romances. None of them had lasted long.

I was particular, and the older I got, I became less interested in spending time with someone I knew wouldn't be a good fit in the long-term. Because this was a long-term town. If you were going to plant roots here, it was wise to read the lay of the land.

Or else move on before you ended up stuck.

Happily stuck in most cases, from what all I'd seen—my brother included. I never thought I'd see Brady happily shopping for baby shit. I didn't get it.

But then again, I'd also spent a good half hour discussing dog food and training with Christian last week. I hadn't seen that on my bingo card for this year.

Then again, everything had changed when I'd found my Francie abandoned in that crappy apartment earlier in the summer.

Christian's dog was a huge German Shepherd named Boomer, so

27

we weren't exactly on the same page as pet parents, but whatever. Dog dads were the one commonality we had at the station. My brother had two dogs, Pancake and Daisy, and Chief Brooks had a dog getting used to her new name. Hell, we were all getting used to Lola since his little girl somehow couldn't pronounce her original name of Sadie. Lola won for the sake of peace and then some.

The dog didn't seem to care. I was pretty sure I could call Francie Bufort and she'd still respond as long as she got her regular meals.

Dogs were easy. Women were not.

Babies were definitely *not* easy. And in this town, dating and sex led to babies at a frighteningly high rate if you were in the right age bracket. I hadn't heard of the town lore breaking biological records yet, but I suspected that would happen anytime now.

Which was why Brady had undergone a vasectomy. Then he'd knocked up Tabitha, something that occurred very rarely after getting snipped.

But medical science hadn't run up against Crescent Cove—and its baby water—before.

Added to that, if one trusted genetics, that meant McNeill men were shooting at a high rate of accuracy. It was just pure luck I didn't have a brood trailing after me around town. I'd had my indiscriminate days like any single man with "piercing" brown eyes (said by an ex-girlfriend, not something I wrote in my nonexistent diary.)

So getting naked with a girl was something I thought about a little more carefully these days. No one had made the cut for a good long while. My mid-twenties was too young to be a dad to anything but an adorable Yorkie.

Which reminded me—dammit—I needed to get more of her *old* food since the new kind produced monster…leavings.

Lucky me, my night was full of more of the same kinds of thoughts, increasingly jumbled the closer it got to dawn. But I didn't doze off for more than an hour at a stretch.

The next day was a fog of exhaustion, then the next, and the next. I kept staying up all night against my will. What the heck was going on with me? I normally slept like a…well, not a baby. But like a man with no troubles.

Until *she'd* moved in next door.

It wasn't like she even came over to bother me. Unless you counted those super short cutoffs she'd been wearing every day to make me insane. We'd been enjoying a stretch of warm September days, and I was pretty sure she had a color for every day. The red ones had about killed me.

She wanted to break my no sex streak, I could feel it. Her plan included weakening me by plaguing my thoughts so I couldn't sleep. Then I would be completely at her witchy mercy.

Like hell.

I was on shift at the station on a typically busy Friday when my brother dropped a bomb on my weekend of, hopefully, sleep. Worse, it was all so he could screw his fiancée.

As if he hadn't done that enough.

Then again, I supposed when she was already knocked up was the best time. What did it feel like without a rubber?

Lucky bastard. I'd probably never know.

I rubbed my itchy eye, dry from days of no decent rest. And I wasn't going to dwell on rubber-less sex when I was already a man on the edge due to Brady's soon-to-be-wife's damn twin.

Twins were always sexy as hell. It was a known fact. Many adult films had been built on that very premise.

Even if Vanessa and Tab weren't identical. Didn't matter. They had similarly attractive attributes, though Van just had something…more.

Something making me insane.

Brady dropped a hip on the edge of my desk, his face open and friendly in a way that indicated I was in very deep shit. Then he picked up the framed family picture our sister Honey had given me at the start of the summer.

Everyone else had family photos on their desk and I'd had a baseball bobblehead doll. Honey, being the only sentimental one in the McNeill family tree, felt sorry for me and made everyone pose outside at a barbecue. The next day she'd plunked the candid shot of our family on my desk with one of Tab's famous cream puffs.

Even Christian had a collage of Boomer photos that looked like the dog was trying out for a military magazine. I used to roll my eyes at the display, but a few weeks after that, I'd found Francie.

Though I carried my picture of her in my wallet. I had a rep to maintain.

"You're scowling in this picture," Brady commented, tapping his thumb over my face in the photo. "We'll have to take a better family shot at the wedding."

"Like I'm going to be smiling when my delirious older brother is getting fit with a ball and chain? Even if she's smokin' hot."

"Watch it." His tone was mild as he set down the frame. "So do you have plans this weekend?"

"Who wants to know?"

"Maverick."

I sighed. "Fine. What do you need? And by the way, I'm not babysitting your child when she's born unless you intend to pay me handsomely. I'm talking big bucks, no brotherly discount, either. You want the best, you're gonna pay, sucker."

His snort echoed through the room so loudly, Christian shot him an irritated glance. Not that there was anything unusual about that. Christian was perennially stern and annoyed when anyone seemed to be having too much fun.

"The best? You are literally terrible with children. You practically develop hives when one gets near you."

I couldn't argue with the truth. "Yeah, but babies love me. I have a winning personality. Now out with it. What do you want?"

"Tab and I are taking an impromptu babymoon tonight."

"Say what? You're not married yet." I leaned back in my chair, lacing my fingers behind my head. "Damn sinners. I can't abide by such shenanigans in such a proper town."

He wisely kept his snicker at a low enough volume not to alert Christian. "A babymoon is a honeymoon you have before the baby comes. Because after you have a baby, there isn't much honeymooning."

"Is a biological lesson next? Can I ask questions?" I sat up and grabbed my notebook and pen. "What are the odds a vasectomy will fail? Do you know exact percentages?"

"Shut up. It's just our last chance to connect pre-kid. You understand, right?"

"*Connect* being euphemism for fuck? Sure." I tossed my pen back on my desk.

Brady sighed and rolled his eyes toward the ceiling. "I pity the woman who gets saddled with you someday."

"What does this 'connecting' event have to do with me and my weekend?"

"We can't bring the dogs. Can you watch them?"

"Both of them?" I frowned. "At one time?"

"Uh, yes. The hotel doesn't allow pets."

"Hotel? Where are you going? I mean, location is nice and all, but haven't you done it enough by now that a mint on the pillow isn't going to improve things much?" I rubbed my chin and considered shaving yet again. I was still deciding if I liked this thicker scruff or not. "Besides, is she even still able to move?"

Brady's brows lifted toward his hairline. "Are you seriously asking if my fiancée can still have sex?"

"It's a reasonable question. She's quite...robust right now."

"Good save," Christian called from his desk while I chuckled behind my hand.

"Robust or not, things are just fine in that department. So can you help out your favorite brother and almost sister-in-law," he rushed on when I opened my mouth to say no, "who made you your favorite Boston Cream cake last week, just because?"

"Damn good cake." I tipped my head. "I wouldn't mind another one."

"I'll see if it can be arranged."

"Did you forget how your dogs rile up my dog?"

"More like the other way around," Brady said wryly. "Never

thought I'd see the day when Mav the stud was carting around a yippy priss of a dog with a pink bow in her hair."

"I'll have you know Francie is irresistible to anyone in any age bracket. Just as I am."

"Sure you want to test that theory in the Cove?"

"Yeah, well, at least I'm smart enough to wrap it up."

"You're just jealous." Brady hopped off the desk and I didn't argue, because I sort of was.

Which was insane.

Why would I be jealous of having to get a dog sitter to have sex with my almost-wife before the baby came? Not to mention the fact that relations as we knew it would end until the kid was 18. That was not logical, and I was nothing if not a logical man.

At least I used to be.

"Do you think Vanessa is like Tabitha?" I asked idly, stopping my brother in his tracks. And my heart. There was no way in Hades I wanted to show that hand of cards yet.

If ever.

"What do you mean?" he asked slowly, locking his jaw. "If this is some kind of pervy twin thing, I will ban you from joint family gatherings until you're too old to even use your dick, you lech."

I had to laugh, ill-advised as it was. "No, not pervy. Not exactly. I don't even know what I'm asking. Just Pocket Plus seems nothing like Tab and I was wondering if maybe she has some hidden side or something. If maybe you knew."

"Hidden porntastic side?"

"I mean, that's never wrong—" When Brady growled, I held up a hand. "Never mind. I haven't slept in days and I'm practically babbling. Have fun tonight. Hopefully, I won't get called in."

"Why would you get called in?"

"A warm Friday night in September. You know, the kind that makes people think of summer before fall's cold snap settles in. People get crazy."

"Yeah, maybe the ducks will come marauding through. Otherwise, I think you're probably safe." He started walking back to his office, then hooked his thumbs in his belt loops and turned back. "Vanessa bought the property next to yours."

"Thanks for giving me an early heads up, jerk."

"You know?"

"Yes, I know." It was my turn to roll my eyes. She was hard to miss or ignore.

"Is that going to be a problem?"

Orgasm bets weren't a problem, right?

I cleared my throat. "For now, it isn't. We'll see what happens in the future."

"Just remember she's going to be your sister-in-law very soon."

"So I can't have a one-night-stand with her and leave no forwarding address—which coincidentally, is next door to hers?" I saluted him. "Got it. Now get out of here."

"Mav," he began.

"Seriously, have a great night. And leave extra treats for Francie, too, in the dogs' overnight bag. I forgot to buy her some."

"Will do. Thanks." This time, he didn't turn back on his way into his office, and he shut the door behind him.

"You're into that pain in the ass, aren't you?" Christian let out a windy sigh. "I foresee a world of trouble for you, McNeill, and not because you have creepy twin fantasies. She's a real ballbuster."

"I can handle her," I said under my breath as Christian slanted me a knowing look.

Everyone knew I was screwed, including myself. At least this weekend I'd be occupied with our crazy brood of pups. No Pocket Plus in sight.

At least that was the plan.

Later that evening, I finally settled all three of the heathens into their respective beds in Brady's soon-to-be vacant apartment. He and Tabitha's new home was almost ready for occupancy on the other side of the lake. They'd been searching for a house for their growing family for months, and the hot real estate market in town hadn't given them many options until finally their perfect place had appeared out of nowhere.

I'd been prepared to let them have my house that I'd been scouting forever, but Tab had gone through it with her witchy friend Luna and declared "the vibe didn't match theirs" and passed on it. Whatever. The vibe suited me just fine. Especially if I didn't look out the window at the hot mess parked next door.

I wasn't sure how she'd gone from an ugly conversion van to believing a rusty short school bus was an upgrade. But the heap was probably half the reason I couldn't sleep. I was just waiting for the complaints from the neighbors to start rolling in.

Francie let out a sharp yip from her pink princess bed as Brady's police scanner went crazy with incoming alerts. I shot up from the couch, nearly upending my paper plate of takeout Chinese as the words "armed robbery in progress" came across the speaker.

On cue, I got a text from Bonnie, our dispatcher, that all hands were needed on deck and I had to report.

Daisy let out a deep *woof* that made Francie trot over to the other dog's bed to ascertain she did not need assistance. Pancake, my brother's other dog, popped up from where he'd crammed himself behind her to sniff at Francie and try to lick her face until she showed him her tiny fangs.

Undeterred, his tongue swept over her ear, and she started barking up a storm that fully blocked out the scanner's squawking.

Some peaceful night this was so far.

I sighed as I stalked into the kitchen to dump my Chinese into some Tupperware for later before I went into Brady's bedroom to get back into my uniform and strap on my gear.

Daisy decided to try to calm the fracas by silencing the yipping with her own more authoritative bark, but all it did was make it nearly impossible for Bonnie to hear me when I called in to let her know I was on my way. She gave me the details—young suspect, potentially armed—and we hung up so I could get my ass over to the Quik Pump gas station.

I opened the treat bag sitting on the counter. Brady had left numerous treats, special toys, plus an older brotherly assortment of notes with instructions I hadn't taken the time to read.

Definitely couldn't do that now.

I tossed treats toward the waiting pups, making sure to evenly distribute them to all three of them. I hoped like hell it would be enough to distract them from destroying the apartment.

"Be back later, girls. And guy. Be good, won't you?" I called over my shoulder as I stepped into the hall and shut the door behind me.

And bumped into Pocket Plus backing out of Tabitha's apartment across the hall with her arms full of...yarn? What the hell?

"What are you doing here?" we asked in unison.

"I'm gathering up my stuff before the big move. And you're—" She frowned, looking me over from head to toe, her gaze lingering on my gun. For once, not the personal one in my pants either. "Where's the fire?"

"You're mixing your metaphors." And I couldn't stick around to talk about it, even if she smelled like ocean air, salt water, and crayons.

The last made no sense, but with Vanessa, pretty much anything went.

Including her wearing an obscenely tight football jersey with the number 69 scrawled across her tits.

"Whatever. Where are you headed?"

"To work," I said shortly, silencing the radio on my hip although it was against protocol. But I wasn't fast enough to prevent her from hearing another alert about the armed robbery.

Her blue eyes widened. "What? How can that be? The Cove doesn't —" Jockeying her yarn, she reached out to grab my forearm in a surprisingly strong grip. "Brady isn't here. You'll be alone?"

"I'm a cop. It's my job. I won't be alone. Christian will—"

"Oh, that fuckwit. Like I'd trust him." If anything, her grip increased. "If that guy is really armed..."

"Don't know it's a guy. Doesn't matter. It's my job." I peeled her hand off my arm, though she fought me. I would've expected nothing less. "Do me a favor?"

For once, she didn't argue. "Yeah."

"Watch the dogs for me. I'll be back when I can."

She shifted the yarn around in her arms, briefly flashing her 69 once more as she swallowed hard. "Okay. Yeah. I can do that. In there? Brady's place?" Her voice sounded strangled.

"Yes." I reached out and tipped up her chin with two fingers, surprised to note it trembled. "Everything's gonna be fine."

"Right. Sure. Go on, be a superhero." She opened the door to a chorus of barks then glanced back with a furrow between her pale brows. "Be careful, okay?"

Before I could respond, she shut the door in my face.

It shouldn't have made me grin as I turned to head downstairs to do my job.

Clearly, I was a sadistic bastard.

FOUR

IT TOOK ABOUT HALF AN HOUR OF LISTENING TO THAT BLASTED SCANNER for me to call in the cavalry. That cavalry happened to be Mav's younger sister and her best friend Mickey, two of my co-workers at my sister's bakery.

Thankfully, Tabitha had hired more employees so the pair of them were off tonight and lived close enough to relieve me as I was rushing out the door.

Pretty soon these dogs were going to file a protest at their parade of babysitters, but it couldn't be helped.

"There's treats on the counter, and their food is labeled and portioned out by dog. I didn't get to feed them but that should be easy enough for you two to handle, right? Right."

"Van." Honey towered over me—not that unusual, since I was extremely petite—and braced her hands on my shoulders. "What's wrong?"

"Nothing's wrong. Everything's fine," I said, echoing her brother.

Even if he was a liar. Even if I felt in my bones he needed me there.

Not just anyone. *Me.* Vanessa Monaghan, who wielded an Apple Pencil and an iPad, not a weapon of mass destruction. Okay, I was good with a piping bag. They were pretty heavy and the tips were damn sharp.

I was officially mentally babbling.

Honey's grip tightened. "Where's my brother?"

"Probably screwing my sister at this very moment."

She scrunched up her nose. "Eww. Disgusting. Not Brady. I know where he is. Where's Mav? He was on dog duty tonight."

I took a deep, so not calming breath. "He's working. He got called in. Nothing to worry about," I added far too brightly.

Her gorgeous features so like her older brothers immediately pinched with worry. "What aren't you telling me?"

"Me? Nothing." I spread my arms wide. "I'm an open book." I ducked out of her hold and grabbed my yarn, now stuffed in a paper bag, on my flight toward the door. "Thanks so much for coming. I'll be back soon. *We'll* be back soon. Thanks, Mickey," I shouted over my shoulder.

Honey's best friend Mickey looked up from where she was crouched over Daisy, rubbing her silky golden ears where she was curled on her side in her bed.

Huh, that was weird. Well, it was bedtime for them, right? Or it had to be close to it.

You had one job—to watch these dogs. He asked you to do it, and that's what you should be doing. You aren't a cop. What do you think you can do, other than get in the way?

I had not one clue. I didn't even know what I was doing right now, other than operating on some indecipherable instinct. One that had come out of nowhere.

I didn't like Mav. Not really. I mean, he was almost family, so I cared. Of course, I cared.

Right. Family. He was basically the same as my creepy great-uncle Stewart, the one with all the chins and bad body odor.

Sure.

"Uh, you're welcome. No problem. Van, Daisy's belly is really pink. Is that normal?"

I frowned. "I guess so? I'm not really sure."

38

Daisy took that moment to kick up her back leg to itch her stomach. But she soon settled.

Mickey stroked her soft ears. "She feels hot."

"Well, the AC in this building sucks. I'm sure she's fine." God, I hoped. But I couldn't really deal with that right now since I had to get in Mav's way and cause him to accidentally get shot and bleed out on the Quik Pump's dingy tile floor—

Okay, I was not allowed to read any more of my clients' novels while I was doing art for their covers and their special fan requests.

Normally, I did mostly paranormal-style artwork, so the stories I consumed on the sly were usually of the fantastical variety. But a big time publisher had contacted me the other day about doing a stepback for a debut romantic suspense author's splashy hardcover. The moody inside cover work was a dream job for me, but then I'd made the mistake of reading chapter one before bed.

Then all thirty-two other chapters before breakfast.

Whoops.

A cop had been the hero, and he'd gotten gravely wounded saving a little boy from being shot. The heroine had to nurse him back to health while trying to find the killer.

I was not about nursing anyone. Even if the hero had been described as looking like Henry Cavill.

That meant I had to make sure all of Mav stayed in one piece.

And I was going back to sketching vampires, gargoyles, and large blue mutant creatures with two penises. At least then, my imagination wouldn't run away with me like it was tonight.

"Listen, call Dr. Thorn if she seems off. He does house calls, I'm almost sure."

"On a Friday night?" Honey seemed dubious.

She wasn't the only one, but I was scrambling for any lifeline I could grab. "He's very hands-on and approachable."

Mickey rolled her eyes, still petting Daisy. "Says you."

Okay, then.

"I'll be back soon. Thanks again." I left before either of them could ask me any more questions.

Not that I had any answers to give. All I could do was follow my gut to Mav's location, my hands tight around the wheel, the radio on silent just in case some awful news report would stop me in my tracks.

I was on a mission. God help us both.

But I couldn't even get near the damn gas station. The road was blocked off and police cars were parked haphazardly, making it impossible for me to even get close in my vehicle.

So I parked around the block and ran.

I was surprised to see the fire department had trucks on scene too. Austin Lancaster, one of the firemen who was close to Brady and Mav, immediately spotted me.

Damn eagle eyes.

I looked around for another hole in the crush of people, but he decided barring a redhead from entry was more important than dealing with the unholy dripping mess I spotted through the plate glass window of the gas station. Everything looked drenched.

"You can't get your gum now, Monaghan." Austin threw up a beefy arm when I tried to do an end run around him, using speed and the element of surprise to—

Well, to end up hoisted in the air, my legs still pumping as if my brain wouldn't accept I wasn't actually in motion.

"Put me down, you behemoth. I have rights."

"You do, and you aren't exercising them in there. Crime scene."

"Was there a fire?" I didn't smell any smoke, thank God.

"No. Someone pulled the fire alarm after they called in a false report. And you didn't hear that from me. Hey, ease off," he said, affronted, when one of my Keds connected with his shin.

The words *false report* settled the chaos in my brain. Enough that I took a deep breath and nudged Austin to put me down. "I'm good."

He lifted a dark brow. "Are you sure about that?"

I nodded and rolled my shoulders, the tension leaving my body. Most of it, anyway. "I had too much coffee today, sorry."

His brow remained raised, but he set me on my feet.

I was about to tuck tail and turn around to leave when I glimpsed

Mav through the window, sitting in a chair as a busty blond Amazon-like woman tended some scrape on his upper arm. He was smiling at her and she was giggling as she dabbed, so he clearly was in no distress.

Threat over. Guess I didn't need to be a superhero tonight either.

Yet I did not leave. No, that would've been too sensible.

I darted around Austin before he could grab me and rushed inside, the bell over the door dinging like one going off before a fight. Even before I opened my mouth, I knew I was about to make an ass out of myself.

Did that shut me up? Au contraire.

"I should've known I'd find you like this." I came to a halt in front of the nursing action—maybe this was a common theme in books for a reason—and propped my hands on my hips. "You asked me to come over to take care of your charges so you could do...this?" I gestured wildly at the Amazon who was staring at me, aghast.

She also had massive breasts. Somehow that seemed like one more insult.

Very slowly, Mav drew his arm away from his nurse and flexed his hand, drawing my gaze to the many muscles currently rippling and stretching with his movement. I hadn't realized what all he had under his uniform. Probably a good thing.

"Vanessa, this is a crime scene."

I crossed my arms. "Your point?"

To his credit, he didn't swear at me. I could tell it was a close thing. "You're going to need to leave."

I gestured to his new friend and decided I might as well dig a hole and just cover myself entirely with dirt.

"She's not a cop. How come she gets to stay?"

His lips thinned, most likely his way of not using a clever string of swear words. "She's an EMT." He leaned forward and braced his hands on his equally muscled thighs, highlighting the scrap of fabric dangling from his biceps. "Are you okay? Are the dogs okay?"

"Don't I look okay? And yes, the dogs are fine."

At least I hoped Daisy wasn't sick. She was very well taken care of under normal circumstances. Mav and I hadn't been in charge for more than a couple of hours.

"You should be fine," his nurse commented with another dismissive glance in my direction before she smacked a Band-Aid on his arm. "If you need anything else…"

"He's just fine. I'm sure he has Neosporin at home."

Neither of them paid me any mind.

After she walked away, Mav slowly rose in a menacing manner that did disturbing things to my nipples. Luckily, they were currently hidden by my crossed arms.

"Go home," he said in an undertone as Chief Brooks' voice grew louder from the back of the store. "I'll talk to you later."

He made that sound like a threat. My nipples tingled inappropriately once again.

"You mean back to your brother's place, where you left me alone?"

"I have to deal with a crime scene."

"Did I call this or what?" Officer Masterson strolled up the closest aisle, smirking. "Where's your traveling eyesore today?"

"Parked at your mama's house."

His smirk remained in place. "You're pushing dangerously close to a trespassing charge. About time I get to cuff you."

Mav stepped between us and got in Christian's face—well, as much as he could when his fellow cop was the size of a giant, as all of the Masterson men were. Still, Mav knew how to glower with the best of them.

"Back off. If anyone's going to cuff her, it's me."

FIVE

NOW THERE WAS A DEFENSE I HADN'T SEEN COMING. AND I HAD TO SAY I approved. Would it be too cheeky of me to stick out my wrists?

Probably. I was tempted just the same.

Things moved quickly after that. The Chief approached and Christian turned to have a hushed conference with him as Mav grabbed my upper arm and hustled me out the door. On the way, he stopped to exchange words with Austin.

All the curse words I'd expected him to aim at me, he fired at his buddy instead. Including saying, "next time, don't let a pretty pair of blue eyes twist your balls in a knot."

Austin just held up his hands palms out and shrugged.

I frowned. He was blaming Austin for my being an ass? That was a first. I was used to taking full responsibility for that one.

"It was my fault."

Mav didn't spare me a glance. "Oh, believe me, I'm well aware, Vanessa."

Many Vanessas, no Pocket Pluses. He must be really mad. Maybe that cuff thing wasn't an idle threat.

A hint of guilt tried to worm its way between my shoulder blades. I could've really messed up things for him on the job, which hadn't been my intention at all. I'd just been really worried and foolish and maybe a tiny bit jealous toward the end there.

Breasts had always been a sore spot for me, and his nurse had been blessed by the boob fairies many times over.

But before I could apologize—to him *and* Austin—he was gripping my hand and tugging me along across the parking lot and then around the side of the brick building to the alley alongside of it. Something little and furry scurried behind a dumpster, but I didn't have time to consider that before he was spinning me around and pinning me against the wall with my wrists above my head.

"Explain yourself," he growled against my ear.

I opened my mouth to reply and realized his hips were pressed entirely too snugly against my back. And things were going on in that region of his body that were not appropriate for a man in uniform.

He wasn't even repentant about being as hard as the brick wall my nose was squished against. He was cocky and, well, fully cocked.

Large and in charge and practically puffing out his chest with it. No part of Maverick McNeill was lacking in any way.

I took a deep breath and wondered what would diffuse this situation so I wouldn't end up losing our bet before he'd even gotten a hand in my panties. Shaming myself should do it.

"I was worried about you."

He released my wrists so fast I had a moment to mourn the loss of his grip. His hands were calloused and strong and authoritative. I didn't mind being ordered around in bed. Far from it. If the dude tried it when I wasn't naked, he'd likely be lacking a nut before he finished speaking, but during sex? Yeah, I had no qualms there.

And while we weren't having sex, somehow everything between us since I'd showed up on his dock had seemed like a precursor to this particular dance.

I had a feeling I'd be finding somewhere new to live soon. He might not even have to do more than speak or look at me in that dark, dangerous way he had, and he'd win by default.

"You were what?"

"Worried. About you." I rubbed my wrists with more than a little

44

COP DADDY NEXT DOOR

regret as I turned to face him, realizing he hadn't stepped back so our bodies were still entirely too close. I craned my neck to meet his gaze and tried to keep my voice even despite the heat in his molten brown eyes. It was past sunset but the alley was well-lit and his eyes were full of emotion. Mostly the kind I couldn't read. "Shocked me too," I added. "Seeing as I basically hate you."

"You hate me?"

"Yes." I shook my head while I said it, doing my favorite Bender move from *The Breakfast Club*. Tab and I had watched that movie a million times when we were home sick from school as kids.

He braced his arm on the wall above my head. "No, you don't."

"Probably not. But I didn't mean to mess up your stakeout."

His lips twitched. "It wasn't a stakeout. I thought it was an in-progress armed robbery. Instead, it was a young kid armed with a water gun and enough bad judgment to pull the fire alarm and shoot off his fake gun at a cashier. The cashier held onto him until we got there, but by then, the sprinklers had soaked everything. Customers were still trying to come in, and it was just chaos."

I reached up to trace a fingertip over the Band-Aid on his arm. "Did he tag you with his water gun?" I asked in the silkiest voice I could manage, despite my still racing heart from hearing him recount what had happened.

Fake gun or not, false alarm or not, the fear inside me had been very real.

I still wasn't quite steady yet. Not even close.

"Not exactly. I crashed into a vintage Pez display and ripped open my shirt." His smile was wry. "Superhero moment dashed."

"I don't think so. Just wish that rip had been a little lower." I let my gaze drop and linger until he did that whole two fingers under my chin deal he'd started doing tonight. He lifted my face and leveled his gaze on mine, making me swallow hard.

"While I want you to promise you'll never do anything close to this again, I'm honored."

"You're honored?"

He nodded. "No one worries about me, even if it was unnecessary.

But a beautiful woman like you racing over here to make sure I'm okay? That's a fucking win, far as I'm concerned."

"It is?" And I'd turned into a parrot. Awesome.

"Absolutely."

"What about the bet?"

"What about it?"

"You hate me so much, you want me to move away. Now you think I'm beautiful?"

"You could still be beautiful even if I hated you. Which I do not. What's between us is much more elemental." He raked his fingers through the longer dark hair falling over his forehead. "You never would've moved if I'd won that stupid bet, and we both know it."

I shrugged. "Yeah, probably not. But you wouldn't win. Besides, you just dared me that I couldn't withstand your magic sex fingers so you could get naked with me without acknowledging how much you want to."

"Is that what you think?"

I crossed my arms smugly. "Not a no."

"I also didn't say anything about making you come with my fingers." His voice had gone seductively low. "My tongue was just as viable."

My heartbeat filled my head. Breathing was now optional.

He exhaled. "But it was a ridiculously dumb idea. As of now, that bet is cancelled."

"Scared you'll lose? I understand. Hard on the ol' ego."

"Hardly. Just it was a childish idea in the first place." He stepped closer and my heart rate sped up even faster. "Neither of us are children. We don't need to play silly games."

"No. So you're not running away from my overwhelming wiles now?"

He licked the inside of his lower lip as his sexy gaze roved over my face. "You see me running, Pocket Plus?"

I was breathing fast enough that my rapid exhalations were practically pressing my breasts against his uniform shirt. Pity they were so much less noteworthy than his EMT's. "We can't get naked. It's against family rules."

Again with the lip twitching. I wasn't sure I was thrilled with his amusement at my expense. I kinda wished he'd go back to threatening to manhandle me—or at least that was what I'd imagined in my perverted brain.

"You keep mentioning sex. Is there any particular reason?"

"Same reason you're hard enough to brand me." I tilted up my chin, pleased when he kept his fingers against my face. "So, are we going to finish this or not? I'm not much for this two-step we're doing. The one we've been doing for a damn long time."

Lazily, he lifted an eyebrow. "Is that so?"

"You know it is. All the way back to when you were icing my sister's cupcakes until late in the night."

"Only you can make that sound salacious."

"It is a gift, I admit it."

"Yeah, well, I'm not much for being led. I prefer to do the leading." He glanced around. "Where's your traveling porn bus?"

I couldn't stop my laugh. "Around the block. Wanna check out my sleeping bag?"

"No, thanks. Let's go. I'm taking you home." He grasped my forearm and tugged, albeit not all that hard because I'd discovered I liked walking slightly behind him.

My vampire with the fangish eyeteeth would be getting one hell of an ass tonight.

Or maybe tomorrow morning, depending how the rest of the evening went.

Saying nothing, he glanced around then opened the passenger door of his truck.

"No squad car? Here I was hoping for the full cuff treatment. Behind the screened partition and everything."

"Night's not over yet. Get in." He boosted me up without me asking and any smart remark I would've tossed back ended with his hand on my ass.

My ass totally approved too.

47

I slid across the buttery soft leather seat and snapped my belt as he shut the door, thankful it was too dark out for him to see my shaking knees.

I hoped.

I wasn't some virgin. It had been a good long while for me—years rather than months—but I still knew how this usually went. But his being the next thing to family made it weird. And hot.

But still weird.

Not to mention, my sister would kill me. She was trying her best to bond with Brady's family, to be tight with them in a way she'd never managed with our parents—because they were stuffy nerds who never looked up from their textbooks—and that didn't include me swapping fluids with Brady's brother.

I had a feeling it wouldn't make our first joint Thanksgiving dinner more special.

Mav climbed in and slammed his door shut, reversing out of the lot at a speed reserved for race car drivers and cops with no fear of tickets.

Or really horny dudes who'd forgotten they were supposed to be babysitting his brother's dogs tonight, not looking to get some himself.

I couldn't fault his thought patterns.

We didn't talk. No banter. No insults. No radio. He focused on the road and drove with single-minded intensity, his broad wrist thrown over the wheel. Broad everything on that guy. Shoulders, thighs, cock —not my usual word for that part of the anatomy, but the dude had some girth.

His phone buzzed through his dash, and he silenced it with a flick without reading the name. Just swatted the call away like a fly.

As if he had more important things to do.

Like to zoom along the road that led up to the highest peak in town, shielded on both sides by more trees than seemed possible. We might as well have been heading into the forest.

I'd never actually been to Lookout Point, since I had no need to star watch or make out with random dudes who didn't have access to an actual bed. But I had to admit I approved of his choice.

I did not want to get railed in front of three curious dogs. Especially one with a pink bow who tended to bark at the slightest provocation.

I preferred to be the one hitting the high notes, thanks.

He turned into the clearing then shot across it at the same high speed, braking just before a drop-off that offered a truly stunning view of the moon glittering over the wide dark bowl of the lake. Then he undid his belt and turned toward me, his jaw seeming utterly rock hard in the shadows. "No more bet. No more games. It was idiotic of me to make that bet in the first place."

"It was. But I still want all those benefits you offered me for winning."

"Like getting to live next door to me?"

"Yeah. And stopping by without a bra to borrow some sugar."

He reached across the space between us to undo my seatbelt. "You make me crazy, you know that?" His voice had gone deeper and huskier, and my quivering thighs had no objections.

"I'd say the crazy is mutual." I wet my lips and tried to gather my scattered wits. "Look, we need some ground rules here."

"We do. First one is no more talking or else I'll cover your mouth with my hand and make sure you can't."

My breath stalled in my throat. We weren't having sex yet. We had to be rational and cover all potential bases before he said stuff like that to me. Or before I spontaneously came in my panties. My past had taught me to never assume anything and never to skip any steps—

"So fuck me already."

That step had not been on the board before right now.

His expression changed in an instant, turning wolfish as I caught a glimpse of those sharp white teeth. I barely had time to breathe before his fangs sank into my neck—

I let out a rough exhale as I realized he had not bitten my neck to drain my blood—no more Mav-as-vampire sketches, thanks subconscious—but had yanked down my shirt to suck on the skin

49

between my neck and shoulder. His other hand found its way into my hair as he tugged me closer, and it wasn't until he yanked that I realized he'd pulled out my hairband. The crazy mass tumbled around my shoulders and into my face. Even into *his* face as he made a noise that verged on a growl and buried his face in my curls.

"You smell like sex. Like fucking on the beach with a bonfire going and waves crashing and the damn best hamburger you've ever had on the grill." He lifted his head, his gaze piercing mine in the darkness. "Like summer never ending and the sunlight always staying right above you. The light never going out."

I couldn't speak. Hokey lines made me crack jokes. But that line wasn't hokey. It felt real and perfect and like we weren't just grabbing what felt good but what was absolutely *right* in that moment.

"You smell wet," I muttered, something I had not realized until that very moment.

Poetry was not my strong suit.

His dark hair was damp and curling with it, the longer pieces on top dipping into his eyes. His shirt was wet too, clinging to his ridiculously toned body. It was too dark to see much, but I knew what he was working with and I couldn't stop running my hands over his body.

"Where's your bulletproof vest?"

"Forgot it." He was already breathing hard. "First armed robbery."

"Better be first and last." I smacked one of his thighs and not just to feel the muscles bunch. Not entirely. "Don't do that again."

"Yes, ma'am. Now keep going with that strip search."

I swallowed a laugh as I started with his shoulders—dear God, those shoulders—and kept right on going, streaking down the front of him, basically feeling him up while I undid his buttons. *All* of his buttons until his shirt was hanging open and revealing his white undershirt beneath.

So very cop-like of him.

I wanted to grab his undershirt between my hands and rip it open, but he had other ideas.

Like yanking me across the front seat right over the console into his lap.

He groaned as I landed just right to cradle his length. Hastily, he jerked back the seat and hiked up my shirt, drawing it over my head and tossing it into the passenger seat. He didn't so much as take a breath as he sculpted a finger over the delicate lace cupping my barely-a-handful breasts. But I would've thought they were worthy of a goddess by the way he was devouring me with his gaze.

A quick flick of his agile fingers and the lace flew open, exposing me—and for the first time ever, I had the craziest urge to cover myself. Not because I didn't want him to see me, but because it felt like somehow he could see entirely too much too soon.

Flirty, wild Vanessa had been replaced with a fumbling, not quite steady version. Somehow he still seemed to want me just the same.

"You're just like I knew you'd be."

When I would've asked what the hell that meant, he leaned up to suck on my nipple, applying a level of suction that managed to empty my head of every single thought. All I could register was mind-erasing pleasure.

He squeezed my other breast in his big hand while he rocked up into me. A light show was going off behind my eyes. It wasn't even an orgasm yet. I was just burning up and over-sensitized in a way I never had been before.

I wasn't even fully aware of reaching down for his belt and yanking it out of its loops. Or of opening the button of his uniform pants and dragging down the zipper before I scooped him out of his boxers, wrapping my fingers around his width.

"Fuck, you're a big boy."

His laughter filled the truck. "*Boy?* You're not that much older than me."

My eager explorations came to a halt as I jerked up my head. "Wait, what? I'm older than you?"

"Tab's just about my brother's age, and he's three years older than me, so I figured—holy shit." He gasped as I fought to get down my jeans and panties so I could tuck that big cock between my thighs—

my very damp thighs—and rub against it like I hadn't gotten any in a very long time.

And I hadn't. Not like this.

"I like cougaring you," I murmured as I bounced against him, not entirely sure I was giving him the right kind of friction but not really caring since it was absolutely right for me.

I'd make it up to him later.

"Can't say I have a problem with it either. Jesus, woman, what do you do with those thighs? Squeeze walnuts for a living?"

"No, I draw vampires like you and monsters with double dicks. Oh, yes, right there." I could barely speak between pants.

He wasn't even inside me yet and I was so slippery with need I could barely keep up my rhythm. I didn't even have a rhythm, not really. It was a lot of rocking and rolling and balancing myself on his tensed shoulders while we both aimed for glory.

Mostly selfishly. We wouldn't win any awards for giving, but we were using each other for our mutual satisfaction quite happily.

Then he upped the stakes by rubbing his calloused thumb over my swollen clit. I shot upward, hitting my head on the ceiling an instant before our simulated fucking became very real, and he surged inside me.

Or I pulled him in me. It was like a force of gravity neither of us had to alter to make happen. It just did.

His groan of pure ecstasy would live in my head forever. I couldn't even moan. Every molecule of my body was focused on the drenching heat consuming me as he drove in and out, one hand still working my clit while the other gripped my hip for balance.

I couldn't help him beyond bracing my hands on his magnificent chest and just riding the wave while the need inside me grew bigger and bigger until there was no withstanding it.

I didn't warn him. I couldn't.

The only thing I managed was to cover his mouth with my own, so the first time I tasted his kiss was as I was quaking around him. His tongue battled with mine and then his arms banded around me as he jerked me up and down in his own pursuit. I would have bruises tomorrow and I welcomed them, just as I welcomed the bloom of blood on my tongue when he nipped me as he reached his own peak.

His noises of satisfaction filled my ears as I slumped against him, our heartbeats slamming against each other through the walls of our chests.

Wild, frantic, crazed. Just like us.

My lips curved almost against my will as he cupped his big hand against my head, turning my face against his shoulder.

Suddenly, reality hit me with a slap, and I shrieked. "You weren't supposed to come inside me!"

His puzzled frown would've been cute, as would've been his sleepy expression, if I wasn't on the verge of a panic attack. "I wasn't?"

I knew the moment he understood. Shock and horror filtered through his expression, and he shoved me back, nearly toppling me off his lap. There was nowhere for me to go except backward into the steering wheel.

Hard.

"You're the one who was rutting against my bare dick. I'm only human."

"Yeah, remember that when you're saying the kid isn't yours." The punch I landed hit him squarely in the gut.

Just then a sharp knock sounded at the fogged up window beside me. Thank God it was foggy, since my arms weren't exactly the best cover for my very bare tits.

"Police! Cease and desist this instant."

SIX

My life flashed before my eyes. Or it would have had I not been fixated on the fact that Masterson had probably just gotten a free look at my girl's tits.

She wasn't my girl. Not really. I wasn't sure if she'd ever allow herself to be *anyone's* girl. Beyond that, it was freaking dark here with all the trees around. I'd chosen this spot intentionally. I hadn't wanted any nosy Covites—a word I'd just made up—to get a freebie glimpse of something they should have to pay good money for on Only Fans.

Not that I knew anything about that site. Nope, not me.

I was the totally innocent dude with my cock literally still inside Vanessa while she'd roughed me up and yelled at me.

And maybe, just maybe, I was still a little bit hard.

I was only human. This woman also drove me insane in the best and worst way all wrapped into one hurricane.

But Christian at the window pounding and threatening definitely killed a boner quick. In fact, he should just stand outside the Lookout Point all season long and people would drive right on by. Then again, it would hurt his ticket count if that were the case. Not that there was a leaderboard in the office, but if there was one, Christian would be in line for the championship title.

"Get the hell back. Give us a second."

The knocking finally ceased and he stepped back, his hulking shadow finally retreating from my truck. But not far.

I gritted my teeth and gently gripped Van's hips to extricate myself from the warm clutch of her body as discreetly as I could manage. She'd gone stone silent and way too pale, tightening her arms around her torso as if she couldn't do anything else. I wasn't exactly feeling good about this situation either, but I was pretty sure something more was going on with her beyond just getting caught naked on my lap.

This situation was plenty fucked up for both of us, but something felt really off.

After cleaning up as best as I could with the napkins in my console and tucking myself away, I reached up to cup her cheek.

She didn't react, just kept rocking herself.

Her eyes locked on mine. "Get him out of here." Her voice was scratchy, like a record that had been played over and over again. "Please."

Rather than grabbing for her shirt off the passenger seat, I leaned up to drag off my button-down uniform shirt and wrapped it around her. She didn't fight with me, just tugged it tight to her chin. I cupped her face and waited until her gaze focused on mine. "I will. Just give me a minute with him, and we'll get out of here, okay?"

She nodded and for one frightening second, I thought her teeth were chattering. The truck was still steamy hot from us and the humid September night, so I knew she couldn't be cold.

I still couldn't imagine tough, smart talking Vanessa ever afraid, but she had been earlier. For me. That still blew my mind.

Why she was so scared right now, I had no idea. Normally, she just flipped Christian off, so it wasn't as if she feared getting ticketed. I didn't even think an arrest for public lewdness would faze her.

But I didn't understand any of this insane night and now wasn't the time to try to unpack it.

Right now, I had to protect my damn job.

"Here, come on, Pocket Plus. Into the passenger seat. Just wait for me, all right? I'll be quick."

Awkwardly, she clambered off my lap and dropped back into the passenger seat, taking advantage of her petiteness to draw her legs up to her chest. She cocooned into herself before my eyes.

I reached out to touch her hair, desperate to bring her back to me —to bring back the feisty woman I'd known all these months.

But Christian wasn't having that and knocked again. "Let's go, Romeo."

I hissed out a breath and raked a hand through my hair. "Be right back, baby."

She didn't seem to hear me. Good thing, or else my nuts would be hanging in her bus as a rearview mirror ornament.

I checked my zipper was where it should be and climbed out, slamming the door with more force than I'd intended. This dude deserved a karmic beatdown for harassing people who just wanted to find some sexual joy in their day.

It wasn't as if my ass had been pressed against the window or something.

And I was officially lust-drunk because typically, I would've agreed with Christian. Public lewdness was not appropriate. People had beds at home, and they should use them.

But I couldn't go home, since I was spending the night at Brady's—

Oh, shit, Brady. The dogs. My head whipped back toward my truck. Wait a second, I'd left the dogs with Van and she'd been with me almost all night. So had she left them alone?

Fuck. Fuck. Fuck.

Yeah, you did that too. How much more can you regret about this night, wise guy?

Christian was pacing back and forth behind my truck, his steps staccato on the blacktop.

Before I could speak, he pointed at me. "You know better."

"Yes."

"Yes? That's your response?"

"I'm not going to make up lame excuses or try to wiggle out of what's coming to me. I know the rules, and I broke them. It's inexcusable."

"You're absolutely right."

"So give me my citation and we'll get going."

Even in the dark, I could see Christian's puzzled expression in the light from his headlights. "There's no reason to be a martyr."

"I'm not. I just need to get outta here." I crossed my arms over my chest and tried not to cast a worried glance toward the truck. "Leave her out of this. This was my idea."

"Man, you're going for full-on hero mode tonight."

"Give me a break, Christian."

"I'm trying to." He took out his old school notebook and slapped it against his palm. "Contrary to popular belief, I'm not a heartless asshole."

I nearly laughed, but I figured now wasn't the time to push my luck.

"If I write this up, the Chief will get involved. It'll go on your official record, and as the newest cop in the department, that won't look good for future promotions."

"Yeah, no kidding. But I did the crime, I'll do the time." I cleared my throat. "On paper. Not like in actual jail."

He let out a short laugh. "I didn't see anything, by the way. I knew this was your truck and had suspected this would occur after," he scratched his bearded jaw, "the incident at Qwik Pump."

I wasn't a man who flushed normally, but my neck was on fire now. Thank God for the darkness. "Just write me up, and we'll get moving."

"That's not necessary. You know, I caught the Chief out here with Bee once."

I glanced at my truck again, torn between wanting the deets—so that I could take comfort I wasn't the only abject moron to get caught with his pants down, literally—and wanting to make sure Vanessa was okay.

I didn't have any clue what was going on with her.

Had I hurt her? Been too rough? I hadn't exactly checked my strength at the end there, and she was so small. I'd slammed her into the steering wheel, for fuck's sake.

I ground the heels of my hands into my eyes, recriminations pouring through me like burning lava. What the hell had I done, bringing her up here? Treating her like some random hookup when she was practically family?

"I'm a fucking moron."

"Not arguing," Christian said pleasantly. "But you're not the first, and you won't be the last. The Chief's been where you are. And so have I."

I dropped my hands and stared at him. "What?"

"High school. Girl of my dreams. Hormones and all that. She got pregnant, and she never spoke to me again." He pocketed his narrow spiral notebook and stared off in the distance. "Make it right."

I watched him take a few steps away, his footsteps crunching on a spot that had been ground into gravel by too many sets of tires. "Wait. What about the citation?"

"I'm not playing the asshole this time," he called back, already climbing into his cruiser.

I was tempted to chase after him. How could he not write me up for something I deserved to be cited for? I hadn't earned any second chances.

Not with the department and not with Van.

How the hell could I make this up to her? Obviously, this had been absolutely the worst move.

Here I'd acted as if she was going to fuck up my life by moving in next door, and now I'd clearly fucked up hers. Somehow. I mean, beyond the obvious of bringing her to Lookout Point for a quick fuck when she deserved so much more than that.

Stiffening my shoulders, I moved back to my truck and yanked open the driver's door, bracing myself for whatever I might see inside.

Instead of the quiet, shellshocked, nearly motionless Vanessa I'd walked away from, she was dressed in her shirt and mine was tossed carelessly on the driver's seat. And she was scrolling on her phone, cackling as if nothing had happened.

"Bet he got an eyeful, huh? Depending on how he liked the view, that might help me with my backlog of tickets. Or not. I'm not exactly my sister in the nature's bounty department." When I didn't respond, she glanced up. "Cat got your tongue, GQ?"

I climbed into the driver's seat and shut the door, then gripped the steering wheel and stared straight ahead at the lake, shimmering with moonlight in the dark.

As much as I was tempted to rush home to the dogs, I couldn't leave Vanessa on her own after whatever had happened. And if I let her stay closed down like this, I had no illusions I'd ever be able to pry open the locks on her vault again.

If I even could now.

"Tell me what happened." I kept my voice soft and forced myself to relax my grip on the wheel.

"What happened? Pretty sure we did the deed and the angels sang and then we got busted." Her casual tone rankled. "What's your take?"

"My take is that more was going on than you admitted."

"Oh, really? As if you coming in my bare pussy in a town like Crescent Cove isn't plenty enough." She tossed her phone on the dashboard with a snap of her wrist.

I shut my eyes. I'd kinda forgotten that part in all the rest. "I didn't mean to. I didn't mean for any of this."

"Yeah, well, don't sweat it. After you drop me at my vehicle, I'll stop at the drugstore and make sure we're all good."

"What?" I stared at her. "What does that mean?"

Her laughter was too high-pitched. "Haven't you ever heard of a morning-after pill?"

"No."

"*No?*"

"No," I repeated flatly. "No pills. Nothing like that. If we made—"

"If *we* made anything, it won't be us handling it, so you don't get to decide. I need to get a damn pill."

"Look, it's your choice. I'm not saying it isn't."

"Thanks so very much."

Fighting the instant panic boiling in my gut, I rushed on. "But I told you I'd stand up. I'm not that guy, Van. I don't know who did you wrong in the past, but I swear to you, I'm not like that. I didn't intend to have sex with you tonight when I left my apartment, but somehow we went to that place. Probably when you messed up my head with all that worried about me crap. And you're so fucking beautiful and sexy and you make me stupid."

When she cut me a sharp glance, I took a breath. "Correction: I make myself stupid from wanting you. It's not your fault. This is my fucking fault, and I take full responsibility."

"Oh, stop it already. You didn't do anything that horrible. We were horny and forgot where we were for a few minutes. Not like plenty of other people haven't done exactly the same."

I didn't say anything. Just like with Christian, I didn't want any free passes. Tonight I was more than willing to marinate in my mistakes.

"Did that fucker give you a ticket?"

"I wanted him to, but no."

"What?" She let out a laugh. "You wanted a ticket?"

"It's my fa—"

"Maverick McNeill, you need to stop. Taking responsibility is sexy as fuck, gotta say, but it's only words until your actions back them up."

"I'm here. I'm not going anywhere. We live next door to each other. We're going to be family. This is my home, and I'm right fucking here." I jabbed the center of my steering wheel. "If it happens to you, it happens to me, and I don't want you to take a pill even though it's completely your right." I scrubbed my hand over my face, shocked that I couldn't breathe through the tension banding around my ribcage. "I just...don't."

"Why?" she asked softly.

"I don't know. I just don't. It probably won't happen, just because we assume it will. Lore or not, it doesn't happen every time. You know how wives' tales are. A lot of embellishment."

She snorted and reached for her phone. "Would you like a photo reminder of my sister and your brother's latest sonogram? They are living proof of that lore."

I couldn't believe what I was about to say. This proved that my lack of sleep was warping my brain. "Maybe if it's meant..."

She sat back, her hands fisting in her lap. "You can't mean that."

"Why not? You were worried about me."

"So that means we are meant to raise a kid when you actually tried to bet me to move away? That's crazy talk. You don't have to what, show up Brady or something here." She flapped her hands like a manic bird. "Not everything is some great romance. We can just fuck and let it go."

"First, I'm a dick who'll leave. Now you *want* me to leave. Which is it?"

"I don't want to deal with this at all. I know how this scenario goes, no matter what kind of pretty words you slap on it."

The band around my lungs rose to squeeze my heart. I didn't move for fear she'd clam up, and then I'd never know what she'd gone through. "How do you know?"

"Because I got pregnant in high school, okay?" The words burst out of her as if they'd been trapped inside for far too long.

I reached over and grabbed her hand, holding on even though it felt weird to touch her that way. Not weird bad, weird different.

I didn't know how being inside her could seem so right, so perfect, but holding her hand seemed impossibly intimate. She didn't pull away, just shot me a look that indicated she might at any time.

"Look, I'm not going for sympathy here."

My heart slammed in my chest. *Just take it slow, McNeill.* "Good. Offering an ear, not pity."

"Who says I need one?" She squeezed her eyes shut. "It was a brief relationship. We weren't in love. I had no clue what that even was. I just wanted to rip the virginity albatross from around my neck."

I couldn't stem my horror. "You got knocked up the first time you had sex?"

"Oh, God, no. It was awful, but it wasn't that heinous." She looked out the window. "More like the third time. Which was on like our third date. We didn't have more dates after that."

I laced my fingers with hers. Still, she didn't pull away. "If I call him an asshole, is that too close to sympathy for you?"

"No, it's the truth."

I bit my tongue on the rest of what I wanted to say. How could I take potshots at a high school student when I'd brought her here for a quickie without even the pretense of a date? I was years out of high school and I'd treated her no better.

My week of little sleep and extended sexless streak had turned me into a damn heathen.

But I could fix this. I *would* fix this. Somehow.

Starting by listening more than I talked.

"What happened next?" I asked quietly.

"Listen, you don't have to do this. We had sex, it was great, now you can drop me off. I won't get needy, promise. I pretty much just wanted you for your body."

It made me laugh. "Same goes. But I'd like to get to know you too."

"Why?" Her obvious confusion made my gut twist. "We both got what we wanted, right?"

I was beginning to think I hadn't even scratched the surface of what I wanted with her. And that would've scared the hell out of me if I wasn't more concerned about her than anything else right now.

She released a long breath. "I know I acted odd before. I'm sure I weirded you out. Hell, I weirded myself out. I just couldn't believe it could happen again." She blew out a breath. "All these years since, I've been so careful. No slip-ups. But I had to go off the Pill last year because it was messing with my system, and I stopped carrying condoms because I didn't need them."

"You too, huh?"

She glanced at me sharply.

"It's been a damn long time since I've been with anyone. Probably why I rutted into you like an untrained dog."

"Well, now, with that lovely description of our lovemaking, the night is complete." She squeezed my fingers. "If that was your untrained dog, what's your prized poodle? That certainly didn't seem unskilled to me, sir."

"Maybe I'll show you someday. After we do civilized things like sharing a meal and some conversation while I admire your eyes glowing by candlelight."

"Oh, Jesus, don't tell me you're a romantic. Amazing cock or not, if I'd known you were one of those, I'd have steered clear." She tapped her chin with her opposite hand. "Tab never said Brady was one."

"Who said I'm a romantic?"

"Candlelight? Hello? I can tell you High School Todd did not care about candlelight when he was feeling me up during study hall."

"High school was some years ago for me."

"Not as many as for me." She smiled convincingly enough that some of the worry inside me ebbed. "The cougar thing is kinda cool."

I shook my head. "You are the strangest woman I've ever met."

"And I like it that way. Why be a copy of someone else when you can be authentically yourself?"

"Got me there."

She tugged at a frayed string in the hole on the knee of her jeans. "When I realized I was pregnant, I went to his house. His dad answered the door. He must've told him to say he wasn't home because he stammered a lot before finally saying Todd had a lot of homework and couldn't come to the door. So I told his dad why I was there."

"Holy shit. You had balls."

She jerked a shoulder. "I decided right then and there that I wasn't going to be ashamed about it. I was only sixteen, but I didn't make that baby alone."

"No, you sure didn't. What happened then?"

"He told me it couldn't be his son's. Then when I finally got Todd on the phone, he also said it wasn't his."

"Fucker."

"Damn straight. He said it wasn't as if I had any proof, and besides, he'd heard I would do it with anyone." She jabbed at the hole in her jeans. "I hadn't been with anyone else. And after that, I didn't touch another guy for two years. Actually considered switching teams since I couldn't get pregnant with a chick, but unfortunately, I like male apparatus even when I don't always like males."

I moved incrementally toward her, and she jerked as if I'd just burned her with a flaming hot poker. "Can I hold you?"

"I'd rather if you didn't. It's easier to say all this when you're over there."

Swallowing hard, I nodded.

"I've never told anyone else." She stared straight ahead.

"No one?"

"Nope."

"Not even your sister?"

"Definitely not her. She would've been aghast. My sister was the life plan girl. I think she saved her virginity until college. She definitely wouldn't have flung it at Todd Miller."

I now had a full name for the faceless dude I wanted to plow my fist into. Over and over again. "She loves you. You supported her with the whole Brady thing."

"Oh, she would've supported me, but I didn't ever really relish the whole hapless sister role. Tab always was the one who had it all together. I was lucky if the dog didn't eat my homework two weeks in a row. And we didn't have any pets growing up."

"What happened to the baby?" I leaned forward until I was in her eye-line. "Whatever happened, whatever choice you made, I won't judge you. I promise. No one else was there, so no one else gets a say."

"I miscarried over the summer." She blinked quickly and then pasted on a wan smile. "Bet you expected something else."

"No. I didn't expect anything."

"It was super early. I didn't even make it out of the first trimester. Never showed. Never even missed a period because mine were always super erratic. If I hadn't taken a test, I never would've known."

"Why did you?"

"Because Tab started throwing up."

"Huh?"

"Not sure if you've ever heard how twins sometimes mirror each other with certain things. It's really weird. Well, I got sick a few days in a row, and I played it off as food poisoning. Then Tab started throwing up, and my gut told me it was something more."

"*Hmm.* Have you thrown up with her baby?"

"No. Thank God. But I did get headaches early on because she was running herself ragged. Ms. Super Competent, who insists on showing us all up because she can do everything flawlessly. Now she's met Mr. Perfect and is going to have the sweetest little family, and I can't be jealous of her because I love her to death and she deserves it."

"Also because you still hate men and are considering going the female route?"

"It is always an option." She glanced at me. "Thanks for not being syrupy. I hate that."

"I'm too impressed with how strong you are to be syrupy. Whatever that means."

She pointed at me. "Now you're verging on it, GQ."

I went for broke and let go of her hand to sling my arm around her small shoulders. She was so petite, so seemingly fragile. But so much strength lived inside her, more than I'd ever dreamed. "Hungry?"

"I could eat." She bit her lower lip. "I called Honey to watch the dogs. So Brady's apartment should still be intact. I hope."

"As in my sister Honey?"

"Unless you know another one."

I rubbed the sudden furious pounding in my temple. "This night is never going to end, is it?"

"Why?"

"You have a sister. Do you realize how much shit she's going to give me when we walk in together?"

"Umm…"

"Trust me it won't be pretty."

"Who said we were walking in together?"

"Me. Because if I'm getting us food, we're eating it together. I have Chinese left from dinner too." When she didn't seem interested, I gave her my most soulful expression. "Please? I could've been injured tonight."

"Man, you're gonna play that worry card to death."

"Possibly. So what do you say?"

"I say if you take out a candle, you're getting struck with it."

It felt so good to laugh. The ache in my head and shoulders bled away almost instantly. "I'll try to control myself."

"Good." She eased away from me to snap on her belt. "I hope Daisy's okay."

"Why wouldn't she be?"

"Honey said her belly was pink, and she seemed itchy."

"Huh, Brady didn't say anything—" As the memory returned, I thunked my head on the steering wheel. "The damn treats. There were notes. I didn't read them because I was running for the call. She's allergic to wheat. Fucking hell." I sat up straight and stared into the lake. "I hope I didn't kill my brother's dog. That would just be the capper to this night."

Vanessa reached out to rub my thigh. "I'm sure she's okay. Let me check in with Honey. I'm certain everything is fine."

SEVEN

EVERYTHING WAS NOT FINE, WHICH WAS HOW WE ENDED UP AT DR. Thorn's vet office at two-thirty in the morning.

We were sitting in the waiting room while Daisy was being examined. Maverick was testing his root strength. If he pulled on his hair any more, he was going to start losing it in clumps.

"I am not turned on by a man with male pattern hair loss, FYI."

Alas, he did not care what I found attractive.

"I can't believe I did this. He trusted me, and I poisoned his dog. I'm not fit to—"

"Okay, shut up. You have whined all night about your screwups, and frankly, it's pissing me off because how can I insult you if you do it first every time?"

He didn't smile, just buried his face in his hands. "I need some fucking sleep before I go psychotic."

"Now I see why you wanted me to drive." I rubbed his back, hoping I didn't sound as awed at that fact as I was. Especially since his jerk of a colleague had probably announced twenty times how I was the worst driver-slash-parker in all of town. "Tab's talked about Daisy's issues before. This shouldn't be a huge deal. Dr. Thorn will give her some meds, and she'll be all set. You'll just have to watch her for a couple days."

"Not me, my brother will. And his pregnant fiancée. Hope you had a nice overnight away. Now monitor your sick dog all weekend. You're welcome. Fuck." He leaned back in the plastic chair and spread his ridiculously long jean-clad legs, making me focus on an area of his anatomy I should not be looking at.

I clearly couldn't be trusted around it.

"Daisy will be fine. And look, you thought Honey would razz you about us being together, and she didn't say a single word."

"She's just biding her time. Once she knows Brady's dog will be okay, she will pounce."

"Oh, c'mon, Honey's sweet."

"Sweet and lethal. You don't know her like I do."

"She told me you guys are super tight."

"We are. I know of what I speak."

I had to laugh as I braced my head in my hand on the arm of the chair. I was worn out, but half of that was from worry for Daisy. It had been a long night on a couple levels, and I had other things to be concerned about too.

At least I hadn't promised him an answer about the morning after pill, though I had to admit, I was leaning toward not doing it.

Why, I wasn't even sure. His impassioned plea for me not to had influenced me, and I didn't want to let him down.

Which was just crazy.

And maybe I didn't want to let *me* down either. I definitely was not in the market for some accidental pregnancy scenario, but I also wasn't a scared, near penniless sixteen-year-old any longer. I was a grown woman with a very healthy bank balance. I'd even invested in property.

Right next door to my maybe baby daddy. How very convenient.

"Mr. and Mrs. McNeill?" A young vet tech with short blond hair approached us holding a clipboard, giving us a tentative smile as we both jerked to our feet.

COP DADDY NEXT DOOR

"How's Daisy?" Mav asked, his concern over Daisy overriding everything else.

Mine too.

"She's doing okay. Allergic reaction as suspected. Sorry we had you wait out here. We've had a bit of a shortage of exam rooms in the back since we started functioning as an overnight emergency clinic for the county. There's such a shortage of facilities equipped with skilled techs and vets that it's been difficult to accommodate everyone."

"Oh, that must be awful. I was surprised how many cars were here so late on a Friday night."

She tucked her hair behind her ear and flashed us a tired smile. "It's been challenging, but we all put animals first. Dr. Thorn especially."

"Yeah, he's been awesome with Francie. My dog," Mav explained as the vet cocked her head curiously.

"Another dog?"

"Daisy is actually my brother's dog. He's out of town, and I was supposed to be watching her and Pancake—" When I laid a hand on Mav's forearm, he blew out a breath and smiled. "Anyway, I appreciate you seeing her so late. She's really going to be okay?"

"She sure is. But you both can come on back now. Dr. Thorn is familiar with Daisy and has reviewed her file."

Mav surprised the hell out of me by reaching out to grab my hand. I was so shocked it took me a second to get my feet moving, but I didn't slide my hand away from his.

Maybe I'd gotten used to the feeling of his fingers tangled with mine in the truck. Or could be, we were just both tired and overwrought after a very long night.

Besides, it wasn't any big deal. Almost family members held hands. Sure they did.

Mere hours after they'd had truck-rocking sex.

Pretty sure that was a *Springer* episode in the making. Was that show even on anymore?

We trailed after the tech into the room at the end of the hall where Dr. Thorn was sitting with Daisy. Her exam had already been done, and the vet was murmuring to Brady's dog in a lyrical Irish accent that I imagined had charmed many.

"Nice to meet you, Dr. Thorn. We really appreciate you seeing Daisy so late and on such short notice." I leaned forward to shake his hand.

He smiled and shook with a firm grip. "Please call me Grant. Late night, Mav? I heard about that business over at the Qwik Pump."

Mav shook the vet's hand, as well. "It's been a comedy of errors tonight, without a whole hell of a lot of actual humor. But all that matters is that our girl is okay."

He crouched down to give Daisy a big hug. Her tail thumped excitedly, if a bit less enthusiastically than normal, and then she shuffled over to make sure she got a hug from me too.

I buried my face in the thick golden fur on her neck then gave her a smacking kiss. "She's a tough nut to crack. This won't slow her down, will it, sweetheart?"

"Nope, not for very long, once these steroids do their job. The Benadryl I gave her already is. She'll sleep well tonight," Grant said cheerfully as he rose and grabbed a couple of papers off the desk. "I'm not going to ask how this happened since mistakes can occur very easily. Just I know how particular Brady is with the instructions he leaves—"

"My fault," I said quickly, shooting Mav a look. He didn't even argue. The guy had bags under his eyes big enough to swim in. "It was just a chaotic night. Wrong treats were grabbed. I feel terrible. But we're so glad she's going to be okay." I bent to drop a kiss on Daisy's head and she pressed her cheek against my belly. Right then, I didn't mind the extra loving. "We can't thank you enough."

"No problem. And no charge," he added as he walked us back into the main office.

I clipped the leash on Daisy and we brought up the rear.

"No way," Mav argued. "This was an out of office hours visit."

"And where would we be without you and your brother serving this town?" The vet clapped Mav heartily on the back. "Take me out to lunch sometime, and we'll be even. Maybe with your brother too, since he's about to leave the single life behind."

"He's not being sent to prison," I muttered behind the now laughing and joking males.

I wasn't normally sensitive about such jokes. But then again, I normally hadn't had a night like this either.

I'd been careful ever since what happened when I was a teen. Tonight I'd played with fire, and I wasn't even taking the steps I could to ensure I didn't get burned.

Maybe Mav was just exhausted. He'd had a difficult night. Once he got some sleep, he'd probably see the wisdom of swinging by the drugstore for extra insurance.

And if he didn't, I still could make that choice.

A few minutes later, we were on our way home with Daisy snoozing mostly peacefully in the backseat. Every now and then, she'd let out a little whimper, which broke my heart, but driving Mav's giant truck required I have all my wits about me.

Needless to say, he hadn't been interested in retrieving my "traveling eyesore" so I could drive my own vehicle.

"Sure you can even reach the pedals there, Pocket Plus?"

"I did just fine on the way over here, didn't I?"

"Yeah. You did." And I would never acknowledge the warm glow his praise gave me, even over something so ordinary.

"Why didn't Christian give you a ticket?"

"He told me he'd caught the Chief in a similar position."

"He sure did. That was the talk of the town winter before last. There was even a sex bet. Oh, hey. Another sex bet." Evidently, we weren't the only ones.

"The Chief made a sex bet with his fiancée? Before she was his fiancée, obviously."

"*He* didn't make it, the town did. They were supposedly 'best friends.'" I did air quotes which made Mav growl for the two seconds my hands were off the wheel. My skin didn't tingle at that rumble deep in his throat.

Absolutely not.

73

"So the town made a bet they were really having sex, and people took sides yes or no. They ended up splitting the pot somehow because Bee was the one who spilled the deets. Or something. I was never real clear on the details."

"That bet still made more sense than the one I made with you."

I didn't argue. It was true.

"This town makes people nuts. Having sex here is basically a lifetime commitment unless you're somehow under the right star or use six forms of birth control or have avoided the water since the beginning of time." I felt marginally better when we turned off the winding dark road to the better lit Main Street of Crescent Cove. "I don't blame you for trying to avoid doing the actual deed, not that me moving away would save your precious dick from being tempted."

He braced his arm against the door and let out a long yawn. "No one's tempted me other than you in so long. Except maybe your sister."

I slammed on the brakes with a screech that nearly had Daisy tumbling off the backseat. "Excuse me?"

The jerk laughed. Actually laughed. "Not like that. Wow, you really think I'd poach on my brother's girl?"

Tentatively, I put my foot on the gas again, after offering a disgruntled Daisy an apology and a quick stroke. It had to be quick because my arms weren't long enough to easily reach her. "You tell me."

"I wanted what he has. I guess I still do." He yawned again and dropped his head back against the headrest. "For a few days, I kind of thought Tab must be the keeper of that slice of nirvana, because he'd never been about that life before her. But then I realized that it wasn't about her. It was about Tab and Brady and them being the right fit for each other. Not every key fits every lock. It's not meant to." He turned his head toward me on the seat, those dark entrancing eyes seducing me without words all over again. "I always did like playing with fire. Playing it safe isn't my speed."

I inhaled shakily and tried to focus on the road ahead. It was late and a fine misty rain had started, obscuring the road just enough that it took all my focus. I was tired and stressed and confused as hell.

My traitorous body kept offering up distracting signals that I had an extremely attractive man beside me in this truck, and if I wanted to, I could pounce on him again. Maybe even explore his body at my leisure.

But we still did not have condoms. And taking a chance again put things into another realm.

"So Christian was actually nice? Is that what you're saying?

"Nice diversion," he said dryly.

"You're tired. Who knows what you'll say before you get some sleep?"

"You do have a point." His hand crept across the space between us and he gripped my thigh. "Say you'll sleep with me tonight."

I smacked his hand and the asshole just laughed. Worse, it was that low, deep, melted molasses laugh that did obnoxious things to my heart rate, and I suspected he knew it. "Hello, we still have no adequate protection. How do you keep forgetting that?"

Did you not hear the man? He wants what Brady has. He wanted Tabitha, but she was taken, so backup Vanessa will do.

Before he could reply, my mouth buried me deeper. "If you think you're going to use me for some breeding kink you've developed, tough cookies, pal."

"Breeding kink?" He doubled over laughing until he was wheezing. Until I couldn't help laughing too because he sounded like a drunken hyena. "What the hell is that?"

"I'm not exactly sure, but I think it involves milk production."

That sobered him up quickly. "Van, I couldn't even give my brother's dog the right treats. Do you honestly think I'm craving a child? What would I do with one? I don't have enough money to hire nannies to keep the thing alive."

I was almost disgusted at myself how swiftly I softened in his direction. And it kept happening. I was beginning to think I was pathologically unable to stay irritated at Maverick McNeill.

"I think you see your brother happy and want some of that."

"Don't you?"

"Yeah." It was easier to admit than I'd expected. "Tab was always the good girl who sat home. I never had to worry I was going to lose her to a guy because she was all about work, period."

"You aren't going to lose your sister. Just like I'm not losing my brother. They're getting married, not moving to Cambodia and never coming back again."

"Yeah." I wrapped my fingers around the wheel. "I guess you're right. It's just going to be different."

"That's definitely true. And with all the marital activities ramping up this month, that's going to be driven home over and over again."

"Ugh. Yes." Now that my worry for my furry family member was in check, a new one was intruding. I didn't do worries, dammit. I hated them. "That damn Jack and Jill shower is coming up soon."

"How's the planning coming?"

I slanted him a glance. "I have a Post-it note with game ideas and I invited everyone."

"Not true. I never got an invitation."

She snorted. "As if you'd come."

"I might. I'm still offended I wasn't asked."

"I'm sure. Write me up as a member of the sucky sister Maid-of Honor committee."

He squeezed my thigh again as I turned the wipers on high to combat the sudden deluge. "I didn't mean I wanted to have sex with you again."

"Oh, thanks."

He chuckled. "Can't please you, can I?"

"You already did earlier, but gotta say, it's much more likely when your mouth isn't involved."

"You only say that because my mouth hasn't been involved with you. Yet." His thumb rubbed against the seam of my jeans, creating sparks along my inner thigh. "I've been sleeping for shit all this week. I blamed you for that too, ever since you moved in next door."

"Sure, that's me. The cause of all the world's ills."

"So I wanted to see what it'd be like to have you next to me. Maybe

76

I could get some damn rest then." His thumb inched higher. "No sex. Though if you're looking for a little foreplay chaser to send you off into dreamland, I could probably be convinced."

"Sounds like you need the foreplay chaser more than I do. I sleep like a damn baby."

He didn't know I was lying through my teeth, and hopefully, he never would.

"Why doesn't this surprise me?" he asked wryly.

Someone who didn't have any issue with sleeping was Daisy, even after my surprise slamming of the brakes. She was still sawing them off when we reached Brady's apartment building. We had to poke her several times to get her up. Mav was about to carry her inside when she roused herself from the seat and dragged herself out the door with a grumble after Mav clicked on her leash.

She promptly showed her displeasure over being awakened by peeing on Mav's tire.

I couldn't hold back my laugh. "What is with you and dogs peeing on you?"

"I prefer my tire over my shoe. Besides, after what I put her through tonight, Daisy owes me a few licks. Or puddles." He tugged on her leash and she trotted behind him to the side door. He locked his truck and we trudged upstairs to Brady's apartment, exchanging glances at the sound of raucous laughter.

He opened the door to find Mickey and Honey in their nightshirts —I must have missed them bringing in overnight bags—dancing on the sofa to *Dirty Dancing* currently on the TV. Pancake and Francie were curled up in Daisy's bed, conked out.

Daisy cocked one ear at the chaos as Mav unclipped her leash, then slunk over to her bed and rolled over on the two smaller dogs until they got the message and moved to their own beds. Then she was out like a light too.

Mav leaned forward to grab the TV remote and silenced the movie, making both girls groan simultaneously. Then Honey hopped down and hurried over to kneel beside Daisy, stroking her soft ears gently. "How's my sweet girl?"

"She's going to be just fine. She's on steroids and Benadryl. Should be no lasting effects."

"I called Brady."

"You did what?" I demanded. "They're supposed to be having fun."

"What they're having is sex, which they've had plenty of considering the baby." Honey rolled her eyes. "But Daisy was his first kid, so he deserves to know Mav was being Mav."

"Um, hello, he had to go to an armed robbery—"

"Van," Mav said quietly.

Honey put her hands on her hips. "Um, hello yourself, since when did you become my brother's defender?"

Since he treated me with more respect about my past than the damn baby's father did.

"Just saying. I was there. He ran out in a big rush with that scanner thing squawking."

Honey whirled to prop her hands on her curvy hips. "Yeah, he ran off, and *you* ran off, so where did you go?"

Heat raced up my spine, and I could feel my red hair screwing me over yet again. There was no hiding your emotions when you were fair with flame-colored curls and freckles to boot. I was probably the color of Austin's fire truck already.

"I forgot something," Mav said smoothly. "She had to deliver it to me."

"Oh, really? Something that took her hours to hand over to you? Since you two were gone forever then only stopped back here long enough to retrieve Daisy and take her to the vet."

"Yes." He didn't so much as blink. "You should be in a better mood after pizza and dance marathons."

Honey plopped on the couch beside Mickey, who'd been silently watching us as if we were a tennis match. "I'm in a great mood, now that I know Daisy is okay. Brady isn't mad, by the way. He was just concerned how the chain of babysitting had gone from Mav to Van to me and Mick."

"He'd just had sex. It was the ideal time to tell him." Mickey leaned forward to pop a pepperoni in her mouth. "Also, I sort of hate that we've talked more about sex in the last five minutes than I've actually had it this year."

"Girl, same." Honey bumped her shoulder into Mickey's. "I should've taken Daze to the vet. At least I would've gotten halfway to a spontaneous orgasm listening to Dr. Thorn's sexy accent."

Mickey laughed. "You know it's fake, right?"

"What? It is not."

"I'm telling you it is. He just uses it to pretend to be charming." Mickey shoved in more pepperoni. "I'm not fooled."

"You're officially a weirdo, Michaela."

Mickey did a dramatic flop back into the couch cushions. "You'll see. One of these days, I'll be proven right."

"By who? The accent authenticity police?" Honey smirked. "Besides, who cares? Dude is hot."

"Says you."

"And I say doth protest way too much."

"Thanks for helping out." Mav lifted his voice over the still squabbling besties. "We're stealing the rest of this pizza."

He snagged a couple of plates from the stack the girls had put on the coffee table and loaded both with some slices. My stomach picked that moment to growl, since I'd forgotten to eat dinner other than a vending machine candy bar when we arrived at the vet's.

He glanced at me over his shoulder. "Grab the 2-liter from the fridge?"

I nodded silently and offered Francie and Pancake some pets before I followed him into the kitchen. He grabbed a stack of napkins and kept going down the hall to the bedroom while I opened the fridge and stared at the contents as if the wilted lettuce, two pitted oranges, and soda bottle held the world's secrets. The girls totally ate my leftover Chinese.

Why was I still here? Why hadn't I asked him to drop me off at my vehicle and headed home before this became weird? It was bound to. We'd had sex, for God's sake, and we barely knew each other beyond the occasional rude comment.

Having pizza and going to sleep together sounded like a couples' activity. Or at least a friends' activity, though I didn't sleep in the same bed as my pals unless there was a severe overcrowding situation.

And none of my friends had exceptional thrusting power and biceps for days. Unfortunately.

When I couldn't stall any longer, I grabbed the soda and wandered down the hall. I'd just give him the soda, snag a piece of pizza, and ask Honey to drop me at my vehicle.

Then he could get some rest.

The words were on my tongue as I walked into the bedroom and found Mav lying on his stomach on the bed, clad in only his boxers. He was digging into the pizza with impressive gusto, but he paused to look up at me with the glow from the TV flashing over his face. His dark hair was a disordered mess, and he had pizza sauce on his cheek.

My foolish heart did a swan dive right into his greasy hands.

"Problem?" He gestured to the TV. "Don't know if you like this show."

I loved *Family Guy*. It was funny and not too complicated for my tired brain. And I really wanted his pizza and to flop down next to him on the bed to eat and laugh and just chill out.

But was anything really that easy? Especially with a dude I'd let come inside me?

That fact kept flashing in my brain like a giant warning sign. Except it was too late for warnings. All I could do now was not compound the situation and hope for the best.

I held out the 2-liter bottle and he grabbed it in his big hand. "Forgot the cups."

He shrugged and uncapped the bottle, taking a long slug before he passed it to me. I did the same and climbed up on the bed to grab a piece of pizza off the second plate.

What was the harm? It was late. I could always leave early in the morning.

"Do you have to work tomorrow?"

"No, I have the day off, thank fuck. I could sleep for a year. If I can." He put away his third piece of pizza and looked longingly at my plate.

I laughed and pushed a slice at his mouth. He took it gratefully then polished it off in just a few bites. Soon after, I ate my second slice.

Comfortable fatigue flowed through me as I stretched out my legs and relaxed into the pile of pillows.

"Aren't you going to get more comfortable?"

"You mean naked?"

"If that's what comfortable is for you." He waggled his brows. "Brady has an old T-shirt you can borrow. Or wait, I have an extra one in my overnight bag." He was up like a shot to rummage through the duffel on the chest at the foot of the bed. He tugged out a soft, worn shirt that smelled of detergent and all the sex pheromones one conflicted chick could ask for and tossed it my way.

Then he turned around to face the TV, giving me privacy to swap mine for his. Even though we'd already had sex.

I am not going to get mushy toward this man. Nope. Am not.

I pulled off mine for his and then tried to shake off the goosebumps I'd gotten on my arms just from wearing something he'd worn. I stood to yank off my sneakers, socks, and jeans and dragged his shirt down as far as it would go.

It was basically a dress on me.

"All set," I said cheerfully, dumping my clothes on a nearby chair.

He turned back and even in the dim light from the TV, I could tell how his jaw locked as he took me in. "That looks a hell of a lot better on you than it ever did on me."

I waved off his praise and climbed back into bed, pulling the covers practically up to my chin. I didn't get what my deal was. Normally, I wasn't shy sexually. And I hadn't been earlier either. But I was still so unnerved by the risk I'd taken, I just couldn't get to that place again in my mind. I wasn't sure I could even if he double-bagged.

Not until I understood how I'd acted so impulsively in the first place.

He grabbed the now empty plates and pizza box and set them on the floor, and then he got back in bed. But he didn't slip under the covers. Instead he stretched out beside me with his head on his palm, close but not too close. At some point, he jerked upright after his arm started to droop, so I brushed a hand over his soft, thick hair and nudged him toward my lap. With a sheet and a light comforter between us, it seemed safe to cradle him there, especially when he immediately drifted off to sleep.

I took advantage of the moment to sketch my fingers over the sharp blade of his nose and his full lips, keeping the pressure almost nonexistent so I didn't wake him. He was sleeping so soundly that I didn't think he would've noticed if I'd pinched him.

Clearly, he needed his rest.

Poor guy. Finally wore himself out enough to get some sleep. Sex did have its benefits, that was for sure.

Even if it scared you shitless afterward.

EIGHT

 Maverick

I WOKE IN HER ARMS, NOT THE OTHER WAY AROUND.

Her small arm coiled around my waist from behind, and as soon as I shifted, I realized her face was tucked tightly against my neck. I wasn't sure how she could breathe.

I was definitely having issues with breathing all of a sudden too. Her firm breasts pressed against my back, and she'd slipped her leg between mine so I could feel the full length of her against me. Her skin shouldn't have been *that* silky.

And she smelled so good. No wonder I'd dreamed of the beach. All she needed was some cocoa butter lotion to complete the theme.

Parts of me really, really liked this situation. But I was ignoring those parts.

Rolling my shoulders, I took stock.

I felt...good, as if I'd actually gotten some decent sleep. My eyes weren't gritty, and my head didn't ache. Which meant this was already a much better day than the rest of the week had been.

Minus last evening before I'd started to second-guess my behavior. Encouraged down that path by Christian Masterson, of all people. What did he know? He'd been single for years, according to town scuttlebutt.

But my gut said I'd messed up with Van in any case.

She expected the worst from men. I wanted to show her we weren't all pigs. Even if I'd acted that way from the jump.

First, with my stupid sex dare, then by mauling her as if I'd just gotten out of prison. Never mind the whole lack of adequate foreplay the very first time we were together.

It didn't even matter that she'd come. She deserved better. The real question was how to convince her of that without scaring her away.

Since even candles posed a threat to her, I couldn't ask her out on an actual date. The mere thought of such a thing had never occurred to me before right now, but then again, I'd never been inside her before last night.

I'd never spent a whole night with her laughing and eating pizza and sleeping so much better because she was beside me than I would have if I was alone.

I'd never smelled her hair against my face. Never tasted her sweet lips. Never had her worry about me or defend me or wordlessly soothe me by rubbing my arm as I tensed up.

Or had her help me off to sleep by nudging my head into her lap. And not even for salacious purposes.

Or possibly get knocked up with your baby, assuming she doesn't head it off at the pass.

That was entirely her right. I'd told her my feelings on the subject —ones I fully didn't even understand myself—so now the ball was in her court.

Whatever she decided, I'd accept it.

Besides, Cove or not, it was highly unlikely she'd get pregnant the first time we were together. Superstition was one thing, but I wasn't the kind of man who avoided crossing in the path of black cats. I'd be more likely to adopt one.

Shit, I really had to pee. I'd been motionless for hours—

I leaned up to see Brady's clock. No way. 11:30?

How could that be possible? And why weren't the dogs begging for food?

I glanced at the closed bedroom door. I hadn't closed that. Had

Van? Were the dogs out there pacing to go pee? I hoped they hadn't gone in the apartment. That would be a deposit my brother wouldn't get back.

Fuck, Daisy would need more meds. I wasn't sure of the schedule for the steroids. I'd have to look at the paperwork Grant had given me.

Maybe the girls were still here. If so, I'd have to compensate them heavily. They'd saved my bacon.

Van let out a snuffling noise behind me, and I stilled, resigning myself to waiting a little longer. She deserved more sleep.

The door swung open, and a very large belly thrust herself into the room, followed by my brother leaning in and peering around the door. His shocked expression mirrored his fiancée's, now that I'd managed to look above the human beach ball to her face.

Hmm, this probably did not look good. Bright side, we were both clothed. *Ish?* I had on boxers. And Van had on panties and my shirt.

Okay, not exactly clothed.

Hurriedly, I put my finger to my lips.

Brady jerked his chin toward the hallway in the universal signal for *get your ass out here.* He probably thought we'd desecrated his bed.

This was most likely the last time I'd be asked to babysit the dogs. I couldn't say I blamed him.

As carefully as possible, I lifted Van's arm and slid out of bed, nearly rolling onto the floor in my effort to preserve her sleep. I made it to my feet without waking her and looked back to find her snoring into the pillow.

Even with the firing squad a few feet away, I couldn't help smiling. She was damn cute.

Especially when she was quiet.

I scratched my head and took a deep breath before nudging them into the hall and gently tugging the door closed behind me.

Brady wasn't worried about being gentle.

"What the hell is going on here?"

Tabitha poked him in the side. "I'd say it's obvious. Don't be an ass."

"In my bed? *Our* bed? Good thing we were getting another one. What the hell were you thinking?"

Irritation burned up my spine. "Can I pee before the interrogation continues or is that not allowed? Since apparently when I wasn't paying attention, you became my daddy. Am I supposed to answer to you?"

The door cracked open behind us. So much for letting Van sleep. "If he's your daddy, then my own sister is gonna be my stepmom, and that's creepy as hell."

Tab narrowed her eyes at her sister. "Really? That's your contribution?"

"You're the ones who stormed in here acting like asses because two grown people were sleeping. We were *sleeping.* Maybe that's equivalent to porn in your current state, and if that's true, I'm very sorry for the both of you." She nudged me out of her way and then gave Brady a hard shove on her way down the hall.

I did not watch her ass twitch under my T-shirt. I was not that sort of man.

Right.

"Is Daisy okay?" I asked, trying to see around them down the hall. It was entirely too quiet in the apartment.

"Honey said she's fine. When I called to let her know we were on the way back early, she offered to take the dogs to her place 'so they didn't witness the bloodshed.'" Tab did air quotes while my brother seethed.

"Guess you didn't realize they'd left during your sex-a-thon in our damn bed. No wonder you were exhausted."

I narrowed my eyes at my brother. "You are a prick."

"Takes one to know." He pinched the bridge of his nose. "The Chief filled me in on some of last night's events. Including the little notation on Christian's log that he located you and Van at the Lookout. Wonder why that was?"

I shrugged. "She wanted to sightsee."

"Oh, I just bet. You just couldn't keep your hands to yourself, could you? Even if you know it's going to cause family strife?"

"Brady, ease off. They didn't break the law, for Pete's sake."

"There's rules of propriety. Especially before the wedding."

Tabitha rubbed the side of her belly and turned on her heel. "Oh, you're just being silly now. I'm going to talk to my sister. Leave us be."

I turned to go back in the bedroom to get dressed. I was not going to be yelled at and accused of crimes I did and did not commit while wearing my boxers.

Brady followed, raking his hand through his hair. "Look, it's not like I don't understand...urges."

"Dude, you are pressing your luck." I bent to pull on my socks and then tugged up my jeans. Luckily, I'd brought some extra clothes in case they decided to stay an extra day.

"I'm just saying I get it."

"Do you? I really don't think you do."

"It's just you know how things are weird around these parts."

"Did you detour into Texas on your way to the hotel? What's with the Southern thing?"

He rolled on as if I'd never spoken. "I just don't want you to make a mistake, that's all."

"Thank you for the concern. But you seemed to handle your 'mistake' just fine."

Brady clenched his fists at his sides. "Why are you fighting me on this? You know you're not father material now. You don't even want to be, which is understandable at your age. And if something happens—"

Something akin to rage bubbled under my skin, which really pissed me off because my morning had started off damn close to perfect. "Why don't you let me handle my own life just like I let you handle yours? How about that?"

"You know, you always do this. Whatever I do, you have to run behind me. I just didn't think you'd do that with Tabitha's sister, man. This isn't the same as getting the same job. You could alter your life and hers forever."

I jerked up the zipper on my jeans and shoved yesterday's clothes into my duffel. "Hope you had a nice night away. By the way, thanks for your concern about last night's situation at the Qwik Pump, which I'm sure you also heard about from your little spies."

"The Chief is hardly my spy. And nothing really happened. You were fine. Everyone was fine."

"Yeah, but Van was worried about me. At least somebody was." I stepped around him and stalked down the hall to the kitchen where Tab and Van were sitting at the small table, drinking tea and talking in reasonable tones like actual adults.

Imagine that.

"I'm taking off." My gaze connected with Van's. "I don't want you to leave if you're not ready to, but if you want to come with me, let's go."

I didn't expect her to stand. "Just give me a minute to get dressed."

Tabitha watched her go. "Don't be too mad at him. He's just puffed up with his new father role. He keeps parenting everyone. Now he's even doing it to his fully grown brother."

"Yeah, nice try to give him that out. He's been accusing me of trying to be like him since I was a kid. And maybe I have done that one too many times. I always looked up to him. Always wanted to be just like my amazing big brother." I smiled wryly. "But looks like that isn't ever going to happen, so I just need to stop trying."

"You can't be like your awesome big brother because you're already awesome, Maverick."

I turned at Vanessa's voice behind me. She was already dressed and ready to go. She was even faster than I was.

When I didn't respond, she rubbed my arm as she spoke to her sister. "I'll text you later. Sorry if this kinda messed up your night away."

Tab grinned and waved her hand dismissively. "You kidding me? This was the biggest thrill I've had in weeks."

"I heard that," Brady called, walking down the hall.

Tab shook her head. "Leave it to my wild sister to shake things up." She leaned forward to tightly hug her twin. "I love you."

"Same goes." Van squeezed her back before she slid me a glance. "Afraid my wild crown is slipping, but we can pretend for now."

At Tab's puzzled expression, Van grabbed my hand and pulled me across the apartment to the door. She waved goodbye and then released a long breath as she stepped into the hall.

"God, family can literally be the biggest drag ever."

I laughed, long and low. "Ain't that the truth."

"Wanna run away together? Like just blow this pop stand. I even have the perfect vehicle. We can live in on the road."

Because I was almost sure she was kidding, I indulged her for a moment. And myself. "You expect me to live in that thing?"

"It gets surprisingly good gas mileage," she said soberly.

"Well, then, what the hell. Let's go." I drew my thumb over the center of her palm. "You cool with living with my dog in tight quarters?"

"We all have to make sacrifices. Depends on how you intend to make it worth my while." Before I could reply, she lowered her lashes. "How are you with car repairs?"

"The best. I have AAA on speed dial."

Her laughter somehow managed to erase the last few minutes as if they'd never happened. I knew I'd go over them plenty when I was alone in my bed, probably not sleeping yet again. But right now, I was feeling no pain.

Other than my growling stomach.

"You hungry?"

"I could eat." She kept pace with me down the hall to the stairs. "Oh, wait!" She gasped and covered her mouth as I looked at her in concern. "Should we wait until the cover of darkness and put on disguises? You know, find some faraway place to get a meal so people don't get ideas about us and get all in their feelings?"

"Absolutely not. I think we should go to the busiest place in town."

"The Rusty Spoon?"

"Sounds great to me." I nudged her down the stairs ahead of me. "Lead the way."

NINE

THE RUSTY SPOON WAS PACKED. THE VINTAGE RED BOOTHS WERE crammed with couples and families along with the occasional singleton. Most of them were more interested in watching us rather than perusing their menus or drinking their coffees or checking out the framed black and white photos of old time stars from years gone by.

The Zombies were playing low on the juke, and small town gossip always took precedence over just about anything else.

I ordered an omelet while sitting with my thigh pressed against Mav's in a booth right up front. Mav ordered his own omelet special with his arm wrapped around my shoulders and his nose nuzzled in my neck.

The Chief's fiancée, Gina aka Bee, so named because she never stayed still for a moment, tried to carry on a conversation with us. The entire time, she noticeably attempted to act natural in the face of this brand new coupling.

She was not succeeding.

"So, yeah, Mitch was desperate for servers, and I had a free afternoon, so I said I'd help." Bee dropped her pad and immediately tried to reach for it, but before she could, Mav bent to grab it.

"Here you go."

"Thanks." Bee let out a breath, red-faced just from bending. "I forgot I'm not in the same shape as I used to be when I did this job." She patted her big belly under her apron. "Time flies."

As she walked away, I shuddered. "Maybe we really should run away. This town is worthy of being in *Stranger Things* with all the babies. It's not natural."

His chuckle rolled over me. "I'm not driving that thing."

"It has a V-8."

"Okay, now you're talking."

"Also, a sleeping bag that has never been used by our siblings."

"Man, getting better and better. Can we get a disco ball for over it?"

"It'll clash with my lava lamp." I took a big bite of my omelet and followed it up with some of my biscuit. Butter dripped down my chin. Before I could wipe it up, Mav was turning my face toward his. He tipped up my chin as his thumb smoothed over my skin and his far too focused gaze met mine.

And there was nothing playful there. No hint of mischief as he did his best to make people talk. Just pure intention.

Or very *impure*.

"Do you have plans today?"

"No." The answer rolled off my tongue faster than my mind could keep up. My brain wasn't having any part of saying no to this man.

I'd hoped to work more on the romantic suspense stepback today. I wasn't happy with my preliminary sketch of the White Chapel alleyway that was part of a pivotal scene, complete with cobblestones on the street and fog whispering around the 1800s-style buildings. Setting was as important as the characters in this story, and I hadn't nailed it yet. The bones were there. But the feel was off.

And feel was everything.

"Good. Me either. Want to do nothing with me?"

"Sure. Do you always eat so fast?" I looked pointedly down at his empty plate so I couldn't wonder if this counted as a date.

It was just a do-nothing day. I'd had those before. Never with a man who could undress me with his eyes one moment and make me laugh like a fool two minutes later, but that was just details.

"I like food." He shrugged and grabbed for the rest of my biscuit. "Maybe we could get a bag of these to go."

"To-go biscuits aren't a thing."

"They can be. We get to decide what's a thing and what's not. We get to make our own rules, no one else."

"You just want to drive my bus."

"I kind of like when *you* drive *my* bus. Err, truck." His grin was quick and lascivious before he swiped at his mouth with his napkin.

I leaned up to lick off the butter streak at the side of his mouth. "Missed a spot," I said, easing back.

But he clamped his hand on my upper arm and held me in place as his mouth made quick work of devouring mine, ending with a sharp bite.

My lower lip vibrated. Not the only part of me that did.

"I missed too many spots," Mav murmured. "But I'm good at correcting my mistakes."

"I just bet. Didn't hear me complaining, did you?" I dropped a kiss on his beardy chin and pushed a forkful of hash browns at him since he'd literally cleaned his plate in record time.

He took the bite and chewed and swallowed, cocking his head thoughtfully. "That's true. I'd imagine you don't stay silent if you're not pleased."

I ate a bite of home fries. They were pretty good. "Finally, the dude buys a clue."

"I've bought a number of clues since last night."

"Oh, yeah? Almost afraid to hear which ones."

His phone went off with a text and he pried out his phone. "Honey wants to know if I can now take back my dog and if Brady can take back his, since babymoon sexfest and any subsequent bloodshed have presumably ended."

"Tell her she can talk to Brady herself until he stops acting like an ass."

His thumbs stopped moving over his phone screen. "You heard him?"

"Not all of it. He pissed me off too much. But when I walked by on the way to the bathroom, I heard some of his 'mistakes' talk." I added finger air quotes.

Mav's spine stiffened. "I'm sorry you had to hear that. He was way out of line."

"I get that he's in a unique situation, and he's just looking out for his little brother."

"He was throwing his weight around, and if I'd ever talked to him like that about his kid, he would've given me a black eye. As he should have. He's a grown man and can make his own choices, just as I can." He blew out a breath. "Not saying every one of mine is always winning, but I follow through. He should know that about me."

"I already do," I murmured, ducking my head when his stare got to be too much.

"You believe me?"

"You haven't given me any reason not to."

"I hope I never do." He went back to replying to his sister. "I told her we'll swing by to get Francie. Brady can do as he wishes with his dogs."

"She's gonna know you two are on the outs."

"Happens frequently, so she won't be surprised."

Even though I didn't know him that well, I could clearly hear how much he hated that fact in his voice. But I had my own sibling to contend with, though we were okay.

At least at this very moment.

"Tab surprised me," I admitted quietly. "She was so cool this morning. Didn't give me any crap about finding us how they did."

"Maybe that's why they work. Always a balance for the crazy."

"Think that's how it goes?"

He jerked a shoulder as he pocketed his phone. "One would hope."

I tucked my wild hair behind my ears, wishing I had one of my headbands to try to control the chaos. But I had some back at my bus, so I could ask GQ to swing by there on our trip to nowhere on our do-nothing day.

Well, other than picking up his dog.

"We should get a snuggy," I mused as I forked up the last of my eggs.

He almost spewed out his gulp of coffee. "A what?"

"You know, for the dog. Since we're going to be wandering all over, I figure hands-free for some of the time might be better. Then we can use her leash the other times. Oh, and I need to go to the yarn shop," I added before he could argue.

"You had an armful of yarn last night. What was it for?"

"I need more browns and pinks. Doing a neutral rainbow baby blanket for Tab, and the shower's soon. Gotta get moving." I sighed and tapped my short, functional nails on the Formica tabletop. "I need to go over my guest list and get decorations. And, um, maybe find a place for this shindig."

"You didn't book a place?"

"It kinda slipped my mind, okay?"

"How many are coming?"

"I don't exactly know. I have a pile of envelopes with RSVPs. I haven't gone through them yet."

His brows pinched together. "Good thing you're hot."

"You think I'm hot?" I waved it off. "I've been busy, all right? I'll figure it out. I always do. I'm great in the clutch. Or so I say while guzzling butterscotch vodka and pulling an all-nighter."

"Oh, man, jealous." Bee stopped beside the table. "I could use a drink after today. My feet are killing me. And my back. And my thighs. God, pregnancy hurts." She plastered on a smile. "Can I get you anything else?"

"Yeah, tell your baby daddy to stop sharing my business with my brother." While I gaped at Mav, he flashed Bee a smile. "Otherwise, we'll take the check. Thanks so much."

Bee cocked her hip as she pulled the check off her pad. "Since he's your boss, why don't you tell him yourself? I'm not your messenger girl."

I couldn't help snorting. *Go, Bee.*

"Also I know for a fact Jared isn't one for gossip, and he has a younger brother himself to boot. So if he told him something personal about you, he probably had good reason."

"Yeah, to start trouble for me."

"He wouldn't do that. This town can be a pain in the ass sometimes with everyone in each other's business, but mostly we all are just looking out for each other. I know you haven't lived in the town proper all that long, but you'll learn." She patted Mav's shoulder and snatched my card when I slapped it down on the bill before Mav could. He was too busy stewing.

"Thanks, Van. I'll bring this right back." She headed up the aisle, her soft-soled shoes squeaking on the scuffed black and white floor tiles. Many pairs of feet came in and out of here in a day's time.

I could only imagine the gossip already circulating about us. By dinnertime, we'd be the hot topic in town—unless we already were. We'd probably been spotted up at the Lookout by more than just Mr. Tightass. It was quite the active spot for residents. I'd just never gotten to partake.

Nice view too. And I wasn't talking about Mav under his clothes, although that was true as well.

"You never told me exactly why Tightass spared you a ticket. Was it just because he figured humiliation with the Chief was better?"

"No. The Chief's been up there too." His voice was distant as if his mind was somewhere else entirely. "Why did you pay the bill?"

"Because you're going to be jobless soon due to you being a known Lookout fornicator." I made a *tsk*ing sound. "Very unprofessional, sir."

His quick grin lit me up inside. "I don't mind you calling me sir."

"Yeah, and I wouldn't mind being called Beyoncé, but reality is a tough pill to swallow. Thanks, Bee," I said quickly, raising my voice in the hope she had not heard that *sir* bit.

Playacting for the crowd was one thing, but sexual innuendos were an invitation to my private life I had no intention of handing out.

"No problem. Don't be too hard on the Chief. He cares."

Mav grunted and thanked Bee and she wisely went to the next

table. He might be a wholly decent dude overall, but he was the poster child for stubborn. I knew that already and I barely knew him at all.

Even if it felt as if I did in a way I didn't fully understand.

"I'm paying for dinner." He waggled his brows. "And breakfast tomorrow."

"Cocky bastard."

Those sharp eyeteeth made a quick appearance in his grin. "Confident, not cocky."

"You really planning on running away with me?"

"Let's see how the day goes." He tugged me with him out of the booth, which gave me the ideal view of his perfect behind.

His chances of that breakfast were good tomorrow, even if full sex would probably not be on the table. But I enjoyed avoiding reality as much as the next woman.

Especially when my co-star in this little bit of insanity was as irresistible as Maverick McNeill.

Our first stop was to get ice cream across the street at Rolling Cones, Ivy Ferguson's ice cream truck stationed behind Macy's coffee shop, Brewed Awakening. Which I swiftly realized was a bad idea without one of my headbands. Ivy tried to help me out with one of the scrunchies on her wrist, but my wild curls could not be contained attractively in a scrunchie. My topknot was akin to a small bush.

A comparison that made Mav laugh uproariously at my expense. But I got him back by making him take me back to my bus before we picked up Francie.

The bus was still a work-in-progress in many ways. The exterior had its share of missing paint and cosmetic defects, but I had faith that with some hard work and dedication, its true beauty would emerge.

From Mav's narrow-eyed stare, I wasn't sure he could see my hazy vision as he studied it from behind.

"You can't see the potential?"

"I forgot my glasses."

"And you call yourself an artist? *Pfft.*"

"Actually, I call myself a cop with artistic hobbies." His smart-assed grin dimmed a little as he tapped the cloudy back windows. "Can you even see out of these?"

"Sure." I shrugged. "The van swap was a little uneven, but there's so much about this bus to love. The canvas awning is retractable along the side, providing the perfect place to get some shade on a hot day. Like on the beach. I have a small portable grill and—motherfucker!"

TEN

VANESSA

HIS DARK EYEBROW SPIKED. "YOUR VOCABULARY IS AMAZING."

I stomped around to the front of the bus and snatched the piece of paper I'd noticed tucked under the windshield wiper. "Does he ever take a day off?"

Mav plucked the ticket out of my hand with a windy sigh. "Yes, and he gave us our free pass already. What number is this?"

"I don't know since I never intend to pay them. I have a bag partially full. He can suck my—"

Mav laid a finger over my lips. "Don't offer him things you haven't given to me yet. I can also write you tickets, you know."

"And you can also never get one single solitary sexual favor from me again."

"Trying to unduly influence an officer of the law is punishable by fine and possible jail time." He stepped closer until the toes of his sneakers bumped mine, taking every advantage of our height difference to gaze down at me with one of his molten stares. "I'd hate to see you cuffed."

"I feel like that is a lie since you keep mentioning them." I cocked my head. "What makes you think I'd be interested in such games?"

"Hope?"

I had to laugh. How one man could be so irritating yet sexy as hell with that boyish streak that ran a mile wide, I did not know. "Keep hoping, pal." I patted his chest just for the chance to cop a free feel. And I felt zero shame over it. "Want to come into my palace?"

"Do I have a choice?"

"Sure. You can stand out here in the blazing sun while I get changed and fix my hair."

"Get changed? You carry a bag of clothes around with you?"

Apparently, he'd failed to grasp the reality that except for the occasional nights with friends or crashing with my sister or at my parents' place in Syracuse, I *lived* in the bus.

Sure, I showered and made food elsewhere, but mostly, it worked for my needs.

Just as I'd mostly lived in the van before. Tabitha wasn't exactly privy to that either, since I took showers when she wasn't home. I hadn't really hidden my living situation, but she assumed I had an actual place I was fixing up and just hadn't shown off yet. I kept talking about the she shed I intended to build on my new property. But I was reasonably sure she didn't get I'd be *living* in it, not just using it for yarn and a cool drafting table and whatever else most chicks put in those things.

Maybe a cabinet for hard liquor.

"It's good to be prepared." I opened the door of the bus and waved him inside. "After you. Make sure you duck."

"Holy crap, I feel like I'm back in tenth grade," he muttered, climbing the steps. At the top, he braced a hand on the ceiling and looked around in a mixture of wonderment and shock. "You actually do have a sleeping bag in here. I thought you were messing with me."

"Nope." My voice was unnaturally cheerful to combat the argument I knew was imminent. "All true. Sit on a cushion. They're surprisingly comfy. And grab a crystal if you feel moved to. All the cushions have pockets with a crystal inside."

He slid me a look. "So you're woo-woo like Lu and Tab?"

"I'm woo-curious." Since he wasn't moving, I chose an orange cushion with sodalite in the pocket and hooked my iPad into the charging station.

Which naturally knocked out my amigirumi vampire from where I'd tucked it.

He picked it up, turning over the tiny crocheted figure, his dark brows knitted together. Then he spotted the small cube next to the bed with its top half tipped off, revealing, um, many more little figures inside.

"Stress relief," I said with more of my false cheer as he rooted through them, though I had not given him permission. He didn't seem to care. "I curl up in bed and watch some YouTube on my tablet and crochet until I can sleep. Some nights it takes longer than others. Plus, I have this blanket to finish making." I pointed to the other cube on the other side of the bed with the blanket spilling out.

He didn't so much as look up.

Evidently, his interests ran to small dolls and animals and handcuffs. What you learned about a person after spending the night and the next day with them, even if all you did was sleep.

Well, we hadn't just slept. But we hadn't needed a bed for that. Or to wait for the darkest part of the night. Just past sunset had been fine.

He pulled out a small frog in shades of green with a tiny crown on its head. "I'm taking this one."

"It's not a dog toy." I tapped my chin. "Though I could make some of those. Too bad they don't like catnip. I can fill it with batting and some of that scrunchy stuff that makes noise and add some scent. Maybe bacon. Though catnip would be easier. Is there a bacon essential oil?"

He plopped down on a cushion across from me and shook his head. "Your mind is a circular and impressive place."

"Thanks."

"I'm not sure it was a compliment, but this frog is cute. The vampire too."

"Glad you think so, since he was modeled partially after you."

"What?"

I nodded. "You were in my thoughts and I had a...vampire-adjacent project so next thing I knew, you and the vampire were one and the same." Against my better judgment, I grabbed my tablet and opened my photos folder where I'd saved a jpeg of Mav the vampire. It wasn't as if I was coming clean about my other drawings.

Yet.

He took the tablet, his forehead dented with more creases by the minute. "You sketched this?"

"Yeah."

"You're really good. Where did you learn to draw like this?"

Briefly, I told him about getting started with fan fiction and all the rest, but I stopped before my hobby turned into a paying gig. Though I couldn't help taking back the tablet and scrolling to one of my favorite monster sketches for some fan art I'd done for an author who'd commissioned it for a book box.

The dude was huge, blue, and had two penises of remarkable girth.

Mav's eyes widened to the point I nearly giggled. "This is what you're comparing me to?"

"I did that years ago. That one's not based at all on you. Sorry. But if the price is right, I can draw yours."

"That price will never be right. So you get paid to do these?"

See, this was what I got for showing off. "Um, sorta. So what do you think of the place?"

"Where's the lava lamp?"

"In transit."

"Sure. Does your sister know you hang out in here a lot?"

In that moment, he sounded exceptionally like a cop. A stern, unbending one. Rather like Mr. Tightass with extra smolder. "My sister knows what I tell her. And I don't tell her much."

"Finally, the truth emerges."

"I'm a grown woman. Isn't that what you said to your brother today?" I winced. "Minus the woman part."

"I get it. I'm all about woman's rights. This town is exceptionally safe—something I take pride in—but I don't feel good about you sleeping in a bus parked all over town."

"Hardly all over town. I use parking lots or RV pull-offs or

COP DADDY NEXT DOOR

sometimes I go for ambiance and park at the beach. You should be thrilled I now have my own driveway to park in."

"Thrilled isn't the word I'd use."

"Oh, right. Eyesore." I couldn't quite keep the hurt out of my voice.

He studied me for a moment. "It's not that bad. Just needs a little spiffing up."

"I have all these ideas and drawings. Let me show you." I shifted around to dig into my cubby that held my bus layout schematics. They were constantly changing since I was always fiddling with them, but he could get the gist from what I had so far. "See, I'm thinking of making a window seat type area by the back doors—"

"What the hell was my brother thinking, letting you bunk down just anywhere?" The question exploded out of him as if he couldn't hold it inside a moment longer.

"Letting me? Uh, he has no say over me or my person."

"It's not safe." His jaw locked. "I saw the kind of flimsy lock you have on this thing. If anyone wanted to break in, you'd have no recourse."

"In the Cove? There's been like one murder here in one hundred years. But you think someone would try to take me out? My biggest adversary is a cop."

"Now I'm your adversary?"

"Not you, jackass. I mean your fellow officer." I shifted to tuck away my schematics. He was obviously in no place to appreciate them.

Mav reached out to grab the papers in my hand, gripping my fingers when I would've yanked my hand away. "You worried about me last night. Now I'm worrying about you."

"Dammit, that's not fair," I muttered, hating that my eyes prickled with heat. "I'm perfectly fine. I've always been fine living like this. I backpacked around the United States, and I never had any issues. You really think I will here?"

"I'll worry," he said softly, squeezing my fingers until I shook him off and put away my sketches.

He wasn't about to let me off the hook that easily. He knee-walked onto my foam mattress pad, leaning over me to take out the drawings

I'd just put away. Before I could respond, he tipped up my chin. "I want to see. And I want you to let me put a better lock on this damn bus."

"Maybe later for the drawings." I eased them out of his hand, and he didn't resist.

I shouldn't weaken in his direction. I couldn't let him sneak past my boundaries and make me care about him when this...whatever it was between us was just temporary and probably wouldn't add up to much.

But that worrying thing was damn intoxicating. I supposed we were alike that way.

So I offered him an olive branch.

"You can put on a new lock if it makes you worry less."

"Thank you." His thumb feathered over my lower lip. "But what would really make me worry less is if you spent the night with me. In my house."

My breath sped up. "In your bed?"

His thumb stopped moving, but somehow that focused pressure right in the center of my lip was even more erotic. "That's up to you." Before I could try to come up with a response, he grabbed the small pillow beside my knee. "This your work too?"

It took me a second to blink enough to actually see it and not just his gorgeous eyes tempting me to throw all caution to the wind.

As if I hadn't done that already.

"Yes." I cleared my throat and touched the flowers embroidered on the pillow in browns, rusts, and golds.

"Late night activity too?"

I shrugged.

"For someone who claimed to sleep like a baby, you have an awful lot of late night hours free for this stuff. And these are so intricate. Must be tiny ass needles."

"One can only stare at a screen for so long."

"Tell me about it. It's beautiful work. You're supremely talented— in more than one way." Still on his knees, he leaned forward to kiss me, his lips soft and hungry against mine. I could taste the chocolate ice cream he'd had and the rich flavor of him mixed with the sweetness made me inch closer, already wanting more. Our tongues barely touched before he was cupping my chin to draw me back. "So next stop is the yarn store?"

"Yeah. And the drugstore, then we'll go pick up Francie." His brow creased and I knew exactly why. "We'll get some condoms," I added, wanting him to know I wasn't going to sneak behind his back and take the morning after pills.

Even if I didn't know why he was against them. Or why I was abiding by his wishes.

Lately, gut instinct was driving my actions straight down the line.

When he shut his eyes in obvious relief, it was my turn to cup his chin. "I don't know why you're so set on not making sure we're covered."

"I'm not either."

"Maybe you're woo-curious too?"

He opened his eyes slowly as a smile curved his mouth. "Maybe. I just think nature should take its course, whatever that may be. But I'm good with condoms."

"Finally, we agree on something."

"Oh, Pocket Plus, I'm pretty sure we agree on a hell of a lot."

ELEVEN

 Maverick

IN A MATTER OF DAYS, I'D BECOME A LAWLESS MAN.

I signed my name to Van's ticket and slipped it back under her windshield wiper just in case Mr. Tightass—err, Christian—wanted to slap another on there for not moving.

I probably should've had her switch to the other side of the street, but the guy was clearly targeting her. Other people had missed the time to swap spaces for odd/even, and she was the only one on the street I'd seen with a ticket.

Granted, she was also the only person driving a mint green school bus with peeling paint and a vinyl rainbow peace sign on the side, but still. Incongruous was not a word meant to describe Vanessa Monaghan—or her vehicles.

We went to Every Line A Story, the newish craft store on Main Street. Surprised to find some woodworking tools in the back of the store, I picked out a cool whittling knife to add to my already healthy collection. Van was happily loading up her basket with yarn and needles small enough my eyeballs wept in sympathy.

The store was eclectic and colorful without being in your face. Each kind of craft seemed to have its own zone. Woodcraft and paper took up the back of the store. Colette, the owner, had several tables of craft books for both kids and adults, and more unique gifts were at the front. She switched up the window with seasonal decor to urge people to come inside. A sewing section with a wall of threads in every color imaginable was tucked along the side, and a sign above an ornate doorway welcomed people to find fiber arts and fabrics on the next floor.

I could tell Van wanted to go upstairs, but she was looking at her armful of sparkling flosses and seemed to mentally check herself from getting more. Now that I understood her a little more with the bus, I figured she was careful not to overbuy for her limited space.

Naturally, we got more than a few speculative looks, especially when she laughed and threw her arms around me at the checkout and I lifted her off her feet. We weren't even playing to the crowd. At least I wasn't. She was as light as air, and I'd discovered I liked holding her and possibly imagining all the other ways her size and agility could come in useful.

"I bet you can get in all kinds of positions," I murmured against her hair as she checked out.

She whacked me in the side. "Pervert!"

She did not use her indoor voice. I wasn't even sure she had one.

Disguising my delight with her was impossible. And eventually, we both had aching sides from laughter as we carted out her bags and headed down the street to the drugstore. I could feel the weight of the other customers' stares on my back and absolutely did not care.

We were having fun, something I hadn't had nearly enough of lately. I had a feeling she hadn't either.

"I feel like getting condoms is encouragement for your behavior," she said as we walked side by side down the crowded sidewalk.

Saturday afternoons were always busy, with everyone strolling by the picturesque lake or shopping and grabbing ice cream. Couples walking hand in hand, often pushing a baby carriage.

Hey, this town didn't hide its proclivities. And neither did I.

I tucked my hand in the back pocket of her jeans as I brushed a kiss over her hair. She turned her head to look at me and our mouths collided, setting off another round of laughter. People gave us a wide berth on the sidewalk, probably suspecting we were drunk or worse, and we stumbled into the drugstore far too loudly.

Especially since we were stopped about five different times by people wanting to say hi, and our purchases were kind of obvious. She let me buy the condoms, and she picked up a bottle of maple-scented shampoo.

At least it wasn't lube.

Then she tossed a jumbo-sized bottle of Advil on the counter. "Back hurts."

"I just bet." The teenager checking us out smirked.

I was tempted to tell him to go fuck himself. But since he was a kid, I held my tongue.

Barely.

Van rolled her eyes. "You men are all the same, whether fourteen or forty."

"I'm eighteen."

"Same difference." She snatched her bag and sailed out of the store without checking if I was behind her.

She leaned against the side of my truck, looking far too pale. "I must've slept weird or something. My back is literally killing me." She bent at the waist and took a series of deep breaths while I frowned and tried to figure out what to do.

At a loss, I rubbed her lower back in circles, which I'm sure also provided entertainment to those passing by on the sidewalk or gawking at us from inside the store. She straightened up and fumbled for the bottle of pills she'd bought, taking them dry.

My phone buzzed and I pried it out of my pocket. It was a text from my brother.

Brady: Tab might be in labor.

Maverick: What? How can she be? It's more than a month too early.

Brady: Yeah, we're freaking out, but her back is hurting badly &

**she thinks she's having contractions. We have a call into her dr.
She needs Van & she's not picking up her phone. Are you
with her?**

Swallowing hard, I glanced at Van, already aching for her.
Hopefully, this was just a false alarm, but she was going to be worried
sick for her sister.

I was trying not to be myself.

Mav: Yeah. Are you at your apt? We'll be there in a few.

Brady: Thanks, man. Look, about this morning.

Mav: Don't worry about it. Not important. Be right there.

I pocketed my phone and moved closer to Van, taking her by the
shoulders. Straight out was best. "That was my brother. He thinks
Tab's in labor."

Her cheeks got even paler, if that was even possible. "No," she
whispered. "It's too soon."

"It may be a false alarm. In fact, I'm sure it is—"

"You don't know that!" She whirled around, rubbing her back
frantically. "We have to go to her. I'm her coach."

"She'll be okay." I rubbed my hands up and down her arms,
unsurprised her skin was prickling with goosebumps despite the
warm day. Fear had a hold of her, and I wasn't even sure if she was
hearing me right now. Between her concern for her sister and her
own lost pregnancy, she had to be a wreck. "We'll make sure of it."

"You can't make sure of it, GQ," she snapped. "It doesn't work that
way. That nature you're so fond of decides who lives and who dies."
She swiped at her cheek, and I shut my eyes, hoping like hell she
wasn't crying.

But if she was, she'd shored herself up by the time she turned to
face me. Now only banked fire burned in her eyes. "Let's go. No time
for chitchat."

She yanked open the passenger door of my truck and had hauled herself inside before I'd taken a single step.

Her strength was inspiring—and a little terrifying.

I circled the truck and got in on the other side, quickly starting the engine and reversing out of the space. It was only a couple blocks to Brady's apartment from here and I made it there in record time, sliding into a spot near the side entrance. Van was already hopping down and jogging inside, not bothering to wait for me.

I wasn't offended. Her sister needed her.

I followed her upstairs and gripped her shoulders while she waited for someone to answer. She swayed against me as Brady flung open the door, his features tenser than I've ever seen them.

"How is she?" Van and I asked at the same time.

Brady *shh*ed us. "She's resting in the bedroom. Other than some pretty serious back pain, I think she's doing better. Her doctor thinks she might've been experiencing Braxton-Hicks contractions, not actual ones, thank God. It's just too early."

Van buried her face in her hands.

I rubbed her shoulder, not knowing what else to do. Over her head, I exchanged a glance with my brother. No one knew about Van's lost child, and considering how difficult all of this would be on her if Tab had any complications—though hopefully, this didn't seem to be one—it felt like they should.

But that wasn't my call to make, and she probably wouldn't feel comfortable telling Tab about it while she was pregnant, anyway.

Brady led us inside and we sat on the living room couch. It seemed too silent without the dogs there.

"Honey still has them," he said as if he could read my thoughts. "We were talking about going to get them when Tab started feeling off. Hey, you okay?" He crouched in front of Van.

She nodded fiercely. "I can feel her pain. It's freaky as hell. Her back hurts really badly."

Brady braced his hands on his thighs and huffed out a breath. "I had a feeling she wasn't being straight with me about feeling so much better. She doesn't want me to worry."

"But you are. And I am. And Van is. It's just part of loving someone." I rose and walked to the windows, unable to stay still.

"Speaking of that…" Brady came to stand beside me. "I was way out of line earlier."

"Now isn't the time—"

"I don't want this between us. I know we've had issues over the years, but mostly, we've been tight. Haven't we?" he prompted as I remained silent.

"You know we've had times we didn't really talk."

"Yeah. Guess I don't want to focus on those."

"Then don't."

"I didn't mean to insult you."

"Yes, you did, and you probably had cause. I'll always be your little brother, and you'll always think you know better than me. Most of the time, you might even be right." I shifted to face him. "But all that matters now is your woman and your little girl."

"Yeah. I just wanted you to know I love you. I needed to say it, okay?" He held up a hand. "Don't give me shit."

"Same goes, you pain in the ass." I pulled him into a hard hug and clapped his back before I stepped back. "Trust me, I've said plenty to you I've regretted."

"I just want you to be happy. That's all. Whatever form that takes." He glanced toward the couch, frowning as he realized Van had taken advantage of our heart-to-heart to disappear down the hall. "She's not easily contained."

"She's not contained at all. But Tab needs her. They need each other. So let them have some time."

Brady lifted his hands. "I won't stop them. Tab knows what she needs better than I do. Whatever that is, I'll give it to her. Seeing her in pain and trying to be so strong… Fuck, it almost broke me." He exhaled. "How am I going to handle childbirth?"

"You can have drugs too, you know."

He let out a low laugh. "Not ashamed to say that I'm probably going to need them. Good thing Strawberry is tolerant of my faults."

"Sure is. Hold onto her. Can't imagine there are many woman as generous as she." I forced a grin.

"I damn well am going to hold onto her. We're getting married soon."

"Well, yeah, early November—"

"We aren't waiting until the day after Halloween. I don't know why we even were going to in the first place. Tab likes the colder weather, but the middle of October is good enough and we can't take the chance of the baby coming early."

"No one says you have to be married before the baby."

The look Brady gave me could've curdled milk. "I'm flexible about most things, but not that. I want my wife to be my wife before my child gets here. Period. So we'll have the shower, then we'll do the bachelor and bachelorette parties or whatever you and Van have planned, and then right after, we're getting married at Mom and Dad's place. Reception there too. Good thing they have that big yard. We thought about asking to use your dock, but it's kind of short for a procession."

"Yeah." I didn't say anything else because my mind was reeling. I hadn't done a damn thing for the bachelor party. I'd just figured we'd go get loaded, and then I'd forgotten all about it. But my brother wouldn't want to be hungover on his wedding day. "How do you feel about strippers?"

Van chose that moment to come down the hall and shake her head. "Keep in mind whatever is good for the goose is better for the gander. So if you're hiring a flesh parade, we will too."

"You don't even have a venue for the—" At Brady's questioning look, I smiled tightly. "Okay, no strippers. We'll just bar hop. It's up to everyone to drink in moderation."

"Oh, gee, is it? I was hoping maybe you'd do something different."

"Yeah, me too, but unless I can actually think of that different thing, we'll drink and be merry." I lowered my voice as Van headed into the kitchen and stuck her head in the refrigerator. "We can still get strippers. Just don't tell the women."

Gripping a soda, she shut the refrigerator door and leaned against the counter that bisected the galley-style kitchen from the living room. The way she was leaning pulled her jersey tight against her tits, and no matter how I tried to lift my gaze to an appropriate level, my neck seemed stuck.

"Since you're newish here," she said to me, "I'll clue you in to my bat hearing. It's probably my number one bodily function."

I had no commentary for that one. What did she mean, I was new here? I'd been here since before Tab had come onto the scene. Maybe she meant new to her prime bodily functions.

I was pretty fond of some of them already. Particularly when she came around my dick.

"And like I said, if you want to perv on naked chicks, go ahead. Just letting you know my sister will also be perving on naked dudes."

"They aren't as easy to come by for women," my brother said smugly.

I raised a brow. I had to think he was trying to act super manly in front of Van, since I'd never expected him to go for strippers. Or else he was so desperate for a distraction from the baby concerns that he was ready to throw himself at some pasties rather than deal with any possible complications.

I couldn't blame him there.

"Trust me, I will find some if you do. I will find a fleet of them. Full nude if necessary."

Brady puffed out his chest. "No one said anything about full nude."

She shrugged and took a long drink. "Don't do the crime if you can't do the time. We aren't going to sit in a kumbaya circle while you whoop it up, pal. So choose wisely."

I patted Brady's arm as if I hadn't started this whole line of inquiry. "Yeah, be careful what you pick."

"Asshole," he said under his breath, but it held no rancor.

"How is she?" I asked Van instead of continuing to discuss stripper tit for tat.

I wasn't going to be able to book any on this short of notice, anyway, since I had no idea where to even find some. It wasn't like the Cove was a bustling city with strip clubs on every corner.

Besides, I'd only seen strippers once, in Vegas for my eighteenth birthday. I'd even gone home with one, fulfilling my most sordid teenage dreams. The fantasy had been pretty great at the time, but I was fairly sure she hadn't been too impressed with me because she'd neglected to give me her number when she ducked out the next morning.

Brady knew my stripper background, but obviously, Van did not. I suspected that was a good thing if I wanted to use those condoms I'd purchased with her.

Luckily, I'd learned a few tricks since my brief stripper days, though last night had not been my finest showing. I intended to make up for it big time.

Van didn't answer right away. Instead, she rooted around in the refrigerator and freezer, this time emerging with a pint of strawberries and a carton of ice cream I hadn't seen the night before. She started up the blender and whipped up some frothy thing that included the rest of her soda. She tested it with a loud slurp of a straw before dumping the mixture in a tumbler.

"She needs a milkshake. Van special." She gave the tumbler one more shake and spoke more softly. "She's really tired. Back still hurts. You better upgrade that bed in the new place, Officer Hot Pants."

I looked at my brother, who shrugged. "Believe me, we are. Definitely not using that bed again."

"We did not have sex in your bed. Though keep saying we did and we will for spite," Van announced before hurrying down the hall to her sister.

I grinned at my brother. "And for other reasons beyond spite."

"Think you might've bitten off more than you can chew there."

"Maybe, but I'll give it the ol' college try."

"I don't mean just her personality."

"Yeah, yeah, you mean playing with fire of the baby persuasion. Let's be real. It can't happen every time people have unprotected sex here, because the overcrowding situation isn't *that* bad."

"You had *unprotected* sex with her? Where is your brain?" Before I could answer, he shook his head. "Never mind. I know exactly where it was."

Since I'd asked myself that same question, I couldn't begrudge him. But I also was not interested in discussing this with him right now—or ever. Hopefully, we'd all move through this blip unscathed, and we wouldn't do something that risky again. "Go take care of your just-about wife. Or chill out while Van's in with her. I'm going to go pick up the furry heathens so our sister doesn't put a hex on us for ruining her Saturday." I pulled out my keys. "I'll be back."

As much as I loved my soon-to-be sister-in-law, all this worry about babies—both in utero and hopefully fictitious—was making my soul itch. I needed some fresh air and sunshine and to hug some dogs who didn't think I was a moron.

At least I was pretty sure they didn't.

"Okay. Hey, while you're out, I don't suppose you'd mind picking us up a few things? We ordered a small grocery delivery this afternoon, but we forgot some stuff and with current events…"

"Whatever you need."

"I'll make a list."

Barely, I resisted rolling my eyes, but then I remembered that my not reading the list Brady had left me for the dogs last night was how I'd made Daisy sick. So I supposed many, many lists was my penance, and I'd accept it stoically.

I was sure I'd get to make many with Pocket Plus later on as we planned the shower and the bachelor and bachelorette parties, and oh, yeah, whatever we had to do for the wedding.

Was it too early to go back to bed? I'd really enjoyed sleeping. Especially with that soft, curvy, warm body pressed into my back.

My front would be fine too.

I smiled weakly at my brother. "Lay it on me."

Five minutes later, I had a list stuffed in my pocket that reminded me of Santa's gift list—it just kept unfurling. But I headed out to the store with a promise I wouldn't forget anything, already wondering how long I could stay gone without anyone thinking I'd run away.

Probably not as long as I wished.

"Call if you need me," I added as I went out the door.

And I didn't even turn off my phone as I said that, so I figured I was now maturing at an extremely rapid rate.

Or else all the responsibility around me was rubbing off. Now that I had a house, I'd probably open an IRA soon and start thinking about rate of return and potential investments. I'd stop thinking about the kind of vehicle I wanted to buy for horsepower and consider what was best for a family.

Somehow I didn't shudder as I jogged down the stairs, but it was close. I was getting ahead of myself. Even if we were in Baby, USA, there were no guarantees.

I probably wouldn't have to think about being a father to anything other than one tiny dog for years to come.

TWELVE

SOMEHOW AFTER A GUY AGREED TO RUN AWAY WITH YOU, IT DIDN'T SEEM proper for said guy to disappear without so much as "see ya!"

True, we hadn't been serious about running away together. I wasn't that silly to believe that. But we'd slept together. Actual sleep had been involved.

We'd bought condoms. We'd flirted. We'd laughed. We'd made the town think we were horny for each other—and it hadn't been a lie.

And in the grand tradition of young males everywhere, he hadn't even stuck around long enough to tell me it had been fun.

Good thing I hadn't been getting attached.

So I did what I did best. I pretended as if I didn't care about him at all.

"C'mon, you're supposed to be entertaining me, not stabbing your hook into that poor innocent yarn." Tab nudged me with her knee.

We were both in Brady's bed, her under the covers, and me on top of them since I was hotter than the sun.

I was furiously crocheting a crossbody bag that I'd left at Tab's apartment. Since I'd just cleaned out my yarn over there last night, this had been the only work-in-progress I had left. I wasn't even sure I wouldn't have to take the whole thing apart later and start over.

But right now, it gave me something to do with my hands.

"Entertaining you? I thought you were going to be sleeping. Isn't that what your doctor said you should do?"

"He said I should rest. Which I am. Besides, as soon as you got here, I felt better."

"Probably because you beamed your pain into my back instead. Is that some new witchy trick of Luna's?"

"Oh, no, did I? And you were on a date. Your first date? I'm so sorry."

"If you don't stop angling for dirt, I'm going to tickle your ribs until you have to pee. Which should take about five seconds in your current state."

"What dirt?" Tab blinked innocently, her blue eyes far too like my own. "I'm just curious. I mean, whoever would've thought we'd end up dating brothers? Cop brothers, no less."

"I am not dating him. I would never date a cop."

"But you'd sleep with one?"

I sniffed. "Dating is another kettle of fish."

"You two seemed so close today. And he stayed right with you—"

"Yeah, until he didn't. Is he here now? No. He split. Vamoosed. For all I know, he's out scouting strippers."

"Huh?"

I sighed. I did not want my sister to know her soon-to-be husband was a pig just like all the rest, but I was fairly certain it came with their apparatus.

"They were discussing the bachelor and bachelorette parties."

"Oh, really? I guess it's necessary since we moved up the wedding."

"What?" My screech could've awakened the dead. "As if it's not soon enough already."

"Brady really wants us married before the baby comes."

I glanced toward her and weakened as she rubbed small circles on her rather massive belly. "Yeah, I suppose that makes sense. So how soon is soon?"

She winced. "Very. Shower in a week or so, wedding at Brady's parents week after that, depending how quickly arrangements can

COP DADDY NEXT DOOR

come together. Good thing we are just keeping it intimate and local people only."

I leaned back against the pillows. "Your sex life keeps me hopping."

She laughed. "We aren't getting married just to have sex."

"Obviously not, since you did it plenty without a license."

"Someone's snarky today. Look, I don't want to get in your business."

I sighed. "Since when?"

"Sisterly prerogative. Just Mav is not the settling down type." She held up a hand. "At least that's what Brady said. Don't shoot the messenger."

I snorted out a laugh. "We screwed up at the Lookout Point. What part of that sounds like 'looking to settle down' to you?"

She did her serious older-sister-by-two-minutes face. "I hope you're being careful."

"Obviously not, or we would've traveled across the country to swap fluids." I shifted onto my side and braced my head on my hand. "He was really sweet to me. Like he listened when I talked. He slept in my lap. He let me wear a shirt to bed and didn't try to grope me."

"Aww." Tab's face softened. "Well, except the no groping. I rather like being groped. Or I did before I was the size of a minivan."

I laughed and gave her belly a soft pat. "You're beautiful."

"Same goes."

"I don't know how to date someone. I haven't since high school." And I didn't detail how spectacularly wrong that had gone, although I probably shouldn't have given up my virginity so fast. Water under the very shaky bridge. "Not that we're dating. Just...I don't know how. And I don't think I knew that until I spent a day with him and discovered I really like him."

"He's a good guy."

"You think he's just like Brady, only taller. And hotter."

"Hotness can be debated, and if he's taller, it's like one inch. Maybe two."

"Let's not compare inches. You've got pregnancy goggles."

She giggled and swatted at me. "I'm not some expert here, but just try not to think about it too hard. Just have fun. If it's for a reason or a season, all good. Unless it ends up being way more than that."

"I think this is the first time in our lives you've had to give me that advice. Usually, I'm the one preaching the enjoy the moment crap."

"And look how it worked out for me." She gripped my hand. "Maybe it'll work out for you too."

"Right, so we can be some seven brides for seven brothers movie of the week deal."

"There's only the two of us, unless Mom and Dad have been keeping something from us."

"Nah. You know they broke the mold after I came rolling out." I tipped my head against hers. "I was so worried about you."

"And I was a wreck without you. You can't go more than a few miles away until this kid is born. You have to promise me."

I linked our pinkies. "Wild horses or fully erect penises couldn't drag me away."

We spent the rest of the afternoon giggling and watching movies and telling stories about our past, the more embellished the better. Brady came in bearing hot French fries from the air fryer at one point, which we gobbled down as if neither of us had eaten in years.

He did not mention his brother. I did not either. I also hid my phone under the mattress so I couldn't check it obsessively.

So lame, Monaghan.

Eventually, Brady announced he'd been called in, if Tab was certain she was okay. She said she was, so he suited up for work.

Tab waddled to her feet to chase after him with about fifty wifely admonitions to be careful and to watch his speed and probably more things I didn't catch. That was the life of a cop's wife—or girlfriend.

Or fuckee. Whichever.

Clearly, I was not cut out for that role, even in a small town like this. Last night had proven that without a doubt. Yet another reason it was good we were just messing around.

Or had messed around. Past tense.

Brady was on his way out the door when a flurry of knocks

followed by a spate of barking, both deep and high-pitched, signaled we had a guest.

The missing Maverick had returned with many paper sacks of food and an assortment of adorable dogs.

I hurried to help him with his bags, and when he mumbled he had more downstairs, I offered to go get them.

He looked at me, aghast. "You can't carry all those bags."

"Watch me."

I left him trying not to drop everything while simultaneously holding onto three leashes and arguing with my very pregnant sister that she couldn't carry even *one* bag.

Why did he have to be so cute while simultaneously being an ass?

Not that leaving without checking in with me was a capital crime, especially since he'd obviously been sent on an errand. Just...I'd missed him.

Lovely. Spend a day with the dude and I missed him after a few hours. Why had I ever come home to live near my sister? I'd heard the rumors.

Hell, I'd seen babyrama expand my own sister's waistline with the quickness. I should run far, far away.

Even if more and more, I wanted nothing other than to stay.

I hurried downstairs and had grabbed the last two full paper bags in the truck bed when Mav jogged down to meet me. He swiftly pried them out of my hands. As I opened my mouth to yell at him, he kissed me so soundly I couldn't even remember why I was annoyed.

Which naturally made him grin as he somehow jockeyed both bags under one arm and snagged my hand with the other.

"How's she doing?"

"Better than you would've been if you hadn't come back here."

He shot me a glance before he opened the side door and nudged me to go by him. "I knew you were the type to choose violence at the slightest provocation." He ran his tongue around his teeth. "Why does that turn me on?"

I had to laugh. "Pervert."

"I think that's going to replace GQ as my nickname pretty soon."

I shrugged. "Hey, earn the title, wear the name tag. Hey!" I glared at him. "You pinched my ass."

"I would never. Scout's honor."

"You were a Scout?"

"Hell no." He urged me up the stairs with his hand on the small of my back, still somehow holding onto the bags with his other arm.

In Brady's apartment, my sister was digging into a jar of pickles while the dogs circled her legs and stared at her with appropriately woe-filled faces. I had to laugh because Francie was leaning up on her hind legs, her pink bow precariously drooping as her little tongue lolled out.

"Figures your dog is the ringleader," I said under my breath, snagging a bag from him and dumping the contents on the counter.

Probably not the best move. A package of dog treats went sailing, ones that Francie apparently recognized because she pounced on them as if they were live prey.

"None of these are for you," Mav said, nimbly grabbing the package as Daisy came to investigate.

"She has a jar of special blueberry peanut butter biscuits on top of the fridge."

"Thanks." He snagged the jar and dispensed treats to all three of them, since Daisy's treats were super healthy and couldn't harm the other two unless they were allergic to the ingredients.

Then he started questioning my sister about her symptoms and making her laugh and just generally being irritatingly sexy as he put away the groceries in mostly sensible places.

I mean, he stashed the toilet paper in a lower kitchen cabinet, but he was just operating by rote by then.

No one was perfect.

He followed up that feat by asking what we wanted to eat and whipping up a super basic stir fry with lots of veggies and chunks of chicken in a delicious sauce.

"Only thing I can make," he said as he noticed me staring, leaning over to kiss me again despite my sister watching us openly while she ate water chestnuts as if they were M&Ms.

Pregnancy sure gave you weird cravings. Pass.

After we devoured dinner, Tab told us to leave. We ignored her, so she went to "rest her eyes" in the bedroom. I checked on her a couple of times over the course of the evening while we binge watched *Reacher* and ate copious amounts of junk food. She was sleeping soundly every time.

And maybe, just maybe, a girl started to get some ideas of a dirty nature. It would be a shame to waste perfectly good condoms.

I came back into the living room after freshening up in the bathroom—minus a shower, which I desperately needed—to find Mav scribbling in a notebook.

"Writing poetry?" I sat on the arm of the couch beside him, deliberately leaning forward so my shirt tightened just right.

He didn't appear to notice. "No, making lists for all the wedding shit we have to do in very little time. I looked at a wedding planning website." He studied his list instead of my breasts. If they were bigger, I wouldn't have to compete, dammit. "Honey, we're fucked."

I reached out to flick my fingers through the ends of his hair. "Fucking sounds nice."

He blinked. Blinked again. Then he looked up, finally buying a very large clue. "Your sister is just down the hall."

"So? Like you never did it next to Brady."

"Um, no, I did not. That's creepy." The tips of his ears turned bright pink. "The stripper doesn't count."

"More strippers. Here I live this wholesome life, and you're coveting sex workers to dance for you."

"They do more than dance. Also they aren't sex workers. Sex is strictly prohibited on the premises. After hours, however..." His Adam's apple bounced. "Are you not wearing a bra?"

"Check for yourself and see."

He swallowed again. "You had one on earlier."

"This is why you make the big bucks." I traced my fingertip over my nipple, biting my lip as it hardened under his stare. "If it'll make you feel more productive, show me your list."

"I'd rather show you something else first. C'mere." He tugged on my hand and I landed in his lap.

I discovered he might be slow on the uptake now and then, but some parts of him were instantly all thrusters operational.

He tugged the headband out of my hair and sent it flying before he fisted a handful of my curls and dragged my mouth to his. While we kissed, hands roaming all over, much as we'd done in his truck last night, he shifted me so I was straddling the bulge in his jeans.

When I moaned, he broke our kiss to clamp his hand over my mouth even as his hard grip on my hip worked me up and down over his erection. The pressure on my clit was just right, and I bit his fingers helplessly as the heat inside me exploded.

His eyes widened as he realized I wasn't just close to coming—I already had. But that burst of warmth had barely taken the edge off.

He cupped my cheek and drew me down for another kiss, his tongue streaking into my mouth as I fumbled between us to undo his button and zipper.

Instead of giving me the green light, he grasped my hand in his much bigger one. The way he dwarfed me was just one more turn-on in an endless list of them. "Let's go next door," he said in a low voice.

"What?"

"To your sister's place. We can leave her a note to text when she wakes up."

"So first our siblings think we desecrated Brady's bed, now we'll move the action to Tab's?"

"Who said anything about a bed? Pretty sure she has a working bathroom."

"I like the way you think."

Pancake picked that moment to trot over to the couch and lean up on his stubby legs to be lifted up. He could jump up if given proper encouragement, but he tended to look for lift service if he could con someone into giving it to him.

"If you come up here, you're staying here until we get back." Maverick's stern speech did not slow Pancake's frantic tail wagging, so he gave the dog a boost. He promptly wedged his way between us and climbed up Mav's chest to give him an enthusiastic tongue kiss.

I couldn't help laughing. "Guess you're popular with both species."

He grinned. "When you've got it, you've got it."

I scrawled a quick note for my sister then made sure the other two dogs were occupied with their chew toys. Pancake had promptly gone to sleep in the warm spot Mav had vacated.

I doubted we'd need long for this. We'd be back in no time.

Once we were next door, Mav told Alexa to play something I didn't recognize, and a moment later, low, seductive jazz heavy on the saxophones filled the room.

I stopped hopping around with my jeans halfway down my ass. "Music? We don't need music."

He cocked a brow in that annoyingly hot way he had. "Got something against it?"

"No, just don't need it." I sputtered out a laugh when he lit an incense cone in my sister's backflow burner. "What are you doing?"

"You said no candles. You didn't mention incense."

I turned my back on him and kept getting undressed. He was not going to deter me with his faux romantic gestures. If that was even what he was trying.

Then he came up behind me and wrapped his arms around me from behind and nuzzled my neck. "You must've really dated some losers if music and an incense stick make you mad."

"I'm not mad. Just we don't need the fuss."

"You sound mad." He nipped the skin between my neck and shoulder. "I told you that turns me on, so it's not having your desired effect."

"No, it's not. You're not turning off the music or snuffing out the damn incense."

His hands crept down to cup my ass, revealed by my lowered jeans. "Don't like the smell?"

The scent held a hint of plum with a smoky darkness that made my head swim. "No, it's fine. It just means—"

"Means we have a little more atmosphere than the front seat of my truck?" He moved around me, crouching to help take off my socks and shoes. Then he yanked my jeans the rest of the way off, nearly causing me to overbalance and topple to the floor.

"The truck had plenty of atmosphere," I said once the giggles from my near fall abated. "The view couldn't be beat."

"Neither can this." His big hands ran up my thighs as he fixated his attention between them. "Do you have some moral objection to me tasting you?"

THIRTEEN

VANESSA

I SWALLOWED HARD. "NOT IN THE SLIGHTEST."

He didn't hesitate. He slipped his fingers through my neatly trimmed curls, biting his lower lip as his dark eyes registered my wetness. He kept going, slipping into me so silkily I couldn't breathe.

His touch bypassed my still sensitive clit, but he dipped his head, lowering his mouth until his warm breath teased my hyper-aware flesh. I shivered and he steadied me with his free hand before he made good on his tasting promise. He flicked his tongue over the tight bud before he licked his way through his slowly thrusting fingers.

I absolutely could not come again this fast. He would think he owned my body or something. As if he could look at me just right and I'd shatter for him.

Worst of all, he wasn't far off-base.

I tipped back my head as he picked up speed, nearly toppling me again as he lifted my leg over his shoulder. "Hold onto me," he demanded in a voice I barely recognized.

I did as he said because there was literally no way I could remain upright while he devoured me unless I gripped his shoulder. Then his neck. And finally, his hair, pulling roughly without checking my strength. He hummed against me while his fingers opened me up and destroyed me stroke by stroke.

I couldn't keep from whispering his name. At least I hoped I whispered. I honestly wasn't sure.

Then I was begging, pleading, and probably threatening him. His response? He lowered my leg and shifted back from me, wiping his mouth arrogantly. Audaciously.

"Get back here." I gestured in case he didn't get my meaning. "You aren't finished."

He shook his head, running his tongue over his teeth. "You'll come when I'm inside you and not before."

"What?"

He leaned forward to lick my inner thigh, humming again. "Not like you haven't come already. I taste it."

I hated that my body betrayed me by shivering as he stood and did that whole looming over me thing while he undid his jeans. The muscles in his forearm flexed powerfully as he undid the button and lowered the zipper, then pushed down the denim and his boxers, kicking them off with his sneakers and socks.

His cock was even more impressive in full light. Thick and long and capable of rendering my brain useless.

Clearly, the bastard knew it as he fisted his length and dragged the ruddy head through my soaked folds. "But I do like when you beg. With your mouth and your eyes." He sucked my lower lip between his teeth. "And especially with this sweet pussy."

I kissed him back because I was pissed off enough that I didn't trust my mouth at that moment. I could tell him off later—after I'd come again. He was just contrary enough to leave me hanging.

He slipped his hands under my jersey, sliding up to caress my breasts while we kissed. His thumbs and forefingers twisted my painfully aroused nipples until I couldn't take another second and ripped away to suck in air.

And call him a few inventive names.

"Take it off."

I took off the jersey and flung it in his face. He grabbed me, hauling me up so that my legs had no choice but to wind around his hips. Even as he walked backward, I grasped his shaft and jerked it almost roughly between us. I almost hoped he came, effectively ending his little game of sexual torment.

Too bad I'd severely underestimated my opponent.

He carted me down the hall, moving with purpose as if I didn't have a grip strong enough to cross his eyes. He marched into the bathroom, turning on the light as he went. With one strong yank, he opened the shower curtain and deposited me in the shower/tub.

I turned to play with the dials. He got in behind me, tugging my earlobe between his teeth. "Stay just like that."

His hard cock brushed between my thighs as I turned on the hot water. Too hot, so that I yelped as it streamed over us. His hands found my breasts, and soon I was feeling no pain as I leaned back against him, on the verge of angling just right so he could slide home.

"Fuck, I forgot the damn condom."

His anguished voice made me laugh even as I felt the same annoyance down to my toes. "Hang on."

"Oh, I'm hanging." He dipped his forehead against the tile wall, looking entirely too pretty for a male despite his extra scruff from not shaving for a few days. His thick dark lashes were starred with water and his mouth looked deliciously soft and used.

Though I was still irritated he'd left me in the lurch, I couldn't resist arching up to plant a quick kiss on his full lips.

His eyes flickered open in surprise. Rather than letting me escape, he fisted my hair and delved into my mouth as if he'd forgotten our other plight entirely.

"I'd be happy here too," he mumbled into my mouth, gripping his shaft and sliding it up my belly. "Wouldn't even take long. Then I'd finish you with my mouth."

"Depends how quick you recover."

"Like lightning when you're around."

I sputtered out water as my giggle turned into full-blown laughter. He pressed his face into my hair, laughing just as hard as I was.

"Or there's always somewhere else available. No risk of babies back there."

From the way his eyes sparkled as he moved back, I might as well have just presented him with a gift-wrapped Kawasaki Ninja. "You are my damn dream woman."

"At least when it comes to sex." I licked his nipple and darted away.

Those kind of activities were for another day.

I leaned out of the shower, water spraying everywhere as I fumbled to get the cabinet open under the sink. It was hard to search from this angle—and definitely difficult to concentrate on the task at hand due to the thick shaft wedged against my back—but I kept my eye on the prize. I leaned forward farther, cursing my sweet, pregnant sister until I located the duck-shaped basket of loofahs.

"That's what you needed so desperately?"

"Well, I haven't showered since yesterday. A good loofah is important." It took all my willpower not to laugh as I rooted through the basket, finally landing on one lonely foil packet. "Score!"

"Hell yes." He grabbed it from me and had himself sheathed before I could take a full breath. Then he shifted us until the full brunt of the stream of water was hitting his back.

Chivalry truly wasn't dead, after all.

He bent me forward, pressing his hand into the small of my back until I was bracing my hands on the side of the tub. He took advantage of the position to suck on my neck while his fingers circled my needy clit. "Oh, yeah, still nice and ready for me."

Without warning, he pushed into me, his invasion from this angle stealing all of my air. I couldn't breathe without feeling him in what felt like every pore of my body. He was so hard and had stuffed me so full I couldn't even moan.

But he was making enough sounds for both of us, praising my pussy so fervently I would've laughed again if my thighs weren't quaking so hard I was having trouble staying upright.

He banded his arm around my middle, effortlessly hauling me up so that I had no choice but to brace my feet on the side of the tub. I had no clue what was up with this position or how he made it feel so damn good at this crazy angle. All I could do was hold onto his forearm and rock back against him in time with his thrusts.

"Rub your clit. Let me watch."

I reacted to his deep, demanding voice without thought. My own fingers were frantic against my clit, and I squeezed around him as the first tremor rolled through me. His hiss against my ear let me know he was just as close as I was.

I couldn't tell him I was on the verge. Couldn't do anything but go limp in his hold as he rocketed up into me one last time and sent my body into overdrive.

He bit down on my shoulder to muffle his shout as I reached my peak seconds before him. As his body shuddered around me, I reached back to cradle his head in my arm. Tenderness swelled inside me while he brushed kisses over whatever skin he could reach.

This time had ended far differently than the first.

He set me on my feet and eased out of me, then he disposed of the condom. After one last lingering kiss, he soaped himself up and did the same for me before rinsing us both off.

My knees were still boneless and I was pretty sure the smirking jerk knew it.

He got out and came back with a towel for me though he stood shamelessly, gorgeously naked, dripping on the bathmat.

"You don't have any tattoos." I continued examining him, pretending I was simply looking for ink and not just enjoying his muscles and all the rest of him.

If only he'd turn around so I could properly inspect his bitable butt.

"Just the one." He angled his hip so I could see the flame near his sin lines. "I got it when I started the ice sculptures."

"You're so talented. I admired them all over town last winter."

"Yeah?" Pride lined his voice. "I always had a thing for fire and ice. It was fun to see I could make actual things out of it, just not sad blobs that melted away far too quickly. I mean, the melting happens regardless, so I take pictures. Sketch my idea, then take photos to save it."

"You keep all the photos?" I used the end of my towel to dry my face and neck.

"Yeah."

I blew away a hank of sopping curls. "Can I see them sometime?"

"Sure, if you'll show me the rest of your sketches for the bus."

I nodded. "I will. I'm having John Gideon and his crew come out this week to start some of the bigger work on the bus, so you should have an idea of what it's going to look like inside before his crew is swarming around next door."

His forehead pinched and I knew he was thinking of me sleeping "outside" again. His concern for my safety was sweet, even if I didn't exactly know what to do with someone caring that much for my welfare.

None of this made any sense.

How could we just stand here basically naked after having sex talking like it was the most natural thing in the world? I wasn't one to have issues with my body—small as it was, my curves nearly indistinguishable, freckles everywhere—because I'd long ago decided I was damn near perfect just as I was.

If someone didn't like me for who I was, then fuck 'em.

Besides, from the way Mav looked at me, I knew he had absolutely no problems with any part of me. At least physically.

"I shouldn't have said it was an eyesore."

"Well, it's a work in progress. Sometimes it's darkest before the dawn." I flashed him a grin. "But while they're working on it, I can stay in Tab's apartment. I'm not sure why she kept hers while mostly living at Brady's for these past months, but maybe she couldn't break her lease. Never asked. Comes in handy for me."

"Or you can stay with me. In my house."

I didn't reply. *Say what?*

Briskly, he used another towel to dry my hair before swiping it over his chest halfheartedly. Since he was more concerned about drying me than himself, I grabbed the last towel on the rack and started rubbing it over his pertinent parts.

If I started with his very fine ass, who could blame me?

I'd rather concentrate on his backside than his offer for me to, what, move in for a few days? Even if it kind of seemed sensible, it was absolutely nuts.

Wasn't it?

My conflicted thoughts must've shown on my face because he tipped up my chin in that sexy way he had. "Did I hurt you? That position was crazy, but you're so flexible."

I forced myself to smile. "And tiny. I know dudes enjoy spinner chicks."

It was hard to think about sexual agility when the super hot, super confusing guy you'd just started having sex with asked you to move in, even temporarily.

Then again, it was just geography. We lived next door to each other. Why not do the logical thing? It didn't have to *mean* anything.

"No," I added. "Far from it. Well, my back a bit." With a wince, I rubbed the ache in the small of my back until he took over the task for me. "Still Tab's fault from earlier, I think. Being a twin is a trip."

"I can't imagine."

"I can't imagine not being that close to someone else, but it's definitely weird. When she was first pregnant, she was a little worried she was having twins—"

I stopped talking. My vocal cords might've gone numb. I was almost sure my brain shut down completely at that moment.

Our gazes connected and held. Then he bent to gather the used towels and shot out of the room, calling over his shoulder that he'd handle the laundry.

Right. Sure. As if *that* was the most important thing to worry about.

FOURTEEN

 Maverick

The following week contained multiple checks in the win column.

The most important was that Tabitha's baby stayed where it was supposed to be. Brady didn't say much about it, but his silence on the subject proved how worried he was. So in the grand brotherly tradition we shared, I made sure to tease him twice as much as normal to keep his mind occupied.

I had plenty of time to taunt him, since Van—and I—were spending a lot of time with Tab now that she'd been put on limited duty at work by her doctor. Her physician was concerned she was spending too much time on her feet, so she'd decided to cut back on her hours. Honey, Mickey, and Tab's other employees were all fully trained now and they were taking up the slack along with Van, who'd started going in bright and early.

I was well aware of this fact since she rolled out of my bed to get ready for work.

Our new schedule of spending evenings with Tab while Brady was at work and then going home to my place once Brady got off-shift seemed surprisingly natural. And most shocking of all? Though I'd always blamed women for being too chatty, she was positively quiet compared to me.

She was worried about her sister too. So I also teased her as much as I could to keep her from dwelling on possibilities, both for Tabitha and for us.

That talk included strippers.

In fact, Brady and I talked about them appearing at the still unplanned bachelor party so many times that Christian requested not to be invited. That way he could be on duty to ticket us for whatever lewd behavior we displayed.

He actually *did* have to be on duty, since the force was so small and Brady and I were roughly half of it. The Chief couldn't go either, for the same reason.

The Chief who laid in wait for most of the week before cornering me in his office under the pretense of asking details about the wedding.

I knew right away that was bogus. No reasonable male wanted to hear about a wedding that wasn't his own.

Even if it *was* his own, I suspected that was a mostly *don't ask, don't tell* kind of situation.

The Chief should know since he and his fiancée were currently planning his own. Yet again, it was vitally necessary they be married before the baby came.

"You know, maybe people in this town should consider getting married *before* having kids. Shotgun weddings are so 1982."

"So says the man caught at the Lookout with his sister-in-law."

"Almost sister-in-law," I said distantly before stretching out my legs. I was seated in the chair opposite Jared's desk and had settled in for a nice long lecture.

Apparently, I wasn't actually a grown man who could make my own decisions without guidance from the equally daft men around me who had also impregnated the women they were with before they were married.

Wait, not also. There was no also.

Had witchy Luna put some kind of weird mojo onto my house?

She'd probably sprinkled fairy dust in the corners while examining it with Tab and opened up my third eye or something so I was more psychic.

But if I was suddenly psychic, that meant I could intuit the future.

You're not intuiting anything, jackass. No condom frequently means two a.m. feedings, especially in the Cove.

"Besides, having a baby doesn't mean you have to get hitched. That's so old-fashioned. You can successfully co-parent without a marriage license."

"Thanks for the update, but I proposed to Bee quite a while ago, and she was not pregnant at the time."

"I'm just saying."

"Yeah, and I'm just saying you know better than to show your bare ass up at the Lookout."

I couldn't argue there.

"Technically, my ass wasn't on display," I muttered.

"Appreciate the bulletin. You're a decent guy, Maverick, and a good cop. I just want you to think about your actions."

"Did you give my brother this same speech?"

"He was never caught up at the Lookout."

I snorted. "Right. Because that's all this is about. Not you and everyone else in town thinking I need to be 'guided.' Even Christian tried to do it, and he's convinced I'm a moron."

"He thinks we're all morons. Half of the time we prove him right." Jared leaned back in his chair and crossed his booted foot over the opposite knee. "This town is special in a lot of ways."

"There's a newsflash."

"We all look out for each other here. That's the best part of a small town. Sometimes that turns into some gossip and drama, but overall, the nosiness is because we care. We're like one big family."

"You forgot the word dysfunctional."

He shrugged. "Who isn't dysfunctional in some way? That doesn't mean there isn't genuine concern and love behind what we do here."

"Along with a load of snoopiness."

"Which you encouraged last weekend at The Rusty Spoon, I heard."

"Did you get pictures too?"

Jared ignored me. "Beyond the basic lure of the small town, this one comes with a bit…more, I guess you could say. I'm not one to put much stock in wives' tales, but I can't ignore the evidence in front of me."

"That this town is hexed?"

Jared wheeled closer to the desk before folding his arms on the blotter and giving me a hard stare. "Is your brother miserable since Tabitha got pregnant?"

I blew out a breath. "No. He's been insanely happy, other than worrying his kid might try to escape its hatch early."

"And do I seem to be in hell since Bee got pregnant? Even though we weren't married yet?"

"No."

"Look around at the other couples in this town. Do any of them who've had an unplanned pregnancy and subsequently gotten married appear to you to be mired in the depths of despair?"

"Depths of despair is a little fanciful, but no." I held up a hand before he could continue. "Fine, fine, I get it."

"Do you?"

"I like Pocket Plus—Vanessa," I corrected, "a lot. It just seems crazy you can't date someone in this town without worrying some town curse is going to strike the chick's uterus."

Okay, so when you didn't use a condom with a woman of childbearing age, I supposed a curse wasn't needed. But that wasn't the point.

"Yet you still forged on. One has to commend your bravery in the face of such obstacles."

"Can I flip off my boss and not get fired?" I wondered aloud.

"In this case, if it makes you feel better, go ahead."

"Not worth it." I pinched the bridge of my nose. "Look, I know I messed up. Not just because this town is woo-curious or woo-leaning or just wooed-out, but because you shouldn't treat a woman so callously."

"I don't believe you'd do that."

"Oh, I have. I didn't take her out, I just took her up to the Lookout—"

"Christian told you about catching Bee and I up there."

"I kind of blocked it out. But if you talk about it again, it's going to take root, so I implore you to take pity on my brain."

He laughed. "Fine. No details on either side. But Bee didn't feel like I mistreated her by taking her up there without benefit of a six-course meal and a string quartet beforehand."

The Chief was making my theory overly simplistic, but still. "How can you be sure?"

"She willingly stayed with me the last couple of years, she says she wants to be my wife, and we actively tried to have this baby. So what do you think?"

"I think you're a lucky bastard. Bee is awesome."

"She is and I am." He cocked his head. "Maybe you'll get just as lucky."

"Nah. Bee isn't that fond of me—" I laughed at his narrow-eyed expression. "Sorry."

"Vanessa is the only person who has ever vexed Christian. She stands up to him like no one else. She might be pint-sized, but there's so much spirit inside her. An unbreakable one."

"Yeah. She's incredible. She makes me laugh like no one else ever has. Like right in the middle—anyway," I cleared my throat, "I just like being around her. For the longest time, I thought she was the biggest pain in the ass. Now I can't get enough of her."

"Fate is a wily mistress."

"Oh, here we go." I tipped back my head and prayed for patience. "Maybe it doesn't have to be that complicated."

"And maybe it's about to get very complicated. Maybe it's supposed to. Did you ever think of that? Now and then, the things we view as our biggest mistakes are actually what lead us where we're supposed to go."

Jared's words stuck with me throughout the rest of the day. I couldn't shake them, just like the dull ache at the base of my skull. The rogue ducks that shut down Main Street at lunch time didn't help, but I dealt with crowd control while the cars patiently waited for the mama duck to shepherd her charges across to the lake side of the street.

Even the ducks in this town didn't use protection.

The tiniest one at the back of the herd was pretty dang cute. He or she kept looking back at me as I shooed them and the rest of the ducks across the street, and I had to stop myself from picking up the baby to—what?

Carry him to safety with his family? Abscond with the duck? Give him a stern lecture like everyone seemed intent on giving me, except his would be geared toward vehicular safety?

Clearly, I was spending too much time with people growing babies. I was turning into parenting material before my very eyes.

I was too damn young to be a dad. So was Brady, but he didn't seem to know it. Even he'd had a few more years to sow his oats than I had.

My oats were dying on the vine, one by one.

I left the duck alone, though I didn't leave the street until he was safely on the grass closest to the lake. Feeling accomplished, I turned back to cross the street to head over to the cop shop when a headful of chaotic red curls caught my eye.

She was coming out of the craft store with her arms full of an assortment of yarn in bright colors, and she was laughing as she walked with her friend AJ who worked there. AJ was carrying even more yarn in just as many colors as her wildly dyed hair. This week seemed to be teal and orange. Somehow it worked for her.

Even with her arms full, Van was animated and obviously excited about something. She kept pointing to a massive purple speckled hank of yarn with her chin. I couldn't help grinning. I'd have to build her a cabinet to store all of that. I had that extra room in my place that I didn't know what to do with yet—

I cut off my thoughts. She'd mentioned building a she shed on her property after Gideon's men were done customizing her bus. That would be plenty of room for her craft stuff. She didn't need part of my house.

Before I could start making mental plans to build an arbor for our pretend wedding in my backyard, I marched across the street and blocked the path of the two women. They continued to talk and laugh until they practically bumped into me where I stood with my legs spread and my arms crossed.

Van blinked and her laughter turned into a soft smile. "Hey, you."

"I'm too young to be a father, but that doesn't mean I won't be a good one."

AJ patted Van's shoulder with a hand with long nails in ten different colors and rings winking on every finger. "Good luck, sister friend." She piled her yarn on Van's stack and vanished back in the direction of Every Line A Story, her clunky boots clicking heavily on the sidewalk.

Van's face was completely obscured by her precarious yarn pile, so I grabbed a bunch off the top. The purple one was distractingly soft.

"You are embarrassing as hell, you know that?" she muttered once I'd cleared enough she could actually speak clearly.

I thought about it for a second and nodded. "Yeah. I'll grant you that."

She released a windy sigh and shifted courses to the café and its small selection of round tables outside. "Now that you've chased off AJ, go buy me a coffee."

"Tall Americano with a double shot?" It probably should've worried me I already knew her coffee order.

Then again, I also knew her first orgasm happened super quickly and then she usually made me work for the second, so knowing her coffee order probably wasn't a stretch under the circumstances.

The circumstances being having inordinate amounts of sex whenever we could manage it. Usually in Tabitha's shower or on her couch or in my bed when we finally dropped into it late at night.

I stacked the yarn on the small table and Van produced a folded up canvas bag to hold it all from a pocket of her denim jacket. Why she hadn't done that before leaving the store, I had no clue.

Macy and her best friend Vee were working the counter. One was smiling from ear to ear and the other was grumbling about a missing truck of supplies.

"Hey there, Officer McNeill." Vee's blond ponytail bobbed as she pushed a tray of pastries at me. "On the house for our town's finest."

My stomach grumbled, reminding me I hadn't had lunch. "Thanks. Can I have two?"

"You can have as many as you want. Actually, I'll wrap up one for Christian too. He never takes a break." She pulled out a bag emblazoned with Brewed Awakening and started wrapping pastries in bright purple wax paper.

"How is Christian your brother-in-law?"

"A question I've wondered often myself. Murphy is far less surly than his brother. Though Christian is all bark, no bite." She put a few extra pieces of wax paper in the bag and pushed it my way. "Take whatever you'd like. Make sure you grab one for Van too," she added with a wink, looking pointedly out the window to where Van sat in the sunshine, scribbling furiously.

Or maybe she was drawing, since she was using her tablet. She was always doing secretive things on there she wouldn't let me see.

Probably designs for the bus. She still kept those close to the vest. I wasn't above plying her with orgasms to get a look at what she was working on.

Not in the parking lot, though. That would have to wait until later.

I grabbed a couple of pastries and wrapped them in the wax paper. For Van, I'd gone with chocolate on top of chocolate with chocolate frosting. "Thanks, Vee. Can you make me a double and a tall Americano with a double shot?"

"Sure thing." She moved to the machines to make the coffees quickly and competently while Macy slammed around a clipboard and rutted through shelves with an assortment of curses.

"Rough day, Mace?"

"Would be a great one if fucking people could do their fuckity

COP DADDY NEXT DOOR

fucking jobs." She gave me a blinding smile. "How's it going for you, Duck Saver?"

There was a name I hadn't heard before. "Just fine, thanks. Didn't know you were watching."

"Oh, I know everything that goes down in this town. Including the big bed your girl is somehow fitting into her bus. Wonder why that is?"

"How can she fit a big anything on that bus?"

Macy tapped her chin. "You have a point. But big's relative."

"Macy! Phone call!"

That it was. It wasn't until Macy had moved on to bark into the phone that I realized I hadn't disputed Pocket Plus was my girl. Why would I? A man would have to be a damn moron to deny she was his.

Even if I'd probably have to pay her off—and with something other than money—to make it so.

"Here you go, Officer." Vee smiled as she slid my coffee order my way.

"Thanks so much, Vee. Say hi to Murph for me."

"Will do. I'd say to say hi to Van, but she'll be in here again in ten minutes when she finishes this. She's addicted to the jolt."

I didn't know what to say to that, so I went outside and joined her at the little table. "You had Gideon put a big bed in your bus?"

She didn't respond, just held out her hand without looking up from her tablet. "Gimme."

I held the drink carrier aloft. "Let me see what's on your tablet first."

She held it to her chest. "You know, I thought orgasm denial was your most heinous crime. I now see caffeine captivity is a far worse one."

I didn't even bother looking around to see who could've heard her. At this point, probably the whole town knew we were doing it, so why bother?

"How do you know about my bed?" She sighed. "Macy. Of course. I didn't realize I needed to get Gideon to sign an NDA to do work on my bus. Did he mention the custom built sex toy drawer too?"

My eyes widened and she laughed hard enough to bobble her tablet. Which allowed me to see the deep green scaly texture of whatever creature she was drawing.

I dropped into the tiny chair not meant for a man my size. Or one filled with that much shock. The legs wobbled as I carefully set down the drink carrier and sack of pastries. "Did that creature have two dicks?"

She sighed. "I have bat hearing, you have bat eyes." She turned the tablet my way and I swallowed hard. "And yes, his dick is pierced."

"He has two. He can afford to bedazzle one."

Her giggle was musical. "His ass is like yours."

"What?"

She flicked to another screen and shifted the tablet toward me again. "It's not made to scale, but the bitable peach shape was drawn from memory of yours. Not that I've bitten it." She licked her lips. "Yet."

"As long as you don't draw other parts of me, we're good."

"Why? Sketch-shy?"

"How do I know you'll be factual?"

"Your fine butt's pretty on point."

"Minus the scales."

She shrugged. "The customer writes monster romance."

"Customer?"

She snatched the bag of pastries. "Ooh, what did you get me?"

I gripped her fingers on the bag and leaned forward until our faces were close. "You have a dirty sideline business."

She shrugged. "Nothing dirty about people getting off. You enjoy it, don't you? So don't yuck someone else's yum."

"Don't yuck—never mind, I don't want to know. Someone writes stories to go with these pictures? Like an illustrated book?" I grabbed her tablet again, and she didn't argue because she was currently sucking the frosting off her pastry. "Your illustrations are in books? Can I buy them at the bookstore? What's the title?"

She smiled benevolently at me between bites of fluffy pastry. I'd found chocolate was a certain mood booster for her. "You're so cute when you're not being annoying."

"You forgot when I'm not seducing you with my wiles."

"That too, but annoying usually is in first place."

"So what's the name of this book? And I want to see your sex toy drawer."

"I just bet you do, Officer Studly. Not a book. It's fan art for a special project."

"What does that mean?"

"But there have been books," she added, neatly sidestepping my question.

"Oh. Wait, what? Books? Like multiples?" I leaned up to grab her cheeks in my hands and gave her a big kiss, not even caring that her mouth was smeared with chocolate. "Damn, my girlfriend is famous!"

I would've kissed her again but she reared back as if I'd decked her instead of complimented her.

"I don't do the girlfriend thing."

"Glad to hear it, since I wouldn't relish the competition." I flashed her a grin that she did not return. "Fine, not girlfriend. We're just friends who fuck. Better?"

A gasp sounded from a nearby table and I held up two fingers in a peace sign in the general direction of the pearl-clutcher.

Van shook her head. "We are a walking disaster."

"Probably why we work."

"Just a couple of weeks ago, you were trying to get me to move away."

"By making you come. Didn't that strike you as a little suspicious?"

She went back to her pastry. "Our siblings procreating has led to heightened emotions in an unusual situation."

"You just admitted you had feelings for me." I snatched a piece of her pastry just to piss her off, and she hissed at me like a cat.

"I do. Angry ones."

"Angry screwing works for me. After you show me some of the books you're in. I told you your work was amazing, and it's on actual bookstore shelves and you didn't tell me. If this pastry wasn't so delicious, I'd chuck it at your head." I wiped chocolate off my fingers and took a drink of my coffee before dragging out my phone. "Under Vanessa Monaghan, I assume?"

"No. Just V. Mon." She shrugged. "I wanted to be discreet."

"V. Mon. Okay."

I searched for her name and found a splashy website with a list of credits a mile long and a portfolio of work that ranged from frightful monsters doing battle to ones clearly meant to be romantic figures. Somehow. Then there was a section with moody period pieces that could've been paintings. I couldn't click on them all fast enough.

"Why didn't you tell me before?"

She seemed more occupied with the last of her pastry than admitting to the staggering talent filling my tiny screen. "I haven't told anyone."

"No one?"

"Well, my agent knows. Both of them. I have one for foreign deals and movies too, though that hasn't come to fruition yet. They buy your option then just sit on it forever without actually making the damn films. But I get paid regardless. So what kind of pastry did you get?" Having finished her pastry, she went back to the bag and started rooting around inside.

"Eat what you want." I was still clicking around her website, truly boggled by what I was seeing. And the word *agent* was whirling around in my brain like the piñata Van had tried to buy for the bachelorette party before she landed on taking everyone to a venue instead.

Not that she would tell me where they were going, dammit.

Besides, throwing the word agent around was intense enough, but dealing with foreign rights? That was some serious upper levels in the art world. "Please tell me your sister knows."

"Nope. Nobody but you."

I jerked to my feet and grabbed the second pastry she'd eaten half of—pretty sure it was Christian's—and stuffed it back in the bag. "We're going to the bookstore. I'm going to buy every single copy of everything you've done I can find. I have empty bookshelves in the spare room just waiting for them."

She struggled to grab her tablet and her coffee and the pastry bag while simultaneously trying to fight me off and laughing. "You've lost it, dude. Didn't know monsters got you so excited."

"You don't just do monsters. You have so much other stuff on your website. Those paintings of what looks like England in the 1800s—"

"Oh, those are what got me my current job. Romantic suspense hardcover with a stepback."

"What does that mean? Eh, never mind, I don't care. Show me when we get there." I kissed her again, conveniently forgetting we had an audience until applause broke out around us.

She shook her head as she smiled at me. "Maybe being your girlfriend wouldn't be so bad."

FIFTEEN

By some miracle, the wedding shower went off without a hitch, even if it got moved a few days later. We held it at a familiar location —my sister's bakery, Sugar Rush. Honey, Mickey and I, along with help from Tab's other employees, Lea and Tiffany, managed to close the place down for a couple of hours on a weekday evening.

It wasn't hard for us to fill the place with all of the people who loved my sister—Luna, Ivy, Kinleigh, who owned a vintage clothing and furniture shop in town, Bess from their building, and even Macy and Vee, among others. Some of her other friends couldn't get the night off, so they'd just sent presents.

Presents were the most important part, anyway.

I supposed most of these people loved Brady too. But c'mon, these shindigs were mostly for the chicks, whether or not they'd had some fancy weedwhacker thing on the registry.

As far as I was concerned, hire lawn care. Who had time to bother with tools to whack the lawn into submission? Not I. Of course I was of the mindset to chop everything down that needed maintenance. Appreciating wild tundra was awesome, as long as it wasn't on my property.

I helped my sister open the many presents, and Brady stacked them in awe-inspiring manly piles while laughing heartily and chatting with the other men who were equally stoked to be at what Christian called a hen party. I was pretty sure he got the name wrong —that was the bachelorette— but I was trying to keep the peace today. He was only there for about a half hour before his shift began, and then Mav would get off duty when Christian went on.

He cleared his throat behind me and I worked hard on ignoring him as I refilled the punch bowl.

"Van, can I have a minute?"

"Did you have me towed? Tickets must get so boring after a while."

"No. You actually put some effort into parking this time. I think this is the first time you are actually within the lines."

It was truly sick that his scant praise warmed me inside. "I tried real hard."

"I'm sure." His lips twitched, barely visible under his thick scruff. "Look, we're off on the wrong foot, obviously. We need a cooling off period."

"Oh, do we? Is that what we need?" I tapped my chin. "Let me guess. You saw my Op/Ed in the paper about wasting town resources on nonsense tickets when there are more important concerns to be addressed?"

"Definitely missed that. I don't often get to peruse the paper since writing nonsense tickets keeps me so busy." He crossed his big, burly arms, straining his starched shirt at the shoulders.

He was truly tall and massive, even bigger than Mav, who was no slouch in that department. Yet I didn't shiver at his height the way I did with Mav's.

Probably good since Mav was the one I was sleeping with every night.

And every morning before work.

And some afternoons, if we had coinciding lunch breaks. That initial box of condoms we'd purchased had long ago been replaced.

Christian wasn't done yet. "But if you're dating Maverick, we probably should forge a truce so it doesn't get awkward."

I still wasn't good with that whole dating label, but even I had run out of names for what we were doing other than dating. If friends had this many benefits under ordinary circumstances, they'd be way past friends and coming around the other side.

"Why? It's been awkward all through Brady's engagement, and you never made an effort not to watch me like a damn hawk."

"You're a loose cannon. I like order." He shrugged as Mav picked that moment to strode through the bakery in his uniform, looking positively edible—even if one didn't notice his sexy glower as he took in Christian standing behind me.

"Masterson, don't you have anything better to do? I just checked. She's parked perfectly legally."

Of course he'd checked. I'd driven Mav's truck to the bakery and dropped him off for work since my bus was still undergoing reconstruction. I suspected he was trying to get on my good side to see my sex toy drawer, but I appreciated the use of his vehicle in any case.

Definitely dating. Keep it up, and you'll be wife-ing it too.

I stuck my cup in the punch bowl and sipped the fruity drink as if I was dying of thirst.

Mav cocked a brow. "Dehydrated?"

I nodded and kept drinking.

At least until he leaned down to kiss me—or so I thought. Instead, he peered at my cup. "Should you be drinking?" he whispered. "You know, in case."

"In case you knocked me up?"

More than a few people stopped *oohing* and *aahing* over my sister's gift unveiling to stare at me and Mav. Including Tabitha and Brady.

And Christian, about ten seconds before he beat a hasty retreat out the door, presumably to head to the cop shop.

Hmm, I supposed I hadn't used my indoor voice.

I didn't give Mav time to answer before I joined my sister and started doing my best Vanna White impression, just with wedding gifts—and a few baby ones, though she'd already had her baby shower.

With effort, I avoided him for the rest of the shower.

After the shindig ended and most everyone left except family, he cornered me by the refreshments table, taking the punch bowl I was about to wash out of my hands.

"Afraid I'm gonna dive in and lick up what's left?" I snapped.

"Testy. No, it's heavy."

"Oh, right. Can't let the little woman carry anything. As if I am not quite used to doing for myself."

"You are, and you do a great job of it. I just want to help lighten the load. Is that so awful?"

I scowled up at him, refusing to be moved by his melted dark chocolate eyes and how he looked at me with so much…care. That was it. He clearly cared, and it was scaring the holy batshit out of me.

"No. Yes. I don't know. Don't crowd me, okay?" I stomped into the kitchen and he didn't follow. I didn't know where he took the punch bowl, but he never brought it into the kitchen.

He probably would use it in an art project so I wasn't tempted to drown my sorrows in alcohol. Little did he know it was virgin rum.

He also didn't help me clean up. In fact, he went to talk to his brother. The two of them were whooping it up so loudly that I was tempted to work out my mad by stomping on both of their feet. I knew just where to aim to cause maximum pain too.

But I just kept cleaning and loading presents into Brady's vehicle until my irritation bled away into quiet recrimination.

I drifted over to the bakery's glass doors to stare out into the night. Across the street, a fall festival had been set up near the lake. In the darkness, bright lights twinkled around the Ferris wheel and colorful ones shone on the different food and game stands. Couples and families roamed around, probably laughing and having a grand ol' time, while I was steaming about nothing.

Suddenly, my stomach roared. I wanted funnel cake. Dipped in chocolate with a chocolate chaser.

"We're taking off." Tab looped her arms around me from behind. "Thank you for an awesome night. Now go home and do handcuff-worthy things with Mav instead of being all snarly."

I turned to face her. "I'm not snarly. And I'd rather cuff *him* right now."

"Dealer's choice. Whatever works." She shifted and her big belly rubbed against mine.

I frowned, something jolting through me at the contact.

"You okay?"

"Yeah." I rubbed the side of my stomach, trying to understand what I'd felt. Probably just static electricity. What the heck?

From now on, I'd only wear shoes with rubber soles. Screw fashion.

"You good?" I asked my sister.

She stared at me strangely and nodded as Brady came up behind her to lay his hands on her shoulders. "I'm fine. Van, you're pale. You're sure you're okay?"

"I'm always pale."

"More than normal." She laid a hand on my forehead. "You feel a little warm. You aren't getting sick?"

Baby flu doesn't come with a fever. At least I don't think.

"Sure. I'm good. Great."

Brady narrowed his eyes. "I can get Mav—"

"No need, he already heard my silent distress call." I rolled my eyes as Mav approached.

Some part of me wanted nothing more than to curl into his arms. I didn't feel sick, but I definitely felt...odd. As if I was having an out-of-body experience from a bad trip, except I hadn't taken anything except five tubes of mini M&Ms.

"We can hang out for a bit." Tab looked between me and Mav as if she feared a rumble was imminent.

Not tonight.

Normally, I'd be into it. Fighting made the best foreplay. But not when I was so out of sorts and wanting to cuddle.

Gah, what was happening to me?

"I'm fine." I smiled as brightly as my crisis of confidence would allow. "Go home and get some rest. Or some naked time, even if I can't imagine that at that circumference. But you know, you do you."

Tab patted Brady's chest. "I let him do most of the work. We figure it out." She gave me another hug. "Call if you need me. Anytime. Day or night."

I sniffled as my eyes prickled. "Same. Keep that kid in you."

"I'll do my best."

As soon as they left, I propelled myself into Mav's waiting arms. He didn't withhold affection or hassle me over earlier, just stroked his hand over my hair and my back to quietly soothe me. He didn't even know what was wrong.

I didn't either.

"I'm scared," I said into the silence, feeling like the biggest dolt who'd ever lived.

"I am too."

I swallowed hard and looked up at him. "How do you feel about funnel cake?"

"Really good." His smile gave me comfort when I wasn't sure if anything could.

And that was even better than a warm, sugary funnel cake.

Well, at least as good.

We walked around the festival dodging friends and acquaintances and eating copious amounts of greasy and bad for you food. Mav kept pace with me, although I suspected his sweet tooth had nothing on mine, especially lately.

We played a game with a soft hammer that required force to make a bell ring. It wasn't just force, but a certain sort of touch so you didn't shoot over the mark. Mav did not manage to soften his enough. But I did and won a stuffed pink giraffe for my trouble.

"Sure you can carry that?" the guy running the game asked teasingly.

Mav leaned around me and flashed him a wolfish grin. "If she can't, I can."

I elbowed him in the gut and he danced backward, holding my giraffe hostage.

When he noticed me sniffing the air near the cider stand, he bought us big cups of hot apple cider with cinnamon swizzle sticks, and we sipped them as we walked beside the softly rippling lake.

"You're cold," he murmured after I'd tossed my cider cup in a trash can. He didn't wait for me to agree before he set the giraffe on the sidewalk and tucked my hand into his jacket pocket, enfolded with his own. "I'd do the same with the other, but we'd probably have trouble walking that way."

"Not to mention carrying the giraffe would be a little tough."

"I could strap it on my back."

"There's an idea."

I laughed and used my free hand to bring his mouth down to mine. Within no time, the usual urgency built between us, heat flaring low in my belly as he took the kiss from leisurely to hungry. His soft lips tasted of sugar and rich apple and cinnamon, all the best fall flavors offset by the crisp wind coming off the water.

All my earlier fears drained away. There was just this cozy, perfect moment.

"I want to take you to bed," he murmured against my mouth.

"Mmm-hmm." I didn't open my eyes. "How about taking me on the grass?"

"In front of the whole town? You really want me to get fired?"

"Sure. I can support us both. Well, depending how good you make it for me. If I'm paying the bills, I have certain standards."

"Oh, do you now?" He tugged me against him.

Playfully, I struggled, and my shoe slipped off, getting caught on the stones that lined the lake pathway. I overcorrected and tried to grasp my shoe.

Then I slipped on the wet rocks.

I couldn't even make a noise as the sky seemed to pinwheel. I grabbed frantically for him, fisting his shirt as his arms locked around me and we nearly fell into the lake together. He hauled me back and clamped his mouth to mine, kissing me with far more desperation than he had even a few moments ago.

"Are you okay?" His hands roamed over me and not for purposes of sexual congress. "Christ, Van, you scared a lifetime off me."

"Especially because I can't swim." I framed his cheeks in my hands, my heart throbbing so fast, I could barely hear him over the wild beat.

His phone went off in his pocket, and he pulled it out with a hand that shook. I couldn't believe what I was seeing.

Big, strong Maverick McNeill was shaking because of *me?*

He scanned the readout and lifted it to his ear. "Tab? You okay?" He glanced down at me. "She's fine. I swear." He chuckled. "No, really. I didn't bury her body in the woods." He turned the phone against his shoulder. "You scared the hell out of your sister too. So freaky. You two are better than 911."

I took the phone and sucked in a deep breath before speaking. "I swear I'm okay." I frowned down at the softly lapping waves of the lake. "But the lake ate my shoe."

Once I'd convinced Tab I was truly fine, we hung up and I scuffed my foot over the gravelly path. The stones were minuscule, but they still didn't feel pleasant on bare skin. "Well, this will be a fun walk back to the truck."

"Go sit on that bench near the sidewalk, and I'll pull the truck around."

I made a face. "Think I can't walk through some grass? Look, I'll show you." I pried off my other shoe and, grabbing my giraffe, took off across the lawn, weaving around the families and couples still wandering around the festival.

More than a few of them watched us with amusement as if we were adorable. Others stared as if we were a circus attraction.

I was pretty sure we were somewhere between the two.

He chased after me across the grass and the sidewalk and even across the street, swearing at me as I darted between cars. "There's a damn crosswalk, Monaghan!"

I laughed breathlessly, dropping my remaining shoe as I full out ran for the truck. The damn giraffe was slowing me down. "Officer Studly, take a night off, why don't you?" I called over my shoulder, letting the giraffe go just as I reached the truck.

He pinned me against the side of his vehicle, grabbing my wrists behind my back so efficiently, I couldn't so much as squeak. "I have my cuffs. Want me to use them?"

"Yes."

He sucked in a breath. "Okay then."

But he didn't. He unlocked the truck and tossed the giraffe into the back. Then he plucked me up and set me on the seat before he bent my leg to kiss my ankle. The sexy look he gave me as his warm lips brushed my skin indicated he wanted to kiss me somewhere just a little higher and more central.

I did not have a problem with this plan.

After he tucked my feet inside, he shut the door and smoldered at me through the glass.

This man was going to be the death of me.

We didn't talk on the way to his place. Or when he drove up his driveway. Or when we went inside and were met at the door by a practically dancing dog that had to pee so badly—despite my having taken her out just before the wedding shower—that she was whining and nearly begging.

She wasn't the only one. I was having trouble not squeezing my thighs together.

"Take off your clothes and stretch out on the bed." Mav slanted me a glance as he grabbed Francie's leash and snapped it, bringing both his dog and me to attention. "And take the cuffs out of the bedside drawer."

I nodded wordlessly as my eyes zeroed in on the cuffs hanging from his belt. "Not those?" I gestured.

"No. I want you to be safe." His gaze bored into mine as he clipped the leash on Francie's collar. "Go."

I went.

SIXTEEN

 Maverick

I HAD NEVER WALKED FRANCIE SO FAST IN MY LIFE.

She started off at her usual meandering pace, sniffing flowers, grass, rocks, and the occasional dead bug. I was not having it.

"Look, dog, I know you're spayed and without access to attractive male dogs, so you don't understand the joys of recreational fucking. I get it. Truly I do. However, I will not be denied my joys so you can wander for forty-five minutes, kill some grass, and then do a tiny dump the size of four Cheerios. Not happening, pal."

Unmoved by my plight, Francie continued meandering at the speed of a lethargic snail.

Despite my pleading and then my curses, my dog would not be swayed. We didn't make it back inside for a half hour, and then I had to give her dinner, because I wasn't sure Van had before the shower. She was pretty good about it, but I wasn't going to risk ruining the mood by checking.

Besides, Francie was tiny. She could afford a few extra ounces on her, especially after her jerks of former owners had gone off and left her for days without food or water.

Feeling extra soft-hearted, I scooped extra wet food into her bowl and topped it with a few pieces of dry kibble and checked that her fountain was working as it should. Then like an overeager teenager, I rushed upstairs, detoured to the bathroom, and then walked into the bedroom, already envisioning Vanessa, naked and wet and waiting for me on the bed.

I got a couple of those things.

She was definitely naked. She was definitely waiting for me—or at least she had been until she'd fallen asleep.

I shook my head at the ridiculous hard-on tenting my uniform pants. Well, that was a waste. I'd be returning to the bathroom to finish that off.

But first I'd cover her up. It was a cool night and goosebumps popped along her shoulder as I ran my fingers over her soft skin. That beachy smell of hers hit my nose and I took a long breath of it, tempted to bury my face in her hair to get more.

Thank God she didn't know I buried my face in the pillow now and then after she got out of bed just to inhale that wild ocean air and bonfire scent that was so very Van.

Just like the monster romance books now proudly lining my bookshelves, all the pieces and parts of her didn't necessarily make sense on their own. But together? They were exactly right.

As I was tugging up the covers, she mumbled something I didn't understand. And then I did and my heart squeezed so hard it was a physical ache.

"Don't leave me, Mav. Please."

I bent to kiss her forehead, my voice surprisingly thick. "Not going anywhere, baby."

As I pulled the sheet up around her shoulders, I decided crawling in with her to get some rest myself was far better than jerking off in the bathroom. Quickly, I stripped down to my boxers and got under the covers beside her. She made a noise in her throat and wrapped herself around me vine-style, instantly settling again with her cold nose pressed against my neck.

Her favorite place to be just recently. She was all about being the tiniest big spoon ever.

Smiling, I shut my eyes and willed my dick to simmer the hell down.

And woke cuffed to my own bed.

I opened one eye, sure I had to still be dreaming. Nope, Vanessa was really naked and straddling me, and one of my wrists was cuffed to the headboard. That said cuff was fuzzy and pink just added to the surreal aspect.

"About time you join the party. Though it was so sweet of you to let me sleep. Sorry, just blinked out." She leaned over me, her small, pale breasts dangling close to my face and jerking me fully awake. "But I'm awake now." She nipped my scruffy chin before dragging her short nails down my torso.

"So I feel."

She rubbed her wet pussy against my clenched upper thigh before trailing her fingers down her belly to sample the goods. She painted my lips with her wet fingertip, making me groan long and low. The taste of her made me jolt involuntarily against the cuff, but I had to say, it was as comfortable as the packaging had claimed.

"You're cute in fuzzy pink."

"That was meant for you, not me."

"Aww, you bought your sex cuffs for me? That's lovely."

"Contrary to popular belief, I don't cuff every woman I meet."

"Probably a good thing, or else you'd end up on Asher's true crime podcast." She dipped her fingertips inside herself again, circling playfully while she cocked her head. "Gotta say, you're far more handsome than the usual psychopath."

"There's a compliment I haven't gotten before. Yet you're the one who cuffed me before I could even use the bathroom, so who's the psychopath?"

Laughing softly, she leaned forward to grip my hard length and darted her tongue over the dark red tip, already dotted with pre-cum. "Don't want to waste another one of these after last night."

She didn't give me time to answer before sucking me down.

Like everything else Van did, she wasn't tentative. She didn't explore me gently, just went for the gold from the first moment. Her rosy lips spread wide around my girth as she slid down my shaft, taking more of me than should've been possible considering every other part of her was small.

Then again, she was clearly an overachiever.

She circled the base of me with her short, purple nails, using just enough pain to drag me back every time I neared too close to the finish line. Her cheeks hollowed and wetness smeared my cock as she bobbed her head and made me strain against the cuff.

With my other hand, I brushed her wild hair back from her face. I needed to see every moment of this.

I wanted to remember every second.

She turned her to head to kiss my fingers and my pulse rate kicked up. "You're so fucking beautiful."

Her blue eyes lasered on mine as she returned her mouth to my length, sucking even harder than before as she cupped my balls in her soft grip. Then not so soft as she drew even harder on my erection, clearly testing my boundaries.

And pushing me past them as her pinky teased me lower and lower while her eyes sparkled devilishly and she tempted me to thrust into her throat. Even fisting the sheet with my free hand wasn't enough to keep my hips from rising, my cock seeking her warm, tight throat without my conscious thought. Once, twice, and her eyes watered, the blue turning glassy.

She doubled down and went even farther, daring me to resist. Knowing it would take all of my strength to try to hold on.

But she didn't realize just how badly I wanted to come inside her. From the first night, I'd been obsessed with just that.

I laced my fingers into her thick hair and yanked her off me, absorbing her whine of protest with pride. She actually wanted me to come in her mouth. She always did, the sexy wench. Something about making me lose control was obviously her catnip.

But this time, she'd be at my mercy, regardless of who was cuffed.

"Get up here," I murmured.

She licked her lips teasingly. "Want to taste yourself?"

"Not nearly as much as I want to taste you. Get on my face."

"You aren't in charge, Officer. Just because you're used to that, you aren't the boss here." She crawled over me and licked my nipple, her gaze roaming my face. "I want to sketch you like this."

I swallowed hard, recognizing that dirty light in her eyes. "Van—"

She scampered off the bed, so confident naked that I couldn't keep my eyes off her. Shoulders high, breasts out, she crossed the room to dig in the bag she'd brought over here a couple days ago, emerging with a stubby charcoal pencil and a small sketch pad.

"Not my usual medium, but I don't want a digital record of this. At least not yet." She curled up cross-legged beside me on the bed and held the sketch pad up to her chest. "If you're not into it, I won't do it. I respect boundaries."

"Except when you forget to get consent for handcuffing me to the bed."

She bit her lower lip. "Oops?"

"Yeah, oops." I couldn't help grinning at her. She was so damn cute, like this impish, sexy sprite, all freckles and sass. And miles and miles of sex appeal.

"Want me to undo you? And put away the sketch pad?"

"Right, so you can do it from memory later?"

"I do have a good memory."

"Uh-huh. I don't want you to uncuff me. Do your sketch and then get on my face. See, compromise."

She pursed her lips while she avariciously studied my very erect, very painful cock. "Yeah, worth it."

I had to laugh. "Oh, the sacrifices you'll make for your art."

"Mind yourself, McNeill, or else you'll end up as a Bigfoot with a monster member."

"Writing that one yourself?"

She tapped the charcoal pencil against her mouth. "Huh. I could, couldn't I?"

Trepidation lanced through my gut. "Uh, no. Don't do it."

Her grin spread as she started to sketch. "I think I just might. Now *shh* so I get the contours just right."

I flexed the fingers of my cuffed arm. And tried not to move while I contemplated how in two weeks' time give or take a couple days I'd

165

ended up secured with my own cuffs to be my bedpost and absolutely in lo—

Uh, in super like with Vanessa Monaghan.

"You're tensing," she muttered, furiously sketching.

I hoped she was sketching the rest of me too, not just my damn dick. Considering the wide swings of her hand, I'd assume so, but you could never be sure with her.

At my bedroom door, my dog scratched frantically. I usually let her sleep with me at night, but sometimes one of us shut the door and she got locked out. If she was scratching, she wanted breakfast or had to pee or both.

"I'm not missing out again because of that dog, so you better draw fast—or learn how to sketch while I'm making you come with my tongue."

She kept sketching, dipping her head over her pad so her hair mostly covered her face and she had to peek out of her curls.

Just her intense focus was enough to have my shaft standing large and in charge. I couldn't help puffing my chest with pride.

At least her Bigfoot would have a phallus worthy of the great beyond.

"Okay, done. Good job, Officer. You barely twitched. No wonder I felt moved to sketch this thing of beauty." She patted my dick as if it was a prized stallion then tossed aside her sketch pad and charcoal pencil.

I started to tell her to put that thing away properly due to its X-rated content, but she chose that moment to swallow the head of my shaft. I forgot anything else but warm wet suction and the sounds of her working me into a frenzy.

Dipping back my head into the pillows, I stared at the recessed lights in the ceiling, grateful she wasn't even slightly shy so I could watch every bit of what she was doing to me. But if I didn't look away now and then, this was going to be over before we'd really even gotten started.

That was not happening.

Just when I was about to demand she do as I'd requested, she drew her mouth up off me and took a long breath. "A deal's a deal."

Shaking back her hair, she crawled over me, her gaze intent. She didn't even hesitate to aim for my mouth, settling herself there without my help until I banded my hand around her thigh and angled her just right.

Damn, she was probably going to kill me—but I was willing to risk it.

I sealed my mouth over her pussy and wasted no time driving my tongue deep. I'd known she'd be on the verge just from almost getting me off. Already I knew her that well. She didn't disappoint me, soaking my tongue within just a few strokes through her swollen folds. But that wasn't enough for me. With my free hand, I arranged her so I could slide first two then three fingers inside her, ruthlessly seeking that place inside her that would make her detonate.

She fought me, squirming away before she couldn't resist sinking down and giving me total access. Even with her thighs near my ears buffeting some of the sound, her moans filled the room. I couldn't watch her bouncing around without losing my focus, so I shut my eyes and sucked on her clit as my fingers turned her into a sobbing, writhing mess.

Her hand wove into my hair and she gasped, pulling me back an instant before she let go.

"Give it to me. You think I don't know how close you are?" I flexed my fingers inside her as I licked my wet lips. "I feel those pulses. I feel how your muscles are tightening around me."

"I want your cock." She lifted away from me, taunting me with her wet, reddened flesh for an extra moment before she retreated.

I jerked my wrist in the cuff and threatened her inventively, but she just moved down my body and rubbed her damp pussy over my cock, over and over again, nearly getting herself off yet again, her tongue caught between her teeth.

"You know you want to pound into me." Her voice was thick, breathless, and she sounded almost as crazed as I did.

Instead of answering, I shifted upward, nearly slipping into her. I stopped myself, but she locked her hands behind her head and stared down at where I was almost inside her.

So, so close.

"You ride the edge."

"You push me there." I gritted my teeth. "You know where they are. Stop teasing me and get one."

"I love teasing you." She reached down and nudged me back, giving me a hard squeeze. "I love too much about you." The last she said almost to herself.

I shut my eyes. She wasn't the only one.

Goddamn Brady and his hormones had gotten me in this position. He was the reason I was trussed up like an overstimulated turkey, thinking things I had no business thinking.

She climbed off me and opened the bedside drawer, grabbing one of the foil packets I was growing to hate. I'd never gone bare with a woman before that night in the truck. Had never even considered it, especially in a town like this.

Now I wanted nothing but. Screw the rules. Screw what might happen.

I just wanted to be inside her, come what may.

When she climbed back on the bed, I grabbed the condom and ripped it open with my teeth. She snatched it back to put it on me, her sure touch messing with my head as much as all the rest.

"I hate it too," she whispered, making me focus on her face even as she drew me into her.

I couldn't do anything but take in every nuance of her expression. Her pupils blowing wide as I filled her, her lips parting as she accommodated me. The way her fingers dug into my thighs impatiently when I didn't move.

I couldn't.

"You wanted me at your mercy," I managed. "Do your worst."

She closed her eyes, trying to shut me out even as she began to move. Wildly, jerkily, her nails scraping down my stomach as if she wanted to dish out pain with her pleasure. To punish me for dragging her out of the place where this was just sex into the place I'd been trapped for days. Probably weeks.

Maybe even from the very first night.

Though it cost me, I didn't drive up into her. I made her work for every bit of what she got. She rode me unsteadily, her frustration mounting as her lips pursed. She was so wet, and she could use me however she wanted. It still wasn't enough.

To get where she wanted to go, it would take both of us. And she knew it.

Her walls tightened around me the faster and harder she bucked against me, but she wasn't getting there. Couldn't.

Not on her own.

"Maverick," she begged finally, her wrecked blue eyes meeting mine.

Resisting her was beyond me.

"Uncuff me."

She scrambled up to grab the key she'd hid under the pillow. As soon as I was free, I grabbed her in my arms and rolled her beneath me, pressing my forehead to hers as I drove into her as if my life depended on it.

She bit off her scream, straining up to take my mouth in a brutal kiss as I finally thrust into her up to the hilt. Without holding back, without being afraid I'd hurt her. I knew she could take it—and me.

Knew she needed to just as I needed her.

Her hands raced up my back as I shifted to tuck her against me. She was so much smaller than me, but we'd been together so much already that adjusting for the differences in our heights didn't require thought.

Eyes locked, I didn't stop stroking into her, sweat dripping into my eyes, the true blue of her eyes my center. Her pupils overtaking the blue as I drove into her just right to make her legs shake. Her pussy squeezed around me and she kissed me hard, her fingers twisting into my hair.

I reached the end of the line inside her, drawing back and sinking home one last time. Her name was on my tongue as I drained myself into the condom, hoping like hell she was with me.

Not knowing if the wetness on her cheeks was hers or mine—or if it was sweat or tears.

Maybe both.

I pressed my lips to her forehead and then her lips, drawing in her air as if it could fill my lungs. She framed my face in her hands, coiling her legs around me so tightly I couldn't have left her if I wanted to.

And I didn't.

"I didn't know what you said before I slept, but now I do," she whispered. "I remembered."

I covered her mouth with my own so she didn't say it aloud. We already knew I wouldn't be the one who wanted to leave.

I wasn't the one who lived in a house on wheels.

SEVENTEEN

I STARTED THROWING UP THE MORNING OF TAB'S BACHELORETTE PARTY.

It had been moved two full weeks later than Brady and Tab had wanted after their scare. Turned out it was really hard to plan a wedding and all the assorted events that went with it when everyone had left most of the details to the last minute.

Not even just me and Mav, but the bride and groom too. They'd both stuck their heads in the sand about all the details, and surprise, surprise, there were many of them. I took on as much as I could, but I was still opening up the bakery in the early morning to take some of the pressure off Tab, who was now the size of the Titanic. Or so it seemed to me, since I'd been a size six since high school.

Not anymore.

Oh, the size difference wasn't much. Anyone else would've said I was imagining things. Of course, I had to be, right? It was far too early. I'd been pregnant before, but not for long. What did I know?

Except I'd known the night of Tab's wedding shower, and that definitely was way too soon according to any doctor's chart.

"We don't need to do this," Tab said as she fussed with her hair in the mirror in the bakery's bathroom. "I'm the size of a house. What do I want to see strippers for?"

171

I had to laugh even though I was leaning against the sink at her side so I didn't fall over. Along with my morning sickness, I was also now so tired that I'd nearly fallen over face first into the croissant dough I was rolling. Twice.

Now I was supposed to laugh and have a grand time at my sister's bachelorette party even though I had a damn good suspicion I was going to need a baby shower of my own in the not too distant future.

Assuming the baby stayed where it was supposed to for the whole nine months. But it was far too early to consider such things.

Even if my brain heartily disagreed with such logic and kept sending nightmare scenarios through with frightening regularity.

Now it was even worse than when I was sixteen, because it wasn't just me who would be dealing with whatever happened, good or bad. Mav would be too. Somehow the idea of him possibly hurting was almost as bad as me.

Oh, who was I kidding? It was worse. So much worse. I'd get through whatever occurred. I might doubt it every minute, but I would. I was a survivor.

I just didn't want *him* to have to face anything bad. He could be an ass and he was irritating and sometimes arrogant and a million other things. But he was mine.

God, I wanted him to be mine so badly, and what was I supposed to do about that?

"We aren't actually seeing strippers."

Tab stopped fussing with her hair. "We aren't?"

"No. We're going to a restaurant called Pleasure Palace because it has a kicking ice cream bar that supposedly includes aphrodisiac ingredients. But I'm pretty sure it's just a marketing schtick." I shrugged. "Closest thing to naked dicks in that joint is peeled bananas for the banana split sundaes."

My sister laughed in delight. "You are so devious. I love it."

I shrugged again and forced myself to halfheartedly swipe lip gloss over my mouth. If even that exhausted me, I could only imagine how fun this night would be.

"They deserve it for all their stripper jokes."

"Mav slept with one for his eighteenth birthday."

"Yeah, yeah, I know. He said it wasn't even that good. She never called him again."

"You're not pissed?"

"That he got some at eighteen? Uh, no. I also got some at eighteen, though not with a stripper."

Tab grinned. "You have the healthiest attitude toward sex and dating I've ever seen. You don't get all twisted up."

I snorted so hard I nearly ruptured something. "You're kidding me, right?"

"No, why?"

"I can barely even *say* the word dating. I'm relationship-phobic. Before I tripped and fell on Mav's penis, I hadn't had sex in almost two years because no one interested me more than my sex toy drawer."

"And Mav's is better than that? High praise." My sister held up a hand. "Please don't tell me. He's about to be my brother-in-law. It's better if I don't know anything about what's in his trousers."

I smiled faintly as I tugged my hair up into a haphazard topknot. "We've been together a month, and we haven't had one real fight."

"Wow. That's great."

"I mean, we squabble all the time, but I think we both get off on that. But the big stuff? The important stuff? We either pretend it doesn't exist or we just…deal."

"Well, the pretending isn't awesome, but it's still all very new. You have time to figure out how to address things maturely."

"You and Brady were mature from day one."

"Hardly. Things look a lot different on the inside, Van." She shifted toward me, adjusting her floral maternity top and letting it float down around her. "How do I look?"

I made myself really focus on her from head to toe. "Radiant," I said finally, shocked as tears spurted out of my eyes.

At least the timing of when I was crying covered up the true cause of my current emotional breakdown.

I hoped.

"Aww, c'mere. What's wrong? Is all this baby and wedding stuff making you itchy?"

I nearly said yes. But I didn't. It was making me itchy because I was starting to consider maybe someday I might want it for myself.

Not necessarily the whole picket fence routine. I didn't know what that was about. I might've grown up in a boringly traditional family, raised by parents who were surprised Tabitha hadn't gotten married before procreation, but that didn't mean I believed in such.

I lived on a bus. Or I had—until I'd unofficially moved in with my almost brother-in-law.

"We don't have to do this. I'd be just as happy spending a night in with you and the others doing a retro movie watch with *The Breakfast Club* and *Mean Girls* and stuffing our faces while the silly guys ogle women in G-strings."

"You're not mad?"

"Nope. He can look all he wants. He's coming home to me. Besides, I'd look at Harry Styles naked if I had the opportunity. Doesn't mean I'm not going to marry Brady."

"What if Harry proposed?"

She tapped her chin thoughtfully. "I'll have to get back to you on that."

I laughed and drew her into a hug, careful not to brush my stomach against hers. Didn't need to stir up any other paranormal events between our bellies, especially when I was so raw.

"You're sure you're all right? You've been acting weird today."

"I'm better than all right. I can't wait for Mav to ask how our strippers were. I'm going to tell him I licked chocolate ice cream off one of them."

Tab howled with laughter, clapping a hand over her mouth. "You're not going to really say that. Are you?"

I shrugged and popped a breath mint in my mouth. Not for the purpose of avoiding bad breath, but because my stomach was threatening to revolt again, although it was nowhere near morning. I was praying I'd be able to stave off the nausea tonight.

And tomorrow morning, since Mav had almost heard me today. I'd had to turn up the music really loud on my phone, and he'd still asked me a few times if I was okay.

Sometimes having a suspicious cop for a boyfriend sucked.

"We'll see how my mood is later. C'mon." We walked into the bakery just as Honey was turning the sign to *closed* on the door. "Hey, you, get a move on. We have partying to do."

Honey sighed and tugged her long brown ponytail over her shoulder. "Gonna be a lean one for me tonight."

I exchanged glances with my sister. "Why?"

"I have got to get out of my house before my mom and I end up on the news."

"What do you mean?"

"She's driving me insane. Stark raving mad." Honey perched on a stool behind the counter and rested her face in her hands. "I've been trying to keep it together while I save up for a down payment on an apartment, but my student loans are so intense and I can't quite piece together enough hours. I'm thinking about taking a couple semesters off until I can get caught up. Maybe find myself a full-time job for a while." She heaved out a breath. "My wardens aren't gonna be happy, but it is what it is."

"Your wardens?"

"My brothers." She shook her head with a smile. "They're both always drilling into my head the importance of my education. God forbid I tell them I'm not certain I'm cut out to be a teacher anymore. The idea of taking out more loans when I'm not even sure..."

"You can take my apartment," Tab said quickly. "We'll be moving into our house soon, and there's still months left on my lease. You can sublet it for a reduced rate. Assuming it won't cause family strife." She narrowed her eyes. "If you think it might, wait to tell your mom until I'm safely married to your brother."

Honey laughed and popped to her feet to give Tabitha a gentle hug. "I'll wait just in case, but you know how much Mom loves you. I think she'd trade me for you as her daughter in a heartbeat. Plus, you're carrying the beloved grandchild." She patted Tab's belly reverently.

175

"No matter what you do, she won't do anything but praise your very existence."

I laughed with them while my mind reeled. If I was pregnant, would it be the same with my child? Would my kid be seen as a blessing in Mav's family? Or would the fact that I was a known chaos goblin who got tickets like I breathed and had a foul mouth and lived in a house on wheels be held against my baby?

I already doubted my parents would be thrilled. They'd grown to accept Tabitha's child because Tabitha was the favored one with a stable business and life and always took care with everything she did. One little blip wouldn't change their fundamental opinion of her.

None of that applied to me.

"Right, Van?" Tab asked pointedly, tilting her head at me.

"Right." I shook myself. "What are we talking about again?"

Honey smiled. "Tab said Bonnie's position at the police department is opening up soon. She's finally committed to retiring."

"Oh, really? That's nice." I didn't know Bonnie well, though I knew she was Bee's mom and an important person in this town. "Do they know who might take it?"

"Brady hasn't mentioned any candidates. I told Honey she should apply. She's taken some elective criminal justice classes as part of her curriculum and could take more if she had aptitude for the position."

"Oh, sure. That's a great idea. I'm sure you'd be an excellent fit." I pushed a few escaped curls out of my eyes. "I gotta get home and change then I'll meet you guys at The Pleasure Palace."

"You should've brought clothes like I did."

"Yeah, I totally spaced on it." I flashed them a quick smile and gave them both hugs. "Don't suck up all the pleasure before I get there."

"Are the strippers going to be naked?" Honey's dark eyes went huge as she groped for her huge moonstone pendant. "I've never seen an all naked one."

"You've never seen a naked man? Holy crap. By your age, I'd seen a baker's dozen. Maybe more."

Both Tab and Honey laughed at me. Nothing new there.

"No. Not a naked man. A completely nude stripper. Actually, I've never seen *any* strippers. Male ones aren't as plentiful." Honey sighed heavily. "I feel like this is another way that men are luckier than women."

"I hate to tell you, Honey, there's going to be no men in loincloths tonight. Not a one."

Honey's crestfallen expression made me laugh out loud.

"None? What exactly are they stripping off then?"

"Nothing. It's an ice cream joint. Just picked that place to mess with the guys because they kept messing with us." I showed Honey and Tab the shop's gilded website on my phone. "But if they're watching actual strippers, I hope they feel guilty."

Truthfully, I didn't really care. Let the boys have their fun. I'd been to shows with strippers before and it never had gotten too crazy, so I wasn't worried. Besides, Brady and Mav were cops. I knew they'd behave. Most of their friends were married or coupled up too.

I had other more pertinent concerns right now.

"I'll catch up with you guys there," I called as I headed out into the early evening, my first destination not Mav's house or even my currently being renovated bus.

Nope, I stopped off at a drugstore a town over to buy a couple of early detection pregnancy tests with cash.

Paranoid much? Nah, not me.

I headed back to Mav's place just as Gideon's crew was packing up for the day. I affixed a smile on my face as I parked Mav's truck. He was riding with Brady today, so he'd told me not to worry about picking him up from work since they'd been on shift together and would go right from work to the "location of the event."

His air of mystery was not lost on me. Strippers. *Pfft.*

But I didn't want such entertainment. I was starving and already looking forward to some ice cream, no need for any extra added aphrodisiac ingredients.

I'd had enough sex for the moment, thanks.

Lucky from Gideon's crew stepped out in front of my truck as I parked in front of Mav's garage. "Great timing." Lucky opened my door and helped me down, though I was quite capable of getting out on my own. "We just finished your window seat."

"Oh, did you? Can I take a peek?"

"Absolutely." He gestured me ahead of him. "Take a look."

I ran around the bus, trailing my fingers along the matte sage paint color they'd done the day before. It was just about perfect. Maybe Mav could add some of his magic for a little extra embellishment.

Or I could. It was my bus, after all.

I hurried around the back and up the steps, sidestepping one of the guys in the crew who was still inside. "Hey, Frank. You guys have been doing an amazing—oh my God." I covered my mouth as I looked around the newly renovated bus. "This is incredible."

"Isn't it?" Frank took a look with me as he wiped his hands on a rag. "We're getting close to done. Just a few touches left to add."

"Oh, yeah? Like what? I can't see there's anything left."

"There's this. Late addition." He laid his hand on a small bookshelf with carved details on top of the shelves and around the base that instantly brought to mind Mav's work. The edges of the shelves were raw exposed wood that looked as if they'd just been carved off a tree and fashioned into a shelf.

I gasped and crouched to run my fingers along the carvings. "This is stunning."

"It is, isn't it? Surprise from your boyfriend. He finished it just today."

A lump formed in my throat. Under normal circumstances, I laughed off the whole boyfriend/girlfriend thing. Not right now. I was far too emotional, and this piece was something I'd treasure forever.

"It's gorgeous. Just like the rest of this is."

I stood and swiveled to take in the soft mints and yellows accented throughout the bus, offset by fun and funky white butterfly wind chimes that jangled merrily and a million different colorful throw pillows. They contrasted perfectly with the ones I'd embroidered myself.

Real wood cabinets were tucked under the windows to offer more storage—and seating, with the pillows on top. And in the back, they'd put in a built-in cabinet in front of the windows that opened up for storage or provided the perfect sketching spot. My sleeping bag bed had been turned into a real one with netting draped around it to offer a little separation, and yet more mini shelves had been built above it.

We'd discussed putting in a sink and food prep area with room for a microwave. But as my pregnancy certainty had grown, the more I'd realized there was no way in hell I'd be living in this bus while my belly was the housing station for a child.

A child I hadn't even had to consider if I was keeping, because this was my second chance. I was keeping my baby. Period.

Assuming I was actually knocked up.

Oh, and that supposed sex toy drawer? Did not exist. But it'd been entertaining to razz Mav about it.

"You guys did such an awesome job with the new flooring and all the built-ins. That window seat is just perfect."

I smiled at Frank and past him to Lucky, who was leaning in because he was far too tall and huge to fit in here with us. I wasn't sure how he fit in here when the bus was empty. "You did awesome, Luckster," I added, laughing as I came down the steps.

"We're glad you like it. It's really cool." With a grin, he plucked me off the bottom step and swung me around before he set me on my feet.

Something about my small stature seemed to make men— especially the bigger ones—want to toss me around. I didn't usually mind, since it was all in good fun. This time, my touchy stomach wasn't into the air acrobatics.

I pressed my hand to it in the hopes of settling everything down. "It is."

Too bad I'll probably have to sell it.

"So when can we start on your actual house?" Lucky asked, prying out his phone to text someone, most likely his wife.

He was always checking in with Tish and their new babies. I'd once looked at his phone at the wrong moment and gotten an eyeful. Not a dick shot, luckily, but let's just say I now knew more about Tish than I'd expected to.

Breast feeding was intense, especially when it involved two babies. All that juggling? I didn't even know how to contemplate all of the choreography.

Hmm, would I finally see some boob growth from pregnancy? I'd have to, wouldn't I? That would be a perk, for Mav as much or more than for me.

If he stuck around. He was all about the heroic gestures in theory, but we'd see what happened when the baby met the carriage.

I shut my eyes and tried to get my chaotic thoughts to simmer the hell down. One thing at a time.

First, I'd take the tests. Then I'd get dressed for my sister's bachelorette party. Then I'd eat lots of ice cream so I couldn't fit in my Maid of Honor dress.

Sounded like a good plan.

"Vanessa?"

"Yeah. Sorry." This whole mental wandering off thing was becoming a problem. "I'm not sure on the house. Soon, I hope. I'll keep you posted. It may just end up a she shed like we originally talked about."

"Okay. But you seemed really convinced the other day you were ready to build."

Was I? I'd thought of changing my she shed plans to an actual small house on a whim. I had the money, so that wasn't a factor. Roots were starting to seem not so scary. Hell, I'd bought property. The roots had already been dug.

I just wasn't sure what to do until I knew if I had a baby on board. Not that I'd get any clarity from that either. Just wanted to be sure what I was working with before I made any big moves.

"Yeah, I'm just—my life is kinda in flux right now. I don't know where I'll be or how I'll be or—" I shifted, catching sight of Mav striding down the front porch steps in his work uniform out of the corner of my eye.

Weird thing was, he was wearing his bulletproof vest though he hadn't worn it to work.

My heart raced. Oh, God, why was he even here right now? Had something happened? Was there an incident?

I rushed toward Mav, colliding with him hard enough that he reached out to steady me. "Going to finish that statement?" he asked coolly.

"What statement?"

"You were answering Lucky." He gestured vaguely behind me.

Lucky had gone back to his truck and was now reversing out of the drive. I was impressed that dust didn't rise from his speedy retreat.

A married man knew when a fight was afoot. He was smarter than I was in that regard.

"Oh."

"Yeah, oh. Are you making plans to move on I should know about? Is that what fixing up the bus is about?"

"Move on? Why would I buy property to move on?"

"It is a question. But you usually dance to your own drummer and the rest of us just watch from the sidelines."

There was no missing the thread of irritation in his voice. Or the hurt. "Why are you home?"

"I can ask you the same question."

I looked back at his truck, where my pregnancy tests waited in a paper bag on the front seat. Ticking time bombs.

"Can we go inside?"

He looked at his watch. "I'm due to meet Brady and the others soon."

"Oh, sure. Right." I cleared my throat. "So nothing happened? Like some incident with someone shooting or stabbing or—"

"Is worrying about my life the only time you're capable of acting like you care?" He delivered his question in a troublingly flat voice that nearly knocked me back a step.

"What's wrong with you tonight? Getting itchy feet so trying to pick fights?" I gave him a sly smile I so didn't feel. "Or just shedding entanglements before you go hang out with the latest round of strippers?"

He gave me a patently bored look. "As usual, you couldn't be more off-base."

I turned to go back to the truck to grab the bag. Last thing I wanted was for him to find the tests before we could talk. Even if he didn't seem to be any place for heart-to-hearts.

Too damn bad.

"Where are you going?"

I opened the passenger door and grabbed the bag, then I turned back to see him standing with his legs spread and his arms crossed as if he was waiting for a suspect to take off into the wilderness at any moment.

Was that how he saw me? As an unpredictable adversary he liked having sex with?

Hell, was that how I saw *him?*

He frowned, his gaze dipping to the bag. "What's that?"

Rather than answer, I pushed the bag at his chest. I couldn't hide this from him. We'd come so far, or at least it had seemed so before this conversation.

Logically, I knew he had his fears too. But right now, I needed his support. His freaking fears could just get in line.

He opened the bag and audibly gulped. "Whoa."

"Yeah."

"Have you been having symptoms?"

Silently, I nodded, hoping I wouldn't break down and cry. Or throw up. Or punch him.

Any of the three was possible in my current state.

"Like what?"

"I threw up a bunch this morning. Had nausea on and off all day." I swallowed hard. "My breasts are sore. I've gone up a fourth of a size."

"A fourth of a size?"

"Just guesstimating there. My pants are tighter. I don't know how much. Maybe it's bloating."

"Or maybe it's baby."

"Or maybe it's baby," I echoed. "Either way, I couldn't just go to the

COP DADDY NEXT DOOR

bachelorette party not knowing. It may be too soon to test, but it should show by now or pretty soon."

He reached down and took my hand, squeezing it firmly. "We'll take it now and find out rather than wonder."

"You only sound so calm and rational because you aren't the baby vessel."

"I can admit that does lend a certain steadiness." He lifted our joined hands to his lips. "But I'm here. I promised I'd be here."

"Because you're trying to be as good as Brady."

"And if I am? Trying to be good isn't a bad thing, is it? But even without Brady's example, I'd still be here." He stopped me at the base of the steps to his front porch and gripped my waist. The pumpkins and bright gold mums we'd picked up at the market last weekend sat on either side of the door. "We're both here. The difference is I'm always wondering how long until you go."

EIGHTEEN

 Maverick

I was about to lose my damn mind.

How could five minutes seem like five hours?

"Is it time yet?" I called through the door while simultaneously texting my brother I'd had a slight delay and would meet him and the others at The Pleasure Palace.

Though the group of others was dwindling by the minute. Bunch of chickens. At the rate we were going, Brady and I would be the only lucky victims…err, candidates.

That this whole scenario was actually my fault was not lost on me. Nope, no siree. And I didn't just didn't mean the one with Brady at The Pleasure Palace.

Vanessa came out of the en suite bathroom, looking far too waxy and pale. Had she looked like that this morning, and I just hadn't noticed in the morning rush?

I brushed her hair away from her forehead and frowned at how warm she felt. "You want to lay down?"

"I could lay down." She pressed her face into my chest. "I'm so tired."

"Why didn't you tell me, baby?" I stroked her hair and waited for her mental punch for daring to call her baby—or physical punch depending how much energy she had left.

"I don't want things to change," she whispered. "We barely know each other. How can we have a baby?"

"We know each other plenty. Time doesn't dictate everything. As for the things we don't know, we'll learn as we go." I cupped her face in my hands and waited until her gaze lifted warily to mine. "Plenty of people have figured this out. They aren't any smarter than us."

"You do have a point there."

"I have many points." I kissed her forehead. "How much longer?"

"Like a minute."

I sat on the edge of the bed. She sat next to me, closer than I ever would've guessed.

"Whatever happens, we'll be just fine," I said quietly. "Look at me and believe me, Pocket Plus."

She sniffled. "You say that now, but the word *pregnant* changes everything, Mav. I won't be Pocket Plus, your pain in the ass anymore. I'll be your baby mama."

You'll be the woman I love. Just like you are right this instant.

I wanted to say it. I *would've* said it if I didn't think it would send her running. That was a very real concern.

"Want me to go look?"

She surprised me by nodding. "Yeah. You can do the honors."

"Okay." I rubbed my damp palms on my pants and rose to go into the bathroom. I took a deep breath and grabbed the first stick I saw on the edge of the sink.

Not pregnant.

I expected relief. Elation. A sense of being born again with a freedom I'd never appreciated enough before.

Instead, I was…disappointed.

I turned around and pressed my forehead into the doorjamb, knowing I had mere seconds to get myself back in line before Vanessa charged in here.

This was a good thing. The timing was all wrong. We could take the time to learn more about each other. What would we do with a squirmy, helpless baby who needed us for everything, anyway?

"Mav? What does it say?"

I swallowed deeply and went out to show her the stick. "Not pregnant."

"Not pregnant?" She frowned. "What the hell? My damn boobs are sore." She stood and started pacing next to the bed. "It's wrong. It has to be wrong."

"We can try again."

"Try again?" She whirled to face me. "What do you mean?"

I shrugged. "If we want a baby—"

"If we want a…" She trailed off and jumped on the bed, walking over to me on her knees to feel my forehead. "You're losing it. You didn't just say we should try on purpose to make a baby."

"Nope. I just said we could. If we're both disappointed, then maybe we should."

"You're disappointed?"

I thought about lying. About playing it off. But saving my ego wasn't worth denying the truth. "Yeah." I let out a ragged laugh. "Surprised me too."

"I'm not disappointed." She fell back on her ass on the bed and stared up at me, her face a mass of confusion. "What the hell? How can I be disappointed not to be pregnant with a baby I'm in no place to have?"

"Maybe you are." I sat down beside her. "Maybe I am. Maybe growing up and taking care of someone else is exactly what we both didn't know we wanted."

She scrubbed her face with her hands. "And the other one says not pregnant too?"

My spine snapped up straighter. "Other one?"

Before she could say anything else, I raced into the bathroom and grabbed the other stick.

Pregnant.

"Oh, fuck." I slammed down the toilet seat and sank down on it when my knees simply buckled. "Fuck. Fuck. Fuck."

"Mav? What is it?" She charged into the bathroom and grabbed the stick from my hand, letting out a noise crossed between a laugh, a scream, and a wail. I couldn't identify it. "Oh my God. I knew it. I knew it!"

I gripped her hips and pulled her closer, pressing my face into her chest. "I can't believe it."

"A minute ago, you wanted to make a baby," she shoved my shoulder, "which is nuts, and now you can't believe it?"

"I can have multiple thoughts at once, and none of them have to make sense."

"Obviously."

My phone buzzed with Brady's ringtone. I didn't answer it. "Dude, life changing events here. I'll strip for your party later."

"Wait, what? You were going to strip for his party?" She narrowed her eyes. "Why would your brother want you to strip at his bachelor party?"

I laughed, somewhat maniacally. "Because we were going to crash *your* stripper party."

"But our party only has ice cream. No point in going to a stripper bar when the bride can't drink." She swallowed hard. "Or the maid-of-honor."

"Huh?"

"We aren't actually seeing strippers." She spoke very slowly. "No strippers. Nada. Except you, apparently? Do you have a sideline I'm unaware of?"

I shook my head. "I got us into this mess."

"Damn straight you did." She kissed the top of my head. "I always knew I shouldn't trust well-endowed men."

"I meant with the stripper jokes. It was supposed to be funny. Brady and I would crash the party and strip along with a few of his friends."

Vanessa's eyes lit. "Oh, yeah? Now it's getting interesting. Which friends are getting naked?"

"The list keeps shrinking. All Brady's friends are scattering like rats. Think it's down to just us as the stripping party crashers. I've tried to get out of it a dozen times."

"Did you pervs get clearance from The Pleasure Palace before you go in there swinging your schlongs? Or is Christian showing up to write tickets part of your act?" She covered her eyes then peeked out between her fingers. "He's objectively hot, but I don't want to see him naked. He's just too anal. But I wouldn't mind seeing Lucky—" She squealed out a laugh as I grabbed her.

"I saw him lift you off the bus." I sucked her lower lip between my teeth. "Mine. All mine." I tightened my hold around her and barely resisted growling. "Both of you."

She wrapped her arms around my neck. "It could be wrong."

"So we'll go to the doctor."

"What are we going to do with a baby?"

"Watch YouTube videos and figure it out?"

"You're going to watch a video to raise a child?"

"Got any better ideas?"

She sat on my lap. One benefit to her being so small was that she didn't weigh much. At least she didn't now. That was going to change.

God, she was right. Everything was changing.

"No. I'm officially idea-less. But our siblings are getting married in a hot minute, because Tabitha doesn't mind being ready to pop in her wedding dress. That's not going to be me."

Some unnamed emotion swam through me, making me just a little lightheaded. But I just tightened my hold on her. "Duly noted."

Her eyes widened. "I mean, that's not—I didn't mean I expect to get married."

"Of course not. You expect to have to put an APB out on me and drag me into court for child support like every other worthless bum."

"No. I wouldn't have to put an APB out on you. I know where you live and work."

I nudged her off my lap and stood. "I should reply to Brady."

"Mav, wait."

In the doorway, I turned and braced my arm against the jamb. "I'm used to everyone expecting me not to step up. With an older brother

189

like Brady, it's not surprising. I've enjoyed proving people wrong for years. I'll prove you wrong too."

Filled with righteous indignation, I turned to go back in the bedroom.

And almost imagined I heard Van murmur, "You already have."

Right now, I had to show my brother I could be there for him too. Responsibilities were coming at me like a freight train. I could either jump on the train or get run over.

I voted jump. I just hoped Van would jump with me.

NINETEEN

WERE ICE CREAM HANGOVERS A THING?

I'd never been a huge drinker even in my rowdiest years, but it felt like a bus had hit me sometime between last night and dawn.

Add in the cement-like feet I'd stuffed into cute heels this morning, and I was dragging. I already missed the Crocs I'd taken to wearing at the bakery. They were like little clouds—at least for the first eight hours of my endless days.

I wasn't sure how Tab did it. I'd only been working full-time hours for a few weeks, and it felt like a million years. And I knew my sister had done far longer than eight hours a day pre-waddling.

At least I didn't have to worry about the bakery today. It was officially closed for the wedding. Tab would probably have found a way to keep it open if she wasn't preoccupied with keeping their little girl under her skirts for at least one more day.

The McNeills were hosting the wedding in their large backyard. Right now, an army of people were making sure Tab was as relaxed and pampered as possible. I wondered if one of our EMT friends could bring an IV bag of drugs to keep her from going into labor. Was that a thing?

All I knew was that the alarm went off way too freaking early. And

Mav had been up before me. I wasn't entirely sure he'd come to bed last night. He'd been in his shop working on something for the wedding after our trip to The Pleasure Palace.

Which we'd come home separately from. I'd tried to keep my spirits up so people wouldn't think I was any weirder than usual. Luckily, my sister had been drooping after an hour, so I didn't have to confess I was feeling the same way.

When Honey dropped me off, Mav was already in his shop. And during the bachelor-slash-bachelorette party, we'd kept to separate sides of the ice cream parlor. The first wave of Brady's friends had been small, then the whole room had been packed with firefighters, cops, and paramedics making massive sundaes. Lucky had crashed the party near the end, announcing he needed the most chill ice cream available, whatever that meant.

And there had been no stripping involved. Amen to that.

I was pretty sure Mav was avoiding me, but I couldn't think about that right now. I needed to get through this wedding without face-planting into the cake or the appetizers or even the main course. My eyelids had an equal amount of cement hanging off of them as my feet.

This first trimester tiredness was no joke.

At least I'd managed to read that much of the baby book I'd downloaded last night before I fell asleep—ironically, of course.

Tomorrow was early enough to deal with Maverick McNeill. Today was all about my sister and future brother-in-law. The fact that I was sleeping with and now procreating with an in-law was also a little gah.

Family dinners were going to be awesome.

Not.

I straightened the belt on my romper, the only thing in my closet besides a hoodie that didn't feel too tight. It would work as I ran around making sure my sister had everything she needed today.

My heels clicked on the wood floors of Mav's kitchen as my phone buzzed in my bag. Mickey was picking me up on the way to the McNeills' place. A large to-go tumbler was waiting for me on the kitchen island. A sticky note in Mav's slashing handwriting told me to drink the tea and skip the coffee.

I sighed as I snatched it off the counter. I really could use a shot of caffeine to keep me going. A memory in the far reaches of my fuzzy brain corroborated the coffee to preggo ration being like one cup.

I was going to expire.

I took a tentative sip of the tea. The hit of ginger settled my queasy belly like a stroke of Mav's careful hand. My eyes stung and I had to blink back tears.

He was always taking care of me, even when he was mad at me. Or even worse, disappointed in how I treated him last night. A rolling catalog of sweet gestures filtered through the fear I'd been trying to hold back since yesterday.

"Dammit, Maverick McNeill. How am I not going to fall in love with you?"

Hadn't I already?

I slid a hand over my still mostly flat belly. Working at the bakery hadn't helped my waistline even before he'd planted a baby in me.

I was about to put the stainless steel to-go cup down when I noticed a smaller Post-it where the cup had been.

Don't forget your dress.

As if I'd forget. Okay, maybe I would have possibly forgotten before I left. But definitely not before I left the driveway.

Maybe.

I tucked the tumbler in the crook of my arm and grabbed my purse, then took the dress out of the closet. Of course it was neatly pressed and laundered under the plastic. He'd probably thought of that too.

And I had not.

Chaos goblin reporting for duty.

Another note was tacked to the dress.

193

. . .

**You'll be beautiful. Take care of you and that little peanut today.
Drink water. NO COFFEE. See you at the house.**
     M

I tucked the note in my purse in the zipper part where it wouldn't get lost. Before I could think that little action to death, I rushed out the door and down the stairs.

Mickey's compact car was idling at the end of the driveway. She popped out and hurried over to help me.

She took the dress by the hanger. "Man, you got your dress dry-cleaned? I thought I only had to do that after I wore it."

To own up to the lie or not.

"My mom would kill me if I didn't." Not exactly a lie. My very proper professor mother ironed her pillowcases, for God's sake. I was just used to being a disappointment.

The pang reminded me of what Mav had said last night. Dammit, I really hated how much he'd been right about how I'd been treating him. We both had that parallel. Only one of us had actually changed in that regard.

And it wasn't me.

"You okay?" Mickey tilted her head.

"Yeah. Just a lot on my mind. Did you talk to Tab yet? She hasn't answered my texts."

"She just asked if I deposited the till last night." She grinned. "Even on her wedding day, she's worried about Sugar Rush."

"That's Tab." I opened the passenger door and dropped down into the bucket seat. "Thank goodness we got a sunny day."

Mickey hung my dress in the back and slammed the door then got in the driver's side. "In this area, it's a miracle. The possibility of clouds or rain or even lake effect is no joke in the fall." She pressed play on her in-dash, and Billy Idol screamed out of the speakers. She gave me a wide smile and the Billy snarl as she sang along.

I couldn't help but laugh as we shot down the street toward Turnbull. Maybe it wasn't exactly a white wedding, but that made it even funnier.

We sang at the top of our lungs as we took the straightaway to the next town over. We turned onto the McNeills' street and had to wait our turn to get down to the house.

The front of the ranch-style home was done up in her wedding best. The usual flowers blooming around the white picket fence had been replaced with barrels full of mums, cabbage roses, and the floofy frond wheat-looking things that my sister had been obsessed with for the last three months.

Whatever they were, I could see the appeal now that I wasn't finding them stuck to my feet. Pancake also loved them and stole them from all the mini arrangements Tab had been practicing on. The shredded remnants had been all over her apartment no matter how much vacuuming we did.

I wasn't sure about using Brooks' Greenery for the wedding, but my sister had been adamant about using local businesses for her wedding. That was my sister, Miss Community. But she'd been right. The older man definitely knew how to make things pretty.

Probably didn't hurt that he was Chief Brooks' dad.

I slid out of Mickey's compact car and grabbed my dress. The cul-de-sac was full of white trucks from various Cove businesses. The Mason Jar was catering the food, and the familiar black and purple van from Brewed Awakening was here with the cake.

Tabitha wanted her team to just enjoy her wedding, so she'd nixed the idea of them making her cake. They were heartbroken at first, until they realized they got two whole days off for prep, wedding, and recovery. That was definitely a win for all of us.

I intended to sleep for two days myself. Especially since I probably wasn't going to get any from GQ until we had some time to kiss and make up.

An older man in a sandy-colored pair of overalls and a plaid shirt was laughing with Mr. Brooks while a terrifying, battle sergeant-like woman with curls held back from her face with bobby pins was directing people where to go.

Oh, crap. That was Mav's mother.

I'd only talked to her briefly at the shower, and she'd been a little intimidating, but now?

Yeah, I was going to give her a wide berth.

I slipped around the truck in the driveway, using the cover of chaos to my advantage.

Hey, look at that, *I* wasn't the chaos for once.

Looking over my shoulder to see if Mickey had followed me, I noticed she'd gotten waylaid by Mrs. McNeill. Oops. Call me a deserter, because I was definitely out of there.

I followed laughter into the main house.

My sister was wearing a cape and sitting on an honest-to-God salon chair in the middle of some sort of home office.

"How did you get that in here?"

A super pretty woman with blond-streaked dark hair turned toward me. "Like it? My husband gifted it to me so I could take care of some of the elderly clients who have a hard time getting into my shop."

"Are you calling me elderly?" Tab asked, laughing. "Oh," she slid her hand under the cape and patted her belly, "Presley is very active today. She's probably just as excited as I am."

"As long as she stays put," I said as I dropped into the office chair behind the impressive desk. I could've put my head right down on the desk and blinked out. Instead, I let my head drop back on the plush leather.

"You okay?"

I opened my eyes. "Yeah, just tired. You keep me hopping, sis. And your back pain is not fun for sleeping."

A tiny bit of a fib, but not much. I had gotten a twinge or two.

"Yeah, I stopped in with my gyno for a special visit to make sure things were all kosher. Doctor said I could go any day, but probably not today."

"Probably?" I sat up and laced my fingers on top of the very proper blotter on the desk.

"Presley Ann can come any day. But I'm getting married before she arrives, dammit."

"I thought you didn't care."

"Blame Brady. He's got me all hyped about it too."

"Well, he did get you into this." I gave the hairdresser a quick smile. "Failed vasectomy."

The woman laughed. "Curse of the town strikes again."

"You too?" I rolled my eyes and popped up out of the chair. "Sorry, I'm rude. I'm Van. The sister. Twin sister, hence the bitching about the phantom pregnancy pains."

The woman took my outstretched hand. "Ellie MacGregor. I can do you next if you want a little shaping."

I reached up to my ever-widening curly hair. "I'm okay." I'd had too many hatchet jobs on my poor curls to trust anyone.

"Ellie is amazing." Tab tucked a glossy curl over her shoulder.

"I actually specialize in curly hair."

"Yeah?"

She nodded, her butterscotch brown eyes friendly. "I can take some of that weight off, but not turn you into orphan Annie."

I winced. "The trauma."

Ellie giggled. "I can only imagine."

"Just worry about the bride. If there's time for me, we'll give it a try." I stood up as Mickey, Lea, Tiffany, and Honey came in wearing variations of my Maid-of-Honor dress.

"Oh, guys." Tab's eyes filled. "You look amazing."

Mickey did a twirl. "I feel so fancy. I've been wearing nothing but college gear for too many days."

"I hear that one," Honey quipped. "And now look at us."

"Let me just put some big rollers in Tabitha's hair, and I can take the next one of you for a quick updo. That's what we're doing, right?" Ellie wrapped Tabitha's strawberry hair around a roller the width of a freaking bat.

197

"Oh, me!" Lea raised her hand. "I was so afraid I'd screw up my hair for the pictures."

"Nah. You're all beautiful. I'll just make you sparkle a little extra." Ellie flashed a smile. "My co-pilot, Paisley, is coming in with the makeup portion. She does hair too."

"Wow." Tiffany tapped her fingers on her purse. "I didn't expect to get the full treatment."

"That's why I didn't want you guys to make my cake. You deserve some pampering too."

The girls made a united front as they crushed my sister. I managed to escape while they were all excited before the mush got to me.

"Where are you going?"

I hunched my shoulders. "Just going to check on the back for you, Tab."

"Oh. Okay. Report back. Maverick has been playing goalie with me all morning. I want to know what's going on back there."

I turned to my sister, who was standing in her cape and a frosty white robe with a very un-Tabitha-like fuzzy hem and cuffs. I rushed back to her and gave her a quick hug. "You already look so gorgeous."

"Oh, what's this?" She rubbed my shoulder.

"Just feeling nostalgic and mushy, I guess." I moved back and patted her belly. The familiar zing made my own system feel even more jangly. "Stay put, little one. We have a wedding planned."

Tab laughed and covered my hand against her satiny robe. "I think she's going to cooperate."

Uncomfortable with the emotions pinging around, I slipped away and swung her fuzzy belt playfully. "Surprised with the robe. Seems very not you."

"Yeah, well, *you* find a pretty robe that covers all of this."

"You did. You look beautiful." And she did. Her cheeks were rosy even without the makeup and her blue eyes sparkled with happiness.

"I feel remarkably calm."

"Because you know you're marrying a great guy."

I might've been mixed up about damn near everything right now when it came to me and Maverick, but I knew his brother was right for my sister. Brady was a rare one.

I was beginning to believe that might be a McNeill trait. It scared me to pieces, but that fact kept sneaking up on me when I least expected it.

Maybe Brady wasn't the only decent guy around, after all.

The sliding door opened behind us, and Maverick filled the doorway. His wide shoulders showed off a snug T-shirt that looked at least ten years old. Maybe something out of his childhood closet.

I had a feeling Mav had been just as hot as a high school student, but maybe he was just a bit more filled out now. And boy, did I enjoy it.

His fond gaze drifted from my sister to me, his expression cooling. The punch of unhappiness rolled through me and made me want to go to him.

To say I was sorry.

That I really didn't know what the heck I was thinking, making him feel crappy about standing up for me and the baby. Well, the teeny tiny speck of a bean growing inside of me that was going to be a baby.

His gaze narrowed on me.

Could he hear the streaming insanity going on inside my head?

Was he feeling it too?

My sister looked between us with a raised brow. "Why don't you go check on the backyard?"

"Right. I'll go check and make sure everything is all set." I gave Tab a quick hug and one more pat. "Go sit down and put those feet up."

"I'm going," she said with a sigh. "I'm so sick of sitting," she muttered as she waddled her way to the recliner.

I crossed to Mav. The closer I got to him, the more his chocolate eyes went from hard to molten. His gaze drifted over my romper to the length of leg it showed off with my heels. I definitely didn't wear these kinds of shoes too often.

"How's it going out there?"

"Why don't you come see? Think you can navigate the grass in those stilts?"

I lifted my chin. "I can run ten miles in heels—at least I used to be able to in my clubbing days."

He folded his arms. "Is that so?"

"Well, what's the fun of traveling the world if you don't have fun?" It felt like a million years ago, but my youth was full of seedy bars, hostels, and probably a few too many close calls with dangerous places.

Being young and invincible felt like a long time ago. And while I liked his interested gaze, I really wished I had my Crocs. But pride had me marching after his long stride.

"Hey, where's Francie?"

Mav looked over his shoulder. "Hanging out with her grandpa." He pointed toward his father who had Francie sticking out of his coveralls. She was happily snuggled under his beardy chin as the barrel-chested man was placing center pieces on each table.

A large white tent was tucked along the back of the property beside a massive oak. Gossamer thin material floated on the light early morning breeze, drawing my attention away from the simple and elegant tables to the tree.

"Oh, Mav."

He reached back to me and I took his hand as we crossed to the tree where two beautiful bird cages were hung on the sturdy branch that shaded a lovely spot on the lawn.

Scars in the bark made me wonder if a swing used to hang right there. Little Mav swinging there on a summer day was far too easy to see. Maybe pushing Honey on that same swing.

Perhaps he'd do it for our baby.

I pushed away those thoughts because they felt too huge. Instead, I focused on the material tacked behind the larger wrought iron cage with the fat cabbage roses in deep burgundy and white tucked into the chain and along the top of the cage. More of the long wheat things were sprayed behind the perfectly in bloom flowers.

The scent of eucalyptus drifted toward me and...was that fabric softener?

"The Chief's dad is pretty amazing. He added the little dryer sheet fans to the flowers to keep the bugs away. There aren't as many this time of year, but the yellow jackets are mean. Don't need them stinging the wedding party."

"Genius." I let his hand go and went right to the bird cage that was hung a bit lower. My fingertips flirted with the edges of the flowers and the sweet fan, but what I really wanted to focus on were the tiny birds inside the cage. "Is this what you were working on?"

"Yeah. Lovebirds. They mate for life."

Happy to have small hands for the first time in my life, I was able to snake my way into the small door. My eyes misted as I noticed the pillow at the bottom of the cage with their rings in it.

The whole thing was at the perfect height for me to grab the rings during the ceremony. He'd thought of everything.

"The other cages have our family."

I swallowed, afraid to ask if I was in one of the cages.

"My dad is the magpie. Typical since he lives for the shiny things in his shop. My mom is the little Blue Jay. Angry and too smart for their own good. My dad drives her crazy, but they love each other." He winced as his mother's voice bellowed from the house.

I swallowed down the lump in my throat, blinking away the emotions that tried to drown me at all the thoughtful touches he'd added. They showed just how much he knew his family.

"See? She's just worried about the schedule. I'm pretty sure the only reason she didn't have a meltdown is that Tab gave her an extra two weeks to nail down the details." He stuffed his hands into his pockets. "She's more traditional than I ever expected."

And she was going to end up with her youngest son's baby mama, who made chaos look orderly.

"Anyway, I don't know too much about your family, but the two owls seemed to fit, and there you are." He slid his palm down my back. "Hummingbird. Tiny and fierce, and they love to eat," he said, his voice low.

I laughed. As usual, even at the height of my overwhelming emotions, this idiot could always make me laugh.

He brushed his lips along my ear. "I hid a tiny egg in there." His arm came around my front, teasing the belt of my romper. He poked my belly. "For our little one."

"It's so perfect."

"I hope to make you something for our wedding day. Different, of course."

I whirled around on him, pushing him back. "Don't talk like that."

"Why shouldn't I?" His expression was intense. "We fit. Even without the baby, we fit better than anything I've ever known. You have to feel it too."

I shook my head.

"You can lie to yourself today because it's Tab and Brady's day. But I know where I stand. With you. Always."

"Mav! I need your help." His mother's voice rose to reach us.

He cupped my cheek. "I'll wait until you believe it." Then he took off across the lawn, leaving me there in the most beautiful spot I'd ever known.

For a moment, I let myself imagine.

And believe.

TWENTY

PUSHING MY FEELINGS FOR VANESSA DOWN AND INTO A BOX TO GET through the day was proving a bit more difficult than usual. Probably because every time I turned around she was staring at me with those huge, confused blue eyes.

I could see the tiredness around the edges, but she was in flight mode.

She talked a good game most of the time, but I had shaken her today. At this point, it was go big or go home. I'd wait for her to come to her senses.

Unfortunately, she was as quick as that damn hummingbird I'd carved last night. Flitting from one person to another as she pasted on a big, bright smile and made sure the wedding was perfect for her sister.

Hell, I was doing the same thing, minus the manic smile—moving tables, putting up tents and displays, as well as a massive photo wall my mother had come up with at two in the damn morning. It was a nice touch and didn't require much out of me other than tearing apart an old wood pallet from my dad's store.

In the end, the rustic entry piece was a statement to Brady and Tabitha. My mother had printed out a shit-ton of black and white photos she'd gathered from the two families on her mini printer. From babies all the way through to their engagement party and shower, she'd managed to amass quite the collection to show off the happy couple. And of course, the sonogram showing the baby took center stage.

The golden child.

I wondered if my own news about our baby would garner as much excitement. Or maybe they'd take up a collection for a nanny because my whole family thought I was incapable of being responsible.

Wincing at the nail I'd hammered in crooked, I took a deep breath. Maybe I'd hammered a touch too aggressively.

"Everything all right over here?"

I flipped around my hammer and wrenched out the bent nail to replace it with a fresh one. "Fine."

"Seems kinda intense for a Brad nail. Don't crack the piece of slate. I don't have a backup."

I blew out a slow breath. "I won't, Ma."

She rubbed the spot between my shoulder blades only she seemed to be able to find. Huh. Funnily enough, Van had found it a few times, now that I thought about it.

Which made my shoulders tense up again. How could she not know how good we were together?

"Girl trouble?"

"It's about Brady and Tab today, not my love life."

"Is that what it is?"

"Ma," I said with a sigh.

"I don't want to know the particulars, but I mean, about the love part."

I dropped my hand and turned to her. "We don't have time to talk about this."

"We always have time to talk. You know you can always come to me. I know your father is the fun one, but I'm the logical one who is a problem solver. You obviously have a problem." She slid her hand down to wrap her fingers around my wrist. Her eyes were so much like mine, dark and intense. But hers had that mama bear fierceness lurking just behind them.

"I can't talk to you with the tacked curls, Ma."

"What?" She touched her hair. "For God's sake, have I been walking around with these all morning?"

"Maybe?"

"You all are the worst."

I shrugged. "I thought it was to keep your hair out of your face."

She pulled the bobby pins out and slipped them in her pocket. "There. Now tell me what's going on in that big beautiful brain of yours."

"It's not a big deal. I have to get this finished and then move on to the sign in table."

"You're wasting more time waffling than if you would just spit it out."

I tipped back my head. Not a goddamn cloud in the sky. At least my brother was getting a perfect day for his wedding.

I exhaled. It wasn't my news to tell about the baby yet. Not with how Van had been acting since we got the results.

"I love a crazy woman." That was the truth and an easier admission to go with right now.

"Well, duh."

I looked down at my mother. "You knew?"

"It's pretty obvious. You McNeill boys don't know how to hide your feelings. Just like your father."

"I suppose that's true. I mean, about Dad."

"It was bound to happen. The minute you started working for the Crescent Cove PD, you started leveling out. I haven't seen you on your motorcycle in months. My heart appreciates it, mind you."

"Kind of difficult to rip down the street when you're supposed to be upholding the law."

"Definitely doesn't apply to many cops, baby. Or the idiots I worked with. It's just you growing up." She patted my chest. "I knew you had it in you eventually."

I frowned. "Pretty sure you told me last week that I was a child."

She patted me harder. "You're still male."

"Gee, thanks, Ma."

She shrugged. "I'm used to it. Brady was always too grown up. Tabitha and that little girl coming made him loosen up a little."

"Made him crazier, if you ask me."

"That's part of being a parent. But he also laughs all the time." She nodded toward Brady who was helping our dad weigh down a barrel full of flowers near the bar. "The FBI showed him the worst of the world and law enforcement for a long time. Bureaucracy will kill your soul. It's something both of us know all too well. Crescent Cove reminded him that he was made to take care of people."

"I guess."

I wasn't sure what to do with all this new information.

"And he wants that for you too. He rides you so hard because he knows what a good man you are. He's your big brother. It's his job to look out for you."

"And to give me shit?"

"Especially to give you shit." She pulled me down into a hug. "And loving Vanessa isn't the worst thing you've ever done, you know." She slapped me on the back. "She'll keep you on your toes."

"That's the truth."

"Please don't wait until she's about to pop before you marry her."

"She isn't—" The lie wouldn't come out all the way, but my mom held up a hand regardless.

"That town of yours is wild."

"It's not like Turnbull is that far away," I muttered.

"Far enough, and I don't want to know anything. Just promise me you won't make me wait forever for a wedding."

"We definitely aren't at the wedding part."

"Yet." She reached up to adjust the sign with Brady and Tabitha's names on the display a fraction of an inch. "You'll convince her. Or better yet, let her come around to the idea first."

"Too late."

She laughed. "I've got to go get dressed. The bridesmaids are going to come over with the pictures from their dressing party to add a little bit of wedding crazy to this." She tipped her head to look at the reclaimed wood display I'd put together in about twenty minutes. "It's really beautiful, Maverick. And those bird cages."

I panicked when her eyes misted. My mother was not a crier. But she laughed and waved me off as I leaned closer to hug her.

"You have a gift. Thanks for helping us make it a beautiful day for your brother."

I didn't know what to say, but as usual, my mother didn't stick around for the emotional stuff. There was a suspicious sniffle before she quickly crossed the side yard to the house.

Luckily for me, I didn't have time to dwell on that huge download of information from my mother. My sister and the frightening pack of bridesmaids was headed my way.

"That looks amazing!" Honey slipped her arm through mine and leaned her head on my shoulder. "Tabitha is going to just die when she sees everything. We've had to tackle her about fourteen times to stay away from the windows."

Lea handed out photos to everyone. "Clip at will. This is just the sweetest thing I've ever seen."

"Thanks." I shoved my hands in my pockets, not sure what to do with all the sweet-smelling females all around me—not counting my sister, of course.

Three months ago, I would've basked in the attention. Now all I wanted was to see where Van was.

Mickey and Tiffany started fussing with all the photos and then my sister jumped in with her own opinions. I took that moment to escape to help my dad and Brady.

"Have you seen Van?"

Brady swiped his forehead with the back of his arm. "I think it was her turn for the primping station. She kept trying to get out of it, but Honey said she finally was on the chopping block. Literally. The hair chick wanted to attack her hair."

My stomach lurched. I loved Vanessa's wild hair. It fit her personality too well.

Untamable in every possible way.

Brady slapped my arm. "Don't worry. It'll grow back."

"Ass."

His lips twitched. "Thanks for doing all this. I saw all your little touches. I didn't know you were doing so much wood carving these days. Tab is going to lose it when she sees those bird cages."

I shrugged. "Ice designs are created in a pretty small window of the year, even around here. I had to do something else or I'd go nuts."

"Well, it's amazing. I really appreciate it."

"Just best man duties."

"It's really not. You went above and beyond." He gripped the back of his neck. "And all I have been doing is giving you shit."

My dad pulled out his tie-dye bandana and mopped his face. "You guys are gonna make me cry over here."

"Shut up," we said in unison.

Our dad laughed. "I'm just glad to see you guys getting along. If it takes a baby and a wedding, then so be it. But we still have a ton to do. Emotions later during the speeches."

I was more than happy to skip the mushy stuff. "What do we have left?"

"Two more barrels have to go near the head table and then we have to take showers or your mother will kill us all."

"I know that's right." Brady grinned. Dirt smeared his cheek and his shirt. I wasn't sure how he'd managed that, but I decided I didn't want to know.

"Well then, let's get it done."

With the three of us attacking the last of the details, and my mom trailing behind us to make sure everything was cleaned and polished, we got everything done and even had time for a beer.

A quick one but still.

The next little while was a flurry of activity. The food, booze, and a metric ton of ice was being hauled in by the catering team. Then my cousins and aunts and uncles arrived hours early. I left my mother to deal with that.

Showering in my childhood bathroom was a blast from the past. I wasn't sure how I used to fit in the skinny standing shower. Part of me wished I could find out just how inventive I could be with Pocket Plus and her bendy ways in this space.

She was tiny enough to jam in the corner.

And that was enough of that. Jacking off with this many people in the house was definitely not advised.

"Don't use up all the hot water!"

"Fuck off," I shouted back to my brother.

"It's my wedding day, goddammit."

I grinned as I gave my face a quick scrub with some of my sister's junk. I shut off the water, but before I could get a towel around my waist, my brother busted in.

"Hey!"

"Whatever. I need to get a move on and Dad is singing to Elvis in their bathroom. I'll never get him out of there." He started stripping.

I rolled my eyes. "I still have to shave."

"I don't care. Nothing you haven't seen." He whipped the curtain closed, and the water came back on.

"Why the hell is the whole family here already?"

"They're probably trying to get into the food early. Aunt Arleen is already driving Ma crazy."

I opened my shaving kit and dug out my good stuff before lathering up my neck while the room was steamy. "How's Tab doing? As best as you can tell, I mean. I know you can't really talk to her with the whole day of superstition stuff."

"She's not the superstitious sort usually, but yeah, I only get to text her until the ceremony. Mom has some set-up for us to take pictures through a door or some shit. But whatever Strawberry wants today, she gets."

I scraped off a strip of beard quietly. I felt the same about her sister. Vanessa could literally ask me to dye my hair purple, and I'd do it right about now.

My brother stuck his head around the edge of the curtain, soap streaming down his ears. "You're gonna make me do all this madness for you too, huh?"

"Probably."

"Bah." He snapped the curtain closed again. "You sure about that? Vanessa is a handful."

"She's my handful." I said it so quickly that I knew it was the truth.

I was already certain how much I loved her, but right then, it clicked how much I wanted it all—the actual real deal of a ring and that baby she was already growing.

Not that I had a clue what to do when it came to raising a child. But we could learn.

There was always YouTube. And hey, maybe even a MasterClass. Or perhaps a For Dummies book.

I shook off my latest spiral. The certainty that I wanted a life with her helped to settle the jangling nerves I'd tried to push down all day.

I finished up and slapped on the stinging aftershave. "Bathroom is yours."

"Finally."

I grinned as I slipped out the door. I'd mostly dripped dry while I was in the bathroom in my towel. I sprinted down the hall to my old bedroom and found my suit on the door.

My mother, always prepared. Thank God someone was around here.

Ten minutes later, I left my room so my brother could get dressed and headed downstairs. All the girls were chattering in my dad's office, their voices carrying out to me.

When I reached the bottom stair, my breath stalled.

Van stood there in her dress, her wild curls slightly tamed in a half up, half down hair thing. The filmy burgundy material dripped off her shoulders and flowed around her hips to the floor. It accentuated her tiny stature and made her look like an ethereal princess.

Her wide, smart-ass mouth was stained to match her dress with some sort of gloss that made me want to kiss it off her, or wear it stamped around my cock.

She was stunning.

I barely noticed Tabitha in her fragile white gown with tiny berry colored flowers that dotted her train.

"You look amazing, Tab," I said once I shook myself out of staring at her sister.

Right then, their twin vibe was more apparent than I'd ever seen before. Both of them glowing in different ways.

Well, actually some of the same.

But they had the same coloring, and while their hair was a little different, the jawline and eyes were so much the same. With Van in heels, they were almost the same height, since the bride was definitely rocking some sparkly Crocs peeking from under the hem of her dress.

Van met my gaze. I ached to drag her close, but it wasn't the time. Especially since the photographer was heading our way.

I moved in front of Tab and took her hands. "My brother's a lucky man."

"You have to say that. I'm a whale in white." She grinned up at me and I pressed a quick kiss on her cheek.

"Just gorgeous."

"Oh!" She touched the side of her belly. "Presley says thank you."

I lightly patted her belly. "You stay in there for a little longer, okay?"

Tab laughed. "We are determined to enjoy every bit of the wedding you all created for us. She'll stay put if I have to stick a cork up there."

"Let's hope it doesn't come to that."

"Bride! I need you to set up with the groom!"

"We have names," Tab muttered. "Coming!" Her voice was sweet and friendly as it carried to the photographer. "Now I have to go try not to see Brady before we do the aisle thing. Not sure how this is happening."

She squeezed Van's hand quickly before rushing off.

"You look amazing."

Van nibbled the corner of her mouth. "You don't look so bad yourself." She reached up to touch my clean-shaven face. "Haven't seen this for a while."

"Yeah. You like me beardy." I pressed my cheek into her palm, then closed my hand over hers when she tried to slip away. "I'm sorry I scared you earlier."

"Not now, GQ."

Before she could back away from me, I gripped her hip. "You can't run forever."

"Mav! We need you over here for pictures." Honey's voice broke the moment.

Vanessa backed away and hurried over to her parents, who were lined up for photos, as well.

Maybe she couldn't run forever, but she was definitely all about running today.

"You okay?" Honey came up next to me.

"Yeah. I'm good."

I'd make sure Van and I both were, even if it took longer than I wished.

TWENTY-ONE

My cheeks hurt from smiling, but it was worth it to see my sister so happy. We tried our best to make the day about her, not just the preggo belly she was sporting.

She'd chosen an A-line dress for the big day. It showed off her bountiful boobs—I hated her a little—and gently flowed around her belly. Her hair was all curls and sparkles with the tinsel-like extensions Ellie had put in her hair to make her glow even more.

Her train and veil were embroidered with tiny flowers and strawberries from yours truly. I'd asked AJ to help me with the project, and we'd knocked it out with a coffee and bitchfest one of the nights Maverick had to work.

I'd needed to add a tiny piece of me to my twin sister's day.

I'd spent far too much time away from her, but I was glad to be home. The wheels on my bus weren't rolling anymore. My roots were firmly growing here.

In fact, I spent more time in Maverick's house these days than my own mini-house.

Couldn't he see that I was getting used to the idea of staying put? Why did people always need words when actions said plenty?

So says the woman who constantly questions both his actions and his words.

And I was not getting mired in that mess right now. Today was for my sister.

I joined the line up at the back door for the processional down the flower-strewn aisle. I would be last out the door before the bride, which gave me a few extra seconds to adjust her veil one last time.

She smiled at me, her eyes suspiciously shiny already.

"Don't you start. If you cry, then I'm going to cry, then we'll both screw up our makeup. And Paisley scares me."

Tab gave me a watery laugh. "No one scares you."

She was so very wrong on that one. "*She* does."

Both of us glanced over to Honey who was slapping away the brush Paisley kept trying to use to powder her face. My future sister-in-law was not one for getting fussed over.

Not that I was either, but I didn't mind a primp here and there. Especially since Mav had definitely been into the end result. Not that it mattered what he thought of my makeup and dress.

Okay, so it shouldn't, but it so did.

And I'd never felt more beautiful than when he came down the stairs and caught sight of me. What would it be like to be wearing a dress like my sister? To have all the butterflies that I could feel going on in my sister's belly?

The twin powers were super activated today. At least that was what I told myself.

I clutched my sister's hand as the music cued up. "You're beautiful, and I can't wait to see your face when you get a load of what they did for you guys out there."

She fanned her face with her other hand. "Do not get me going."

"Oh, who am I kidding? You're only going to see Brady."

Her eyes filled. "Yeah."

"I'm so happy for you, Tabby cat."

"Okay, you can stop now." Her voice was thick with emotion.

I cleared my throat. "Okay, okay. I'm done." I could hear my future mother-in-law barking orders.

Wait. Not mine. Tab's mother-in-law.

Yours. You know you want it to be yours too.

I ignored the little voice that was getting louder every day. It was just the wedding fairy dust sprinkled everywhere. It made people crazy. It was obviously having the same effect on me.

"You're up, Vanessa."

I followed Honey as we got closer to the door.

Paisley stopped by me and gave me a satisfied nod before sighing at my sister. "You are trying out my waterproof mascara to the best of its ability, ma'am."

"We should have gone with clear." Tab waved her hands in front of her face.

"Oh, right. You redheads with your blond lashes."

My lips twitched as I sailed through the door, my head held up high. I tried to ignore the twinge in my back. I wasn't sure if it was due to me or my sister.

Fake it 'til we make it was the rule of the day for both of us.

The afternoon was warm with just the hint of crispness on the air. The perfect day to celebrate love.

And I wasn't even throwing up—for one reason or another.

I wobbled slightly when I saw Maverick at the end of the aisle. The wind lifted the gossamer material draped over the massive tree branch, making it flutter prettily. The bird cages swayed gently, and the sound of bells drifted my way.

He was so tall and gorgeous in his suit. The unrelieved black and white against his tanned skin made my heart race. His slightly long hair fluttering in the breeze made my fingers itch to grip and stroke.

We locked eyes, and good Lord, I was in trouble. My heart pounded in my ears, and the bells became a distant hum until I broke the staring contest.

I swallowed hard and forced myself to take in the moment. The rest of the guys were dressed in suits, with a few of them in their dress firefighter gear since the wedding had been relatively last minute. Adam Parish and Austin Lancaster, two of Brady's firefighter friends, stepped in to cover the bride-heavy side of the wedding party.

There was no way Tab would've considered not including include her whole staff. We'd all become such a tight unit over the last year. Even me, who didn't want to really get involved with sticky entanglements, had ended up befriending the women.

All of these people showing up to support my sister made my eyes misty.

And finally, Brady was standing stiffly at the end of the aisle. Nerves radiated around him as he looked around me for Tab. I was the last one—the maid of honor.

At least a maid for a few more months, anyway.

Stop with those kinds of thoughts already.

My mother was seated in the front row, and I wiggled my fingers as I passed by. She wasn't overly demonstrative, but even she had a tissue clutched in her hands as I walked over to stand with the other bridesmaids.

The wedding march started and everyone stood. Then Brady leaned forward, his hands covering his mouth as Tabitha came down the aisle on my dad's arm.

Actually, she more like floated down the aisle with her flowing dress and veil. Her bridal bouquet was simple with the white and burgundy cabbage roses in full bloom.

And then there wasn't a dry eye in the crowd as Tab giggled into a sob, and Brady laughed as he broke protocol and went down to get her. He cupped her face, kissing her before we could even get close to the wedding vows.

The crowd whooped. Lucky, with one of his twins on his hip, lifted a fist. "That's how you do it."

Luna Beck was officiating, and she took a few steps forward. "All right, you crazy kids. Let's actually do the vows part first!"

Brady let her go and took her from our dad. My father was grinning and just as drippy as the rest of us as tears rolled down his cheeks.

I took the bouquet from my sister. "You're so beautiful."

She sniffled and hugged me before turning back to Brady.

The vows were simple and heartfelt. Neither of our families were very religious, so they went with traditional vows.

Tabitha sniffled as she reached into the bird cage for their rings. She leaned against Brady as she stroked the tiny wooden egg beside their rings. She scooped it up with the rings and tucked it into her palm.

A memento for a lifetime.

Both of their voices were thick with emotion as they pledged their love and devotion before all their friends and our families.

"I now pronounce you man and wife," Luna said with a big grin. "You can officially kiss your bride this time."

Not that Brady even heard her. He had his wife in his arms and was kissing the stuffing out of my sister.

"May I introduce Mr. and Mrs. McNeill," Luna added with a laugh.

After a raucous round of applause, I was being hugged by everyone. My parents came forward, along with Mav and Brady's, and then all of us bridesmaids crushed into a puddle of hugging and crying.

Eventually, I found myself getting passed to the guys in the wedding party. First, to the too pretty to be real Adam and the adorably beefy Austin, who teased me about running into the gas station that night. I let him have his amusement, now that I knew that night had led to our whole lives changing.

I still couldn't quite believe it.

Even the Chief gave me a quick hug. Finally, I ended up in front of Mav. He lifted me off my feet, and I grabbed onto his shoulders. He kissed me under the tree adorned with all of his thoughtful gifts.

And I let him, because there was really nothing else I wanted in this world right at that moment.

He put me down just before we were dragged over to the tents in the surge of people. Our hands stayed locked as long as possible.

Half of Crescent Cove had to be in attendance. Between the police force and the firefighters and the EMTs, it was a wonder anyone was actually on duty.

But of course I knew who one of them was. Christian was

definitely not into having any of the wedding emotions sprinkled on him. I was sure he was finding someone on Lover's Lane to bother.

And for once, it wasn't going to be me.

Liz McNeill lifted her voice and instructed everyone to take a seat in the tent. A seating chart had been a ridiculous undertaking, so the place was a free for all.

Half the men got waylaid at the bar. We'd gone the easy route with beer, wine, and spirits from a local winery, as well as cider from the nearby Happy Acres.

The twinge in my back increased. I tried to find my sister in the crush of guests, but she was still surrounded. I caught a glimpse of her radiant face and forced myself to relax.

Today was only meant for happiness.

I tried to push down my own nerves about early pregnancy problems. I'd just found out, for God's sake. I was fine. My hand went automatically to my middle. The baby was fine.

Everything was fine.

I was passed around for another round with the bridesmaids as the wine started flowing. Luckily, the wedding had been built around an alcohol-free bride, and I was able to avoid the bubbly without being obvious about it.

Just as I managed to loosen up, another blast of pain radiated down my back. A familiar hand gripped my hip.

"Hey, are you okay?"

I clutched Mav's arm. "Where's my sister?"

His eyebrows snapped down over his midnight eyes. "They're just about to do the first dance."

I twisted around. "Where?"

"There, near the cake table."

I whipped around to see my sister swaying with Brady as they talked quietly.

Beside them, the three-tiered cake was almost as wide as Tabitha. The fat, nearly over-bloomed roses were echoed in the frosting along with a waterfall of strawberries along the bottom layer next to a pair of dog statues that looked as if they were taking a chomp out of the cake.

As cute as it was, I couldn't shake the knee-shaking fear. They were okay. Was it me?

Terror clutched my throat. Mav noticed and grabbed a water off one of the tables. "What's wrong?"

I shook my head.

"Vanessa? Is something wrong?" he asked me more directly, a hint of his cop voice slipping through.

I focused on his sharper tone and forced myself to slow down my brain and my heart rate. I couldn't spit out words, my attention still on my sister. She was rubbing her belly, but she was forever doing that.

"I have a feeling Tab is going to go into labor. I think. Maybe."

He leaned down closer to me, his breath on my ear. "Twin thing?" His hand slid over to my belly. "You sure?"

I pushed it away when all I wanted to do was hold on. "I'm not sure of anything."

He sighed and drew me back to one of the tables as the music from the DJ grew louder to signal first dances were commencing.

"Ladies and gentlemen, I'd like to officially introduce Mr. & Mrs. McNeill to the party!"

Claps and catcalls filled the tent. Tabitha's smile was wide, and the sound of her laughter soothed me. She was clutching Brady's hand, but other than that, she seemed like her usual self.

Maybe I was imagining it.

Brady whispered something in her ear, and she flushed before he drew her gently into his arms. I could barely hear a note of the song. My head was full of fuzz and my spine felt hot under my skin.

Tab tripped, and one of her Crocs came off. Brady bent to get it, and she let out a startled yelp. Just before she could go down, Brady swooped her up into his arms.

"Strawberry?"

The attendees surged forward.

I tried to push my way through the mass of people. There were far too many emergency personnel in attendance, and they all instinctively shot into action.

I was too damn short.

"Mav!"

He lifted me like a damn football and pushed through the people.

Austin and Adam had circled the crowd and met each other behind Brady and Tab.

"Not the time, kid!" my sister yelled.

"Don't think the kid much cares, ma'am," Austin said as he gently helped to get Tab back on her feet.

Lucky and Tish cleared a table and grabbed the tablecloth. Lucky rushed over and the cream tablecloth hit the ground just before Tabitha.

Tabitha grabbed for Brady who was right behind her, bolstering her. My sister arched her back, and a quick screech had my heart thundering harder between my ears.

"Gotcha. Here's Van." Mav tugged me along and we pushed past my shocked parents, going to either side of them.

"Thank God." Tab clutched my hand. "Oh, I don't want to do this here."

"Not sure we have a choice." I sniffled and rubbed her lower back.

"I think we can still get to the hospital. This is your first baby, right?" Austin knelt beside her, his gaze fixated on his watch. "You have a little—"

Tab shrieked again.

"Okay, maybe not." Austin slid a look at Brady. "Your wedding day and your baby's birthday look like they're going to be the same day."

Brady slipped an arm around my sister's shoulders. "I don't care. As long as the baby is okay."

"All right then." He twisted around and seemed to spot someone in the crowd. "Burke. You're up!"

Finally, I looked away from my sister. "Who is Burke?"

"EMT. Best one in our unit."

I nodded and put my focus back on my sister. "Hey, we did the classes and everything for this. We're prepared, Tabby cat."

"Just like nothing?" Tab's eyes wheeled as she stared at her bent knees. "I'm in my wedding dress!"

"Hey, you were only going to wear it that one time."

Tab laughed. "That's true." She slammed back against Brady. "Oh, shit."

Brady pressed his cheek to her temple, frustration wrinkling his brow, but he didn't stop holding on. And I guessed that was better than anything else in this world.

He stood up, again and again.

Actions were always more important than words.

Fear flashed on my sister's face as another contraction hit.

"Hey. I know we wanted that little duck as your focal point, but it's gotta be me."

Tab nodded and stared at me as we breathed slowly through the tail end of the pain. It exploded up my spine, but I gritted my teeth into something akin to a feral smile.

I'd take it for her.

I'd take it all for my sister if I had to.

But when it came to my own birthing experience, I was taking every drug I could possibly get and then some.

The tall, buxom blond who had tended to Maverick that night at the Qwik Pump knelt beside me. "You guys are doing great."

Ugh. Did it have to be her?

The woman's gaze locked with mine, and there was nothing but kindness in her cat-like green eyes. "She's young and healthy—" She shot a look at Tabitha. "Right, Mom?"

Tab's eyes suddenly flowed over with tears. "I'm going to be a mom."

Burke nodded. "You sure are." Tab's gaze bounced around to the people behind us, but the EMT squeezed her knee. "Nope. Just worry about what's going on here." She glanced over at Austin who popped to his feet and started asking people to back up.

I'd totally forgotten everyone around us, but instantly, I felt better when they all dispersed.

Between contractions, my sister shouted for people to take food and desserts home.

A nervous bubble of laughter cracked the tension locking my spine as Mav reached over to clutch my free hand. We made a trio around my sister with Burke at the bottom.

I didn't want to think about what she was looking at or that she'd ripped all my sister's underthings. So much for the pretty lingerie we'd picked out.

I turned to whisper to Mav. "Do not let anyone ruin my panties, you hear me?"

He narrowed his eyes. "I'm assuming except me?"

"If it's La Perla, goes for you too, bucko."

Adam came up to us, his face perfectly blank. Had he overheard us? If he had, that should momentarily distract him from my sister's hoohah.

Yeah, now he's thinking of yours, genius.

He cleared his throat. "The ambulance is on its way, but it will be about ten minutes."

"Pretty sure we'll have another passenger by then," Burke said ruefully. She gave my sister a nod. "We get to start pushing now, mama."

"Oh, God. I'm not ready." Tab's chest heaved, sparkles and lace contracting as she tried to push away from Burke. "No way. I was supposed to be at the hospital. At the pretty pink room at the birthing center. I had music picked out!"

Brady lightly rocked her side to side. "We have a DJ right behind us."

Tab elbowed him. "Don't be logical."

"We have pink flowers," Mav offered up.

Tab grabbed him by the tie and pulled him closer to her face. "Fuck your pink flowers."

"Okay." Brady shifted her against him. "We're going to have the best wedding story of the town, right? That's enough."

"I'm tired of being the talk of the town," Tab grumbled before her body stiffened.

"Here we go." Burke smiled brightly. "I've done this a dozen times in the Cove. We're going to be fine. Everyone likes to have babies out of the hospital. Actually, it's a bit more odd to actually *have* them where they're supposed to."

Tab growled through the contractions, and I could only hold on. I might have a broken hand by the end of it, but we were going to get this baby out of my sister.

God, if my sweet sister had a stubborn baby, what kind of heavy machinery would be required to pry my kid out of me?

Maybe I'd have to start wearing throwaway underwear just in case by month seven.

She slumped back on Brady as the latest one passed. "Okay, Hot Cop, you can take over."

"I would." He hugged her against him, his hands on either side of her belly. "I'd do this if I could."

In a flurry of shouts and inventive and inspirational ways that Brady would never touch her again, Presley Ann McNeill was born in Mav's parents' backyard.

The sky was intensely blue and a perfectly warm breeze blew under the tent as Presley's first cry cracked the air.

The ambulance arrived just as Burke placed the wiggling, cream-tablecloth-covered baby on my sister's chest.

She clutched the baby close, and her other hand slid up to cup the back of Brady's head as they both cried and laughed. Wonder and relief warred on my new brother-in-law's face as he rocked both of his girls in that way parents seem to know instinctively.

Arms helped me off the ground and I melted back into my father's familiar fresh laundry scent. I turned around in his arms. "Congrats, Grandpa."

He patted my back awkwardly and I burrowed into him harder. Both my mom and dad weren't really good at the giving comfort thing, but right now, I'd take what I could get.

After my sister was put on the stretcher, I laughed as Luna handed out sparklers. We had to send off the bride and groom one way or the other.

Might as well be in style.

Tabitha cried and cuddled her baby close as she was wheeled down the winding lane that led to the front of the house where the ambulance was parked. Brady was right by her side, oblivious to the last of the wedding guests lighting their way.

His future was definitely heading forward.

I glanced at Mav standing alone, watching his brother walk away. I only hoped our future would do the same.

TWENTY-TWO

 Maverick

AFTER THE INSANITY OF THE WEDDING, VISITING BRADY AND TABITHA AT the hospital seemed positively anti-climactic. None of us lasted long during visiting hours, but we all stopped in to make sure Presley was perfect in every way. The entire family was exhausted from the wedding preparations and the adrenaline crash of the wild and very public birth of my niece.

I still couldn't believe how it went down.

I was an uncle.

And soon to be a father.

I wasn't sure how that happened either. I mean, I knew. I was there and the steamed windows of my truck were the proof. The rest was held inside Van and the spark of my future.

A few months ago, the idea of a baby had been as foreign as learning another language. Who needed German when you had to read *What to Expect When You're Expecting*?

I'd been reading it in my squad car now that I was on my own, since Brady was taking his paternity time. The baby was officially four days old, and I'd barely seen Van. She and my mother were taking shifts helping Tabitha every day.

I tried not to take it personally. I knew a lot of things were on her mind right now. Some of it was work. She'd gotten a phone call at the hospital and had been preoccupied ever since. If she wasn't at Tab's or the bakery, she was hunkered down in her bus, sketching late into the night.

The last two evenings I'd had to go over there and drag her to our bed—yes, ours. I didn't freaking sleep well without her. I usually found her curled around her iPad with her digital pencil lost in her curly hair.

Almost as if she shoved it behind her ear and passed out mid-thought.

The only time I could sneak under her defenses was when she was tired. She would curl into me so trustingly and let me carry her home. Exhaustion from the first trimester and pulling double duty at the bakery and Tab's house was pushing her to the edge.

Not that she'd let anyone see that.

But I did. And it was more than just worrying about her out there alone in the very secure bus. Between John Gideon's crew and my own research on the best locks for her setup, she was safer there than in most houses.

But I wanted her next to me at night. Not even wanted, I needed her there. While I could bury my face in the beach-scented pillow, it just wasn't the same.

I kept fighting against the fear she was pulling away from me. A lot was going on, and I wasn't the center of the damn universe. At least that was what my mother kept telling me.

Someday it might stick.

Loving a strong and independent woman was not for the faint of heart, that was for damn sure.

I glanced at my watch. Three hours left on my shift and then I could go home and twiddle my damn thumbs.

Great. Maybe I could convince Tab to come out to dinner with me between work at the bakery and seeing her sister.

I parked on the street near the park and decided to take advantage of the sunny fall day with an old-fashioned beat walk. I didn't get very far. The front of Kinleigh's halted me in my tracks.

The handcrafted bassinet in the window hit me like a bolt of lightning. Maybe that was exactly what I needed to do to show Van I was all in.

I wasn't the master carpenter that August Beck was, but I could make something for our little one that was one of a kind. My fingers itched for my notebook as ideas flooded through my brain faster than I could catch them.

I crossed the street to Every Line A Story. I picked up a backup sketchbook, eraser, and pack of willow vine charcoal, happy to find my preferred sketching medium now in stock.

Lucky break.

"Oh, hey, Maverick. I see you found my new supplies."

I placed my mini stack on the checkout counter and smiled at Colette, the owner. "Yes. I usually have to special order it. I can't believe you carry it."

Her quick fingers tallied everything up on her vintage register. The old school *cha-ching* never got old. "Van asked me to stock it last time she was in. Mentioned she saw it in your workshop and wanted to pick some up for you."

I paused with my billfold open. "She did?"

"Of course. She's always looking at the supplies in here. She always asks me for the most obscure floss for her embroidery work. I think she's working on something new."

Imagining both of us working on something for the baby kicked up the corner of my mouth. At least maybe what she was doing was for the baby.

I pulled out a twenty. "Makes two of us."

Collette cashed out and tried to hand me the change. I just shook my head. She smiled wider and dumped the few dollars in the jar for art supplies for Crescent Cove High. "The art club thanks you. Oh, speaking of..."

I narrowed my eyes at her.

She shrugged. "I gotta shoot my shot."

My chest tightened. "Oh, I'm..."

She flushed. "Oh, gosh, not that. I was wondering if you'd be

227

interested in doing a workshop. The art club is fascinated by your ice carvings."

"Oh." Surprise and delight hit me. "Yeah. I would love to."

"Not that I wouldn't ask you out if Van hadn't snapped you up." She winked at me as she handed me my receipt.

"Yeah, she's it for me."

Colette sighed. "The good ones always get snapped up fast."

I laughed. I had nothing to say to that one without getting myself into trouble, so I quickly took my leave.

I was tempted to stop into the bakery, but the line was out the door, so I detoured down the block and across the street to the path around the lake. Some of the Crescent Cove Tigers were tossing a football around on the common ground while the girls gathered to watch and flirt.

The town was expanding. They'd added an extension onto the high school last year, and now they needed to do renovations on the elementary school to make room for larger classes.

When I'd grown up in nearby Turnbull, the Cove had been a dinky town that barely had a football team. Now they were getting some state attention.

Pretty soon the Chief would have to hire on a few more part-timers to fill the holes. Especially when all of us were expanding our families and didn't grab for overtime as easily.

I took a seat on one of the benches by the water to be able to watch the guys playing as I sketched out the idea that had come to me.

Soon, I lost myself to the drawing. The hummingbird I'd carved for the wedding made a reappearance, along with a bunny and deer.

The foot of the bassinet took on a woodland story-style setting. I'd always been attracted to birds and small creatures while carving. Instead of worrying about something new, I brought the pieces I'd put in the bird cages into the design.

I pulled out my eraser and changed the head of the bassinet to hold the hummingbird now as well as a penguin just behind her. That wasn't exactly a woodland creature, but it made me grin.

I remembered reading about Emperor Penguins as a kid. Well, my dad had read to me back then. Having a dad who bore the brunt of the rearing with my mom being career FBI for most of my life had been weird to my friends.

My dad had been the one to carpool, go to my games, and cook dinner. I wondered if I would be the same kind of father. Especially since Van secretly was more of a badass career woman than I'd originally thought.

The once playful drills by the high school team on the common ground suddenly turned into a shouting match. I slapped my notebook shut and left it on the bench as I ran over to break up the fight.

I didn't notice Austin was picnicking with his little sister, Joey, until he ran over to back me up.

I hauled the blond kid with spiky sweaty hair off the burlier Black kid who was trying his damnedest not to take a swing at the punk.

Austin jumped between them when the shorter hothead tried to go for another round.

"Hey, watch it." I pushed the blond back a step. "What's your name?" My tone was firm enough that the blond kid finally got it through his head I was a cop.

He pushed his hair back, looking around at the group of people who were gathering. "I wasn't doing nothing."

"Anything," Austin muttered as he crossed his arms.

"What?"

Austin rolled his eyes. "Never mind."

The taller Black kid lifted his chin. "Mitchell just needed a reminder that I'm the quarterback, that's all."

"Not for long," Mitchell snarled.

I glanced at the other kid. "You are?"

His jaw tightened. "Kimmel. Josh Kimmel. I don't want any trouble. Cody," the sneer in his voice was evident, "just thinks because he moved here from Syracuse that he's going to be taking my place. Not happening."

"We'll see." Cody Mitchell rolled his neck and puffed up his chest.

I sure didn't miss my high school days. "Don't make me call Coach

229

Conners. I'm pretty sure neither one of you wants to be benched for the upcoming game."

"C'mon, K. It's not worth it." Another kid came up to us. He'd been standing off to the side with a tiny redhead who reminded me of Pocket Plus minus the extra fire.

Kimmel's brows snapped down. "I'm good."

Austin picked up the football that had been discarded and tossed it to Kimmel. "Good luck at the game Saturday."

Cody swore, then backed up and ran toward Main Street.

Austin sighed. "Do you want to go after him?"

"Nah. I'm assuming there wasn't any real beef here?"

Kimmel shook his head. "No, sir."

The other kid spoke up. "Cody's mostly all right. He's just butthurt because Coach didn't immediately kiss his ass like they did at his old school."

"You a senior?"

Kimmel nodded curtly.

"Cody too?"

Kimmel sighed. "Yeah."

"New school in senior year sucks. Being the bigger guy sucks too. Part of being captain." I tipped up my chin a little because the guy had at least an inch or two on me. If I was Cody, I wouldn't want to be on his bad side. "Go on, get out of here."

Relief dented his prideful stance, and he backed up with the ball clutched in his huge hand. "Thanks."

His friend slapped his shoulder as they both loped across the grass to the group of girls clustered together.

Austin pulled his sunglasses out of his pocket. "Remember being young and dumb?"

"Christ, I would never go back."

"C'mon. All those girls dying to talk to the QB?"

"I was in shop." I laughed. "Brady was the football guy. I was better at fine motor skills." I waggled my eyebrows.

Austin tipped his head back and laughed. "I just bet." He shook his hair back with some fanfare. Asshole knew there were girls looking at him. "I guess my work here is done." He nodded to the girl texting furiously on the plaid blanket a few feet away. "And now Joey will be on that thing for the rest of the afternoon talking about what happened."

"She's, what, a freshman?"

"Don't remind me."

I laughed. "That kind of gossip is too much to keep to herself, man."

Austin rolled his eyes. "Save me from the teen years, man."

My friend had stepped up after his parents' died a while ago. Now he was raising his sister as a pseudo single dad.

At least I had time to get used to the idea of being a dad, and I wasn't going to be on my own. I also didn't have to deal with a teenager right off the bat.

"Beer next week?" I asked.

I had achieved bad friend status lately while I'd been pouting about Van. I could be man enough to say that was what I'd been doing.

Which meant it was time to be proactive about Vanessa Vail Monaghan.

"Yeah. That'd be good. I could use some time out of the house."

"Same, man. Oh, and thanks for the assist. Careful the Chief doesn't see you. He'll try to recruit you away from the fire station."

"If the town council keeps carving at the budget, I might be hitting him up."

I laughed because I knew Austin would never leave the firehouse. But that was the one drawback of a small town. We might be growing, but the firehouse was originally built with volunteerism as its base.

The older firemen were aging out, and the younger guys wanted a steady paycheck, not more work on top of doing a forty-hour week at a day job.

"Yeah, our budget pulls from the same pool, remember? We don't even have enough squad cars half the time, between mechanical issues and whatnot." I shook my head. "And that's with a smaller force. Can't wait until the Chief hires more officers."

Austin laughed. "Fun everywhere, man."

"Ain't that the truth. Catch ya later."

Austin nodded and I went back to the bench where I'd left my sketch pad. A duckling was sitting on top of it.

"You better not shit on that, bird."

As I got closer, I noticed that the fuzzy bird wasn't quite a duckling. Evidently, teens were going to be my problem for the day all around. "Can I have that back?"

It quacked at me.

"How about a bribe?" I toed open the hidden compartment of corn stashed next to each of the benches. It stopped people from feeding bread to the ducks, which actually wasn't good for them.

When the duck quacked louder, I tossed corn on the ground and he or she hopped off my sketchbook. Luckily for me, there were no additional duck droppings.

Then again, I guess I'd have to get used to shit in my life with a baby on the way.

I grabbed my pad and hurried up the hill toward Main Street. Hopefully, I could still catch Van at the bakery.

She was just swinging out the door as I was crossing the street.

"Pocket Plus!"

She turned at my voice, a little harried. "I gotta head to Tab's."

"No, what you need to do is eat. I bet you haven't had lunch today."

"I…ate." She wouldn't look at me.

"A pack of Ritz crackers doesn't count."

She blew out a breath and crossed her arms over her middle, then she lowered her voice. "It settles my stomach."

"And now?"

"Okay, I could eat. Pancakes maybe?"

"Pancakes it is." I urged her forward with a hand at her lower back. "How are you doing?"

She shrugged. "Fine. Presley doesn't believe in sleep, so we're all tired."

"From what I read, it could take some time to get on a schedule."

"Read?" She tipped up her head to look at me as we walked. "What are you reading?"

232

"The book. You know," I lowered my voice, "the baby bible."

Her cheeks pinked up. "Oh. I keep falling asleep when I try to read it between…everything."

"You can't keep working yourself to the bone, babe. Something has to give, you know. And I don't want it to be you falling over in exhaustion."

"I know. Tab needs me right now."

"Does she? Brady is there."

"I know but—"

"But nothing. You need to let them get a routine going. And if Tab knew everything, she'd say the same."

"I'm going to tell her. I just want to wait a little longer. Besides, everything should be all about her right now."

I gripped her by the elbow and gently urged her away from the foot traffic that was getting thicker on the sidewalk. We were right near Brewed Awakening. "Yes, but I'm all about you." I shifted toward her and laced my fingers over the small of her back. "You're my priority."

She laid her hands on my chest, her short nail tracing around stitching of my name patch on my vest. "I've never been someone's priority."

"Well, get used to it."

"Maybe I could get used to it." She nibbled on her lower lip. "What if I like it too much?"

"Then I'm doing my job."

"I'm not a job, Maverick."

"No, you're just my whole life. Eventually, you'll believe it." I kissed her forehead. "Now let's get you fed. I'm starving."

Her stomach grumbled. "I guess I am too."

"Good." I hustled her across the street and opened the door of The Rusty Spoon, nudging her in ahead of me.

Polly, one of the full-time waitresses, waved us inside. We took a booth at the back of the diner, Van shoving her huge bag onto the bench seat.

"Usual?" Polly asked from the counter.

I nodded and she came over with two glasses of water and an iced tea for me.

"What'll it be? Special is meatloaf and garlic mashed potatoes with green beans a la Mitch."

"A la Mitch?" Van blinked. "What's that mean?"

"Means Mitch's flavor of the week. This week, there's a lot of garlic going on."

"Oh." Van wrinkled her nose as she laced her fingers on the table. "Silver dollar pancakes, bacon crispy and lots of butter, please."

Polly nodded. "Officer Studly?"

Van grinned at me, her blue eyes sparkling. "Yes, Officer Studly. What'll you have?"

I ignored them both. "I'll have the hot open-faced turkey, please."

"Fries or…"

"Oh, he'll have the fries," Van said quickly. "Extra gravy."

"You got it."

Once Polly left, Van pulled her water glass in front of her, twisting it in the shallow puddle of condensation. "Now that I actually have you here, there is something I want to talk about." She glanced around, pitching her voice low. "I have some names I want to run by you."

"Isn't it a little early for names? We don't know what we're having yet."

"Say it a little louder, pal."

I took a sip from my iced tea and set it aside, then I leaned forward. "What names?"

She dug into her bag, coming out with a sparkly notebook with a unicorn pen. Was that a horn or a…

You know what? I didn't want to know.

She flipped the pages. Even from here, I could see that her chaotic handwriting filled the lines with a staggering amount of bullet points. Then she pushed the notebook my way.

I frowned down at the names. "What are these?"

"I picked out three different doctors from the birthing clinic where Tab went. Well, where she was scheduled to go, anyway. She really likes this doctor." She pointed to one name. "But she was a bit stuffy for me."

"Okay. But the other two? We can try them both. Find out which one you like more."

She frowned. "Oh."

"Well, we'll be working with them for a while, right?" I drew a nine on the table with my finger.

"That's smart."

"I do have moments."

She rolled her eyes. "Whatever, McNeill." She pulled the notebook back to her side of the table and stuffed it into her bag. "I'll call and make an appointment."

"Good. I want to be there."

"You do?"

"Of course. I'll be there every step."

She pressed her lips together and swallowed thickly. She was saved from reacting to my statement by the arrival of our food.

When was she going to get it into her head that I wasn't skipping out on this?

Not even just because it was my responsibility, but because I loved her. And this new life we were starting was just the beginning.

Somehow I resisted the urge to bang my head on the table. Being patient sucked.

She slathered her pancakes in butter and syrup with relish. I hoped for her sake gestational diabetes wasn't in her future. She'd probably kill everyone during the next eight plus months if anyone tried to deny her food in any capacity.

I had to stop reading that book before bed. The facts were jamming up my thoughts followed directly by the minefield of things that could go wrong.

Blissful ignorance was sounding good right about now.

She popped a forkful in her mouth. "I guess I should tell you I'm a millionaire then," she said around the bite.

I paused with turkey and gravy dripping from my fork. "Excuse me?"

She swallowed. "Yeah. Crazy, right?" She pointed at me with a piece of bacon. "Lawyers are a pain in the ass."

I nodded mutely. She couldn't have said what I thought she'd said.

"I had to talk to my lawyer and my agent and about three other lawyers from the publishing house. I can't believe they said yes to my terms. Makes me wonder if I should have asked for more."

"Wait. Back up. Million?"

She took a sip. "Oh, right. Well, you know you never actually get a million dollars from a publishing deal. It takes forever to pay out and then there are taxes—"

"You're only giving me half the story."

"Oh. Sorry. I forget that you can't download my brain sometimes."

That was a horrifying thought, but my life would be much easier if I could.

Probably.

"I got tapped to do a graphic novel for a romance author. The one with the magic double peens? Yeah. They want to branch out to do graphic novels. Maybe even anime. Wouldn't that be wild?"

Polly came back to check on us and asked if we needed anything.

Van took a bite of her bacon as I tried not to fall out of the booth. "Could I have some more water?" she asked. "Maybe a big glass of milk?"

Polly nodded. "Sure. Be right back." She frowned at me. "You okay, Mav?"

Van patted my hand. "He'll be okay in a minute."

"Okay, then." Polly shrugged and turned on her heel.

I put my fork down. "I'm sorry. Did you say million? Just checking one more time."

She nodded. "With an option for a sequel if it does well." She picked up her fork and stabbed at her pancakes. "These are amazing. Want a bite?"

I shook my head. "I knew you were incredible from your website, but holy shit, Pocket Plus."

"I know. This is my first seven-figure deal. It's pretty crazy."

Her first seven-figure deal as if there might be more. She was *that* talented.

"Wow. I'm so happy for you. And for me, that I know you."

"Even in the biblical sense." She snorted then picked up the butter for another layer on the bottom pancake. "I didn't want to jinx it. You're the first person I've told. Well, other than my agent. He said he's sending me flowers so don't get jealous, okay?"

"He can send you all the flowers he wants if they come with that kind of check."

"Right?" Her blue eyes sparkled. "We should go home and have sex. After a nap."

I laughed. Life with this woman would never be boring. "Sounds like a plan to me. And this time, I won't fight you if you want to pick up the check."

TWENTY-THREE

VANESSA

HALLOWEEN IN CRESCENT COVE WAS A THING TO BEHOLD, AND NOT just because Macy—and her team—at Brewed Awakening had perfected a candy spider that melted like a flavor shot into hot coffee.

And not just because the damn thing looked freaking real sitting in the foam before it disintegrated.

"C'mon, you're not trying my spider? I figured you of all of the chicks here wouldn't wuss out." With a shrug, Macy nudged the creation back her way. "Fine. I'll get high on my own supply."

My regret was real. "If only I could."

I frowned down at my surprisingly delicious cup of caramel apple cider, debating with myself.

Did I dare share my news? I wanted to, even though it was early. I was still nervous. But my doctor's visit and some research online had smoothed me out a bit. I was perfectly healthy, and a lot of women who had early miscarriages never miscarried again. My twin had just given birth to a beautiful little girl. That had to be a good sign.

And I was doing my due diligence by forgoing most caffeine. That had to count for something.

I darted a quick look around to make sure no one in the busy coffee shop was standing too close. Not that I'd keep this under wraps for long.

Especially since I could swear my waistline was already expanding. It didn't seem possible, but if it wasn't from baby growth, it was the street corn Mav had made again the other night. I'd had three, maybe four servings.

Followed up by a bowl of pistachio ice cream.

I was calling them cravings because I was hungry, and if I could claim it was for the benefit of the baby, even better.

But when I opened my mouth, Macy held up a hand. "Don't bother. You've got the Cove look about you."

I narrowed my eyes. "Is that a good thing or bad?"

"Depends on your point of view, but you're glowing, so I can't see the bad." She leaned over the counter and spoke softly. "I'll have a special decaf version of your Americano double shot next time you stop in."

I sniffled. "You're too sweet to me."

"Are you being an ass?"

"No, hormones." I waved a hand at my face then let out a laugh. "Well, I'm kind of always an ass, but I've been waiting for you to make me my special drink. It's like I really belong here now. Like I have a place." And the tears that had threatened a moment ago actually pooled in my eyes, mortifying me.

Macy shocked me by not shaking her head in disgust at my female display. Instead she grabbed a spider off the tray of them and plopped it in my cider. "It'll take longer to melt this way, but the end result will taste just as good. Happy Halloween."

I grinned as if she'd just presented me with a brand new iPad as I pried out the candy spider.

"You're supposed to wait til it melts—" Macy sighed. "Never mind. I remember those days. I would've eaten the paper cup. Enjoy."

"Oh, I will," I mumbled, already getting hints of almond from the flavor shot burst in the center. It didn't exactly go with the cider, but it was good nonetheless.

Macy was a damn genius when it came to coffee and what went

COP DADDY NEXT DOOR

with it, not to mention all things spooky, as evidenced by her decorated front windows.

Purple gauze and lacy cobwebs dripped from the ceiling offset by strands of orange pumpkin lights. Tiny white lights seemed innocuous until you looked closer and realized they were fashioned to look like bones. Gelatinous blood spatters covered the glass in somehow artful shapes. And of course, Macy's favorite character, Michael Myers, watched from the side of the window, the soulless eyes of his mask peering out at everyone who passed.

I shivered in delight as I studied the decorations. I needed to get some for my bus.

For tonight.

I shivered again for a whole different reason. I'd been turning an idea over and over in my mind, and somewhere between the doctor's visit with Mav and today, my resolve had strengthened. I could do this. I *would* do this.

Actions meant more than words, always.

He had the night off. I had the night off. I was still able to perform any number of lewd sex acts, and what better gift to give your boyfriend when you propose to him?

Holy Michael Myers, I was going to attempt to become a married woman. But I wasn't wearing white. No way in hell was I pulling that off when my belly was the size of a basketball as my sister's had been.

Maybe I'd go with tie-dye or Day-Glo. Something truly memorable.

Outside of the coffee shop, I stopped and tapped a blood red fingernail to my lips. *Hmm.* I wanted Mav in a tux—so I could enjoy getting him out of said tux. I guess I couldn't show up looking like bride of Chucky.

I spotted Kinleigh's vintage shop and hurried across the street. Maybe she'd have an idea. Was there was a way to combine classy with sassy? Unique with elegant?

If it could happen, Kinleigh was the best place to start.

"Wait a second, you're buying a wedding dress before you've gotten engaged?"

"He'll say yes to me. How can he not?"

In truth, I wasn't quite as certain as I appeared to be. I mean, sure there was the baby, and he was an honorable guy. But I wanted him to marry me for me, just as I was marrying him because I loved the hell out of that man—forever and ever, amen, there would never be another for me.

Period.

Kinleigh smoothed a hand over her sleek fall of auburn hair. Redheads seemed to be all over this town. Maybe we were magnetized here just like babies were.

"I have to say, I like your confidence. Wish I'd had an ounce of it before I was married."

"Well, you should have." I sucked down most of my cider in one gulp. It was so good. "You pinned down that stud muffin August, and he's a long, tall bite of sexy."

Kinleigh blinked a couple times before laughing. "Yeah, I suppose he is."

"Trust me, he is, and he adores you. So be confident, girl. Be confident anyway, but take comfort that he knows exactly what and who he has in his life." I released a long breath. "I'm not buying a dress yet. I'm just wishful shopping. Is that a thing? I didn't even want to be married before. Maybe it's hormones—" I swallowed hard. "Or PMS!"

She smiled knowingly. "Or maybe it's happiness. Marriage is far less scary when you know he's the one." She led me over to a rack of vintage gowns. "Since you're just getting ideas, want to veto these right off the bat?"

I drank the last of my cider and pitched the cup in the trash. "Yeah. I'm too short for these. I want to show some leg. And some back."

If my breasts cooperated, I might even have some cleavage to speak of. Praise be.

"You know, I think I'm going to send you elsewhere."

I frowned. "Is this my *Pretty Woman* moment? I can pay." Could I ever after landing my big deal.

She laughed. "No, of course not. I like you, Van."

"You do?"

"I do. You inspire me. Just I have a friend who is more in sync with your vibe, I think. She'll come up with something amazing for you."

"Quickly? I want to still have some shape left. I mean, I'm not running down the aisle for Thanksgiving, but—" I blew out a breath. "I need to ask him first and see how he feels before I plan the whole shindig and tell him when and where to show up." I bit my lip. "Huh, maybe I'm becoming a planner?"

"It sure sounds like it, but yeah, you should probably get his input. At least a little."

"His input can be scary."

"Well, he is male."

I nodded sympathetically. "Very much so. But he deserves to get to help plan this deal too. Unless he just wants to elope, which gotta say I wouldn't mind." I closed my eyes for a minute, imagining a Just Married sign and tin cans jangling off the back of my bus.

The idea had merit. And his dad loved Elvis. I was pretty sure someone else in town had gotten married in Vegas. I'd do my research and add it to my list of possibilities.

"Eloping solves a number of logistical problems. And pains in the ass."

Surprised to hear the usually prim and proper Kinleigh swear, I laughed and opened my eyes. "So where are you sending me?"

She moved back to the counter and grabbed a pad, jotting something down before tearing off the paper. "Have you heard of Vintage December? It's a newer shop in town, just off Main Street. December is a goddess at finding exactly what her customers need. And she has a funky sense of style like you do."

I glanced down at my denim miniskirt, lime green patterned tights, and chunky Doc Martens. My earrings were dripping bloody cleavers. "I guess funky fits. Thanks," I added as I took the paper. "I'm going to try to wait to see her until I actually have a fiancé. This was just a whim."

She grinned. "Probably a wise plan."

"Thanks again." Impulsively, I rushed around the counter to give her a big hug, though she towered over me. What else was new?

She hugged me back, pleasure radiating in her smile as she shifted away. "For what it's worth, he'd be an idiot to say no to you, and Maverick isn't an idiot."

"No, he's definitely not. I've been the idiot who kept saying no to him." I bit my lip. "Not that he proposed. Dragging his feet there, just like his damn brother. No wonder my sister had to take control."

Kinleigh flushed. "Some men enjoy when a woman takes control."

"Oh, he definitely enjoys that. Hmm, maybe I'll get out his handcuffs—just in case." I grinned as Kinleigh's flush turned into a four-alarm fire right up to her hairline. "See you!"

I practically pranced out the door. Then came to a stop as my gaze zeroed in on my bus parked damn near perfectly against the curb.

And the obvious piece of paper tucked under the windshield wiper.

"Motherfucker! Not again!"

About half of the townspeople passing by on the sidewalk turned to look at me, aghast. Mothers covered their innocent children's ears. Hell, even Arlo the duck—so named by me—lifted his head from pecking at whatever the pet store had put out in a dish for him.

I was officially the town potty mouth. Did I really think I would make an appropriate wife for a cop?

Yes. Yes, I damn well did. Because no one would love that cop more than me. Besides, he'd do his job better because he was going to be sexually satisfied every night and some mornings too.

I marched toward my no-longer-an-eyesore bus. However, the other cop he worked with was going to get an earful from me. I snatched up the ticket, ready to blister the ears off anyone who had the misfortune of being nearby.

And saw a damn smiley face written in pen with the words *Happy Halloween* and a little broom. Or a stick.

Happy freaking Halloween? Had Christian had a psychotic break? Mav had mentioned he'd taken a few days off last week, which was uncharacteristic for him. Maybe he'd gone to the beach, discovered there was more to life than work, work, work.

Maybe he'd even—*gasp*—gotten some.

I knew good sex certainly put a pep in my step. Part of why I was so perky today, hopefully imminent nuptials aside. Mav had given me some extra glow this morning before he'd made me pancakes.

I mean, the guy was basically perfect. Unless he turned me down, and then I would not be responsible for my actions.

Speaking of, I should make sure he knew he had plans tonight before I went to kick cop booty. Because something was clearly wrong with Christian, and it was my duty as a Cove denizen to find out what he was doing—and who.

Van: Got plans tonight, Officer?

Mav: Hoping to bewitch you.

Van: Oh, that's already happened. I'll be waiting for you at eight. Come find me. *wink*

Mav: Oh, I'll come, all right. See you then.

I rushed down the street to the cop shop, wondering if I should just let things lie. It was Halloween and I had a man to seduce—and hopefully get engaged to—which required prep work. Shower time, shaving time, makeup time, illicit lingerie time. I also had to decorate the bus with a few important accoutrements. At least we didn't need to worry about condoms anymore. Though realistically, we'd obviously never needed to. Our kid was determined to be born.

I hoped that remained true.

Before all the arrangements, I needed to talk to my sister. I'd left her out of too much important stuff lately, but I was on sisterly thin ice right now. I wanted her to know what was going on. Besides, I was so happy I could burst.

You know, in between being scared witless.

So I really didn't have a ton of time to be hassling Christian. I could be benevolent in my current fully sexed state. If the guy was happy, good for him. Free love was a beautiful thing.

I needed to put my rainbow peace sign decal back on my bus. Assuming Mav hadn't tossed it out when Gideon's crew was repainting it. The man I was marrying was a wily one.

My eyes narrowed on the door of the police station. A closed sign hung front and center.

Closed? Since when? There were cars in the lot. Not many, and I knew Mav and Brady both were off-duty today, but Mr. Stick Up His Butt should be there. And there was another sedan I didn't immediately recognize. Hey, had Christian drawn a stick to represent his personality?

Another puzzle to add to the list. In the meantime, I was going in. The cop shop wasn't supposed to close. What if I needed assistance, for Pete's sake?

I rattled the door and it opened without hesitation. Hmm. I rushed inside, headed around the corner to the small break room—and shrieked.

Two people were on top of the damn table. Or partially atop it. Close enough.

And they were not doing a crossword.

Hands were roaming. Hair was mussed. Clothing was askew—and a bountiful breast was out of its holster.

Dear God. It couldn't be. Not Honey and Christian freaking Masterson.

TWENTY-FOUR

I WHIRLED AROUND AND PRAYED TO BE BEAMED UP TO ANOTHER PLANET.

This wasn't my reality.

This was *not* happening.

More shrieking swiftly commenced, the kind that could pierce an unsuspecting eardrum and make me wish I'd just gone to the bakery to see my sister. Who was currently missing an employee who'd been exposing her breast to the mouth of a man who obviously knew what to do with it.

I needed to lay down in a dark room.

I needed to tell Mav.

Oh, God, I could never tell Mav his sister was being...fondled by his fellow cop.

And moaning. Just no.

"I'm not starting my marriage with secrets, dammit," I announced to the wall, since there was no way in hell I was turning around anytime soon.

"Marriage? What marriage?" Honey sounded breathless, but still... aroused. Should I know how my soon-to-be sister-in-law—maybe— sounded like on the verge of happy times? Nope. Definitely not.

"This is payback," I muttered. "Just because I got pregnant up at the Lookout, now I had to be scarred by seeing breasts I shouldn't be seeing, at least not until we're at a sleepover. Which is probably what my bachelorette party will be since I no longer stay up past nine p.m."

"Pregnant?" Another screech, this one accompanied by a tackle hug from behind by a now thankfully dressed Honey. "Really? Are you sure? Oh my God, did Mav faint? He had to faint. Why didn't he tell me, the jerk? We just went to lunch yesterday."

"Pretty sure you're keeping some things from him too," I said pointedly, turning around to hug her properly. I really did love the girl, although she had questionable judgment for days.

"No, I wouldn't."

"Um, hello?" I didn't look over her shoulder to where the man I'd intended to berate had wisely turned around to adjust his clothes. And probably other things, which if he was built to scale, probably would be worthy of one of my ginormous aliens.

Abort! Abort! Inappropriate thoughts seeking landing clearance.

But Honey was now fondling me—my belly to be exact. "You're still a pancake. Are you sure? It's so soon."

"Yes, I'm sure. We went to the doctor already."

She squealed. "And what about marriage? Did he propose? I'm going to kill him for leaving me out of everything, I swear. I'm supposed to be his best friend." She stopped talking and peered down at me, her mouth tugging downward. "Well, I guess not anymore, now that you're here."

"Aww, you're still his best friend. We're so new."

"And getting married? And having a baby?"

"Why wait?" I asked jauntily, nudging Honey aside when the Redwood she probably would've gotten fully naked with, chose to walk past us as if we did not exist.

"Um, hey there. What were you doing with Honey?"

He ignored me and went back to his desk while Honey poked my side about two hundred times.

"I asked you a question, jerk."

"I'd say it was obvious. Now if you don't mind, I have work."

"Oh, do you now? You have *work*." I went up on my toes to grip Honey's shoulders. "Didn't you just interview here?"

"Yes."

"Just today?" I gasped and shook her a little.

"No, yesterday." She bit her lip and lowered her voice. "But we know each other. We've been…around."

"You've been around? Is that a euphemism for fucking?"

"Knock it off," Christian snapped from his desk. "Not all of us do that immediately."

"Oh, right. She had an interview yesterday. Reasonable wait time. And what if she gets the job? What then? You know the Chief will never go for fraternization when it's so important to keep clear heads —and hands." I used mine to cover my face to try to forget what I still could not *unsee*.

"You can't tell Mav. Or Brady. Or anyone. Please." Honey made her plea into about ten syllables, and suddenly, I realized how young she was.

Fully an adult, but young. Five years younger than me. Or maybe four now because I was pretty sure she'd recently had her birthday.

Still, far too young for Christian Masterson.

"You know what it's like," Honey continued urgently, dropping her voice to a near whisper. "You make an impetuous mistake and next thing you know—"

"Next thing you know, he's going to be your colleague. You're just finally getting out of your mom's house. Don't fuck it all up before you even start your new life."

Part of me was berating myself for not being cooler about all of this. But that part of me was being stomped on by all the protective instincts inside me for Mav's baby sister who he loved so much. He would not take kindly to Christian taking advantage of her.

She might be an adult capable of making her choices, but he was still the older one. The supposedly wiser one.

What the hell had he been thinking?

I whirled back to him and raised my fist with the ticket in it. "And what was that Happy Halloween bullshit about?"

Christian's face was an unreadable mask when he shifted my way. Michael Myers had more expression than he did right now. "What are you blathering about?"

"The ticket you left on my bus."

"I didn't leave a ticket. Mav stopped by earlier for a few minutes. He probably did." Christian smirked. "Problems already in your happy home?"

I opened up my fist and smoothed the ticket against the wall. Of course. That was Mav's handwriting. I was just so conditioned to think the worse when I saw a ticket on my windshield.

Without saying any more, I rubbed my fingers over the ticket to save it and then shoved it into the zippered pocket of my purse.

"Aww, that's the sweetest thing I've ever seen. Saving Mav's note."

I scowled over my shoulder at her. "I'm not keeping your secret."

Her face fell. "But you have to."

Inwardly, I knew I did. I'd been in Honey's shoes before, and I knew her brothers were hard asses with her—out of love, but still. Just how could I not tell Mav? Did that count as betraying him since it involved his coworker too?

"I'll tell them," Christian said stoically, seeming as if he'd rather face a firing squad.

Couldn't say I blamed him. I didn't envy his role in that conversation. But I had to admire him for standing up. Maybe that was really what was in the water in the Cove. The urge to do better and be better for the love we found.

Honey growled. "Absolutely not. They're my brothers, and you aren't to breathe a word of this. All we did is kiss." She rubbed her mouth, smearing her lipstick even more. "I mean, basically."

"Kissing traditionally involves just the mouth. That was clearly second base."

"Second base? What are you, twelve?" Christian's voice was slicing and cold.

"And what are you, abusing your position?"

Honey hissed out a breath. "I'm not talking to either of you." She marched over to the break room table, snatched up her cardigan and her purse, then waltzed out with her head held high.

Leaving me and Stick-Up-His-Ass alone.

"Look, Honey is important to me, but I don't want to lie to Mav."

"I understand that." Christian's voice was tight. "I don't want anyone to lie. I'm taking full responsibility for my mistake."

Jeez, where had I heard that before? There were far too many honorable men in this town. It was starting to get annoying.

And I needed to be planning my night with Mav, not interfering in his sister's woe-begotten love life.

God help the girl.

"Chemistry just happens." I spoke to my feet. "You can't control it."

We wouldn't discuss how I'd always thought Christian had the equivalent attraction level of a ficus. He was a good-looking guy, but his personality? Not so much.

"No, but you can control what you do about it. This won't happen again. You have my word on it."

"You don't owe me your word. But you do owe Mav and Brady— and Honey—your honesty." I walked to the door. "Just don't hurt her. That's all I ask," I said over my shoulder.

"Too late," he said quietly as I let the door swing closed behind me.

Before I could change my mind, I hurried over to the bakery. Tab's windows were also done up for Halloween with festive bats, skulls, and cobwebs dripping over the door. A vampire swinging from the ceiling nearly hit me in the head as I rushed inside, but I knew to duck —and managed to swerve around Mrs. Gunderson as she aimed right for me with the light of good gossip in her eyes.

"Vanessa! Is it true?"

"No," I said as I beelined for my sister, not knowing what juicy morsel she'd happened upon but not in the mood for a chatting session in any case.

"I'll catch you later, don't think I won't!" she called.

"Not if I see you first," I mumbled, grabbing my sister's arm and towing her into the back while she laughed and sputtered.

Once the door to the store room closed behind us, I turned and gripped her upper arms. "We have a situation."

Tab's blue eyes narrowed on me suspiciously. "What did you do?"

"Me? Why does everyone always assume I've done something? Why, here I am, trying to get engaged and everyone figures I'm having an illicit affair or something."

Tab crossed her arms as I paced away to the back door. "That was last month."

I had to look back with a grin. "True."

"And, um, what's this about trying to get engaged?"

"Yeah. I'm gonna propose tonight. He better say yes. If not, I'll probably kill him. How are you with a shovel?"

"Fair." She patted her still slightly rounded belly. "And I have to work off this baby weight, so why not?" Then she giggled and bundled me into a hug. "I'm so excited. You really want to get married?"

"I really do. It's probably hormones."

Tabitha's eyes filled as she gave me a smacking kiss. "I knew it. I swear, I knew it."

"Well, it's not really a leap in this town." I swallowed a few times until the tears threatening finally abated. I did not want to be a weepy mess today. "And you know, that whole condomless sex thing probably didn't help. Every time after, we were good, but too late, the baby had been planted."

"Presley will have a cousin almost the same age. How cool is that? It's almost like we planned it." Tabitha hugged herself as I wandered off to poke at the bat windchimes tinkling over the back door. "Is Mav excited? He better be excited."

"He is. From the first, he's been onboard." I moved on to the witch candy jar on the counter and startled as her green eyes flashed and she let out a loud cackle before her mouth dropped open, revealing some candy. I plucked the wrapped pieces and grinned. "How cool."

"This town has turned into Halloween central, thanks to Macy's influence. Figured we might as well join the fun. There's another of those witches by the cash register. Just put it out there today. I swear, Presley tried to look at it this morning, but Brady thinks I'm nuts."

252

"Yeah, well, our kids are gonna be gifted. Or are already. For fuck's sake, not again." I pocketed my candy and rubbed my thumbs under my eyes.

"You okay?" My sister rubbed my shoulder.

"Yeah. I am. Just still a bit unsteady with the kid thing." I released a watery laugh. "Not that I don't want it," I added hurriedly. "Just maybe I want him or her a little too much."

"Is that possible?" She tipped her head against mine, still rubbing my shoulder in rhythmic strokes. When I didn't speak, her voice lowered. "I know about high school, Van."

Something crackled open in my chest. Not with fear or dismay, but with relief. Thank God she knew. I didn't want to say the words. To even speak it into existence again.

"I read your diary," she added with a hitching laugh. "I shouldn't have. But I knew something was up, and I was afraid for you…"

I turned toward her and buried my face in her neck. "I should've told you back then. I wanted to so much. But I was scared and ashamed and just a general wreck."

She held me tightly, just letting me talk.

I finally told her everything, and the whole time, she kissed my hair and waited me out. Through my tears and my embarrassed laughter and the parts I could barely say.

She was just my best friend, my twin, loving me silently through every bit of it.

"It's been so long and I just shoved all of it down. But this thing with Mav brought everything bubbling up again."

"Understandable. Are you going to tell him?"

"I told him the first night we were together."

Tab's pale brows shot up. "Really?"

"Yeah. I freaked out on him after our first time. Because that's the way to start a relationship, right?" I laughed, shaking my head. "He wanted to know why I reacted that way, besides the obvious terror of forgetting to wrap it up in a town like this." My lips curved. "And he listened to the whole story, Tab. He asked questions. He held my hand. I mean, where did he even *come* from?"

"Turnbull." Tab grinned. "And he has an equally amazing brother. Lucky us, huh?"

"Yeah, lucky us," I echoed. "Just now I'm scared I'm going to lose all of this that I can't believe I even found." I forced myself to smile again. "I guess you found it, huh? Score one for the big sister."

"We find what we're meant to when we're meant to, and not a minute before." She brushed her fingertips over my wet cheek. Wet yet again. "You're going to be an amazing mom."

"Oh, God." The tears poured out and there was just no stopping them now as I clung to her.

A few minutes later, when we were both sloppy from crying and rocking and laughing in the way that we always do, she eased back and cocked her head. "What's this about a situation?"

"It's not about me for once." I winced. "How are you at keeping a secret?"

"Pretty good."

"Yeah, I guess so, since you never let on you knew about mine. This one is epic. Huge. And it involves both our guys, so you have to swear you won't tell anyone. It's not mine to tell, but God, I gotta share it with someone before I burst."

"If it's more stripper talk—"

I snorted out a laugh. "Nope." I lowered my voice and darted a glance at the closed door before rushing over to lock it just in case someone tried to interrupt us. "It's about Honey."

TWENTY-FIVE

 Maverick

I HAD ENTERED FULLY WOO TERRITORY ON THE DAY OF THE YEAR WHEN the veil was thinnest. I supposed that was appropriate.

"Come on in," Luna said as she waved me inside as if she'd expected me to show up on her doorstep this afternoon.

She probably had.

Shockingly, the only Halloween decoration was a black cat figure that stood sentinel at the front door. As soon as I entered, its real life doppelgänger ran down the stairs to wind around its mistress's legs.

"This is Levi. He likes you."

Since the cat was paying me no mind, I wasn't sure how she'd come to that conclusion.

"Oh, good. I like cats." I dipped my hands in my pockets, feeling like a moron.

Not unusual for me around some of the powerful women in the Cove. Including my own.

I followed Luna and Levi into her spacious living room done in all creams and blues, a soothing space that fit her personality and her Zen ways. Silk and satin in the same muted colors whispered around her from the long, caftan-thingy billowing around her ankles.

I half expected chimes to tinkle from an unseen breeze.

She plucked up her baby Milo from his swing and nestled him to her chest. To my utter relief, he did not attach himself to her boob, just snuggled in for a snooze.

I knew I'd have to get used to such things soon enough, but I was still in the learning phase.

Besides, maybe Van wouldn't want to breastfeed. My own mother hadn't. Or rather, she'd breastfed my brother and then given up when it came to me and Honey. I didn't know why. I didn't even want to know that much, truth be told.

Levi curled up in a fluffy blue bed next to Luna's chair and settled in for a nap of his own.

I sat down on the couch across from them as Luna rocked her baby and studied me intently. "How are you?"

"Good." I had no idea how to do this.

"And the new mom and her sweet little one? And your brother?"

"They're all fine. Really, really good. The baby sleeps a lot." I didn't add that she'd needed many diaper changes the few times I'd seen her recently. Luna probably knew all too well how that worked, considering her son wasn't even a year old yet.

God, I was surrounded by babies, and I wasn't running for the hills. Clearly, something supernatural must be afoot.

"As she should. And how is Vanessa?"

"Good." I locked my fingers together in my lap and then yanked them apart. "Uh, how are you?"

"Good." She smiled serenely. "You seem stressed."

"Um, yeah, a little. Well, not stressed, just..."

"Out of your depth, Officer?" She crossed her legs at the ankle and tilted her head. "It's okay to admit. Your aura is navy, by the way."

Here we go.

I took a deep breath. "Aura?"

"For some people, they process emotions as colors, and I can see them physically. You're very true blue. Dependable, hardworking, honest. Sometimes too honest. You think this is a load of bunk."

"Not bunk, exactly," I hedged.

"The strongest magic is love. You believe in that."

256

"Yeah. Only recently though. I mean, I believed in it for other people, just not me. I knew my brother's feelings for Tabitha were—are—real. I just never met anyone who made me think it might happen for me."

"And now you have."

"Yeah."

"And you very much love your child already."

My head jerked up. "How—what—who told you?"

Milo shifted and let out the cutest baby yawn before he cuddled into his mother.

"No one. I imagine it's too early for the announcement but the lights inside her are very strong already." Luna smiled gently. "I'm not psychic, but judging from what I feel, you don't have to worry for her. She's going to be just fine. She's strong, your Vanessa."

My throat tightened and I cleared it, trying to make the lump go away. "She is. But she's afraid because she lost a baby before."

"Yes."

"You knew that too? How?"

"I didn't know it, but her fear is all around her." Luna rocked her baby back and forth, keeping her voice even. "The way to combat that is to make her feel your love. And your faith. You have to have enough for both of you until she gets with the program."

"Okay. Okay, I can do that." I worked on just breathing, in and out. Hearing the confirmation that Van was so scared—though I'd already sensed it—locked me up inside. I hated that I couldn't battle all her demons for her, even the unseen ones.

Especially the unseen ones.

"I just want them to be safe."

"And they will be, with a strong protector such as you to defend them." Luna stroked her baby's head, and his blond lashes fluttered in sleep. A pang of yearning hit me so strongly that I would've needed to sit if I wasn't already.

"I just don't understand where all of this came from. These feelings in me. For her, for the baby. Like they came out of nowhere. I never really thought about having a family before and now it's all I think about. Is it seeing my brother settle down? Or is it this town?"

"Love is the strongest magic," she said again. "But it's new for you, so you don't trust it yet. Speed has nothing to do with it. You think love has a timetable?"

"Yes. No." I frowned. "I don't know. I'm just not this impulsive normally. She is. She's a damn whirlwind. I want to marry her," I said suddenly, rubbing my hands over my thighs. "Like…now."

"Now now?"

"Yeah. Tonight, if she'd have me. But she won't. Is that why it seems so vitally necessary?"

"Maybe. I'm not some all-knowing being, Mav. Unfortunately." She laughed and gazed down at her sleeping child. "Sometimes I wake up in the middle of the night, confused and nervous like anyone else."

I hissed out a breath and started to stand. "Yeah, I'm sorry. This was another impulsive move."

"Doesn't mean it's wrong. Sometimes wisdom comes in flashes. Sit and tell me what else you need."

"She likes the sparkly rocks."

"Oh, jewelry?" Luna's lips curved. "Many women do."

"No, not that. Not yet. I need an engagement ring since Brady took our grandmother's for Tabitha, but I haven't seen the right one yet. I did do some looking yesterday at lunch."

"Does the deli now sell rings as a sideline?"

I managed to laugh. "No, I looked online. You know how this town is. If I got caught checking out baubles at the jewelry store—"

"Everyone would have you married in no time. Which you will be, so why does it matter?"

I narrowed my eyes on her. She looked like an ordinary woman. She was beautiful and blond, yes, and she practically radiated happiness and serenity, even more so since she'd become a mother. "You're not the least bit green. But man, you put Yoda to shame."

Her laughter flowed out, warm and rich. Milo didn't so much as blink. "Thanks, I think. So what sparkly rocks do you mean? Oh, crystals," she said after a moment. "You're cute."

"Funny, Van says that about me in the same tone. I don't think she actually means I'm cute. More like very male."

She laughed again. "Yet she's going to marry you, so I'd say she does. What kind of crystals are you looking for?"

"If I say big, will that get me the cute moniker again?"

"Well, big is always nice." Her eyes twinkled. "But not important when it comes to crystals. They're not like diamonds. Small ones can pack as much or more punch."

"I'm not going to make any inappropriate jokes."

"Feel free. I have a husband, you know. Caleb's best friend is Lucky. So, trust me, I've heard it all."

"Lucky is my nemesis."

She cocked a slim blond brow. "Is he now?"

"Yes. He's like a huge Nordic god. I'm not a jealous guy, but let's just say, he's lucky he's married."

"Very happily married to boot." She laughed. "No worries there, he only has eyes for Tish. She'd de-ball him otherwise."

"Yeah. I know." I shook my head. "This love stuff is nuts."

"Tell me about it. So you're looking for protection stones. And ones to enhance love. Am I right?"

I hadn't fully even realized what I was looking for yet, but as always, Luna just seemed to know. "Yeah. I just want her to have stones she can carry with her, kind of touchstones, I guess."

"Of course. That's very sweet—and she will appreciate them more than she would flowers or candles."

I shuddered. "Don't say the word candles. She's against them."

"Van is unique."

"Tell me about it."

"Give me your wallet," Luna said suddenly, and I handed it over without a blink.

She shifted the baby so she could cup her hand around the leather for a moment. Then she smiled. "Ah, yes, my instincts were on target with you. I just wanted to make sure. Even the casually witchy need to have a system of checks and balances. But your energy is very true blue." She returned my wallet. "Write these down."

I pulled out my phone and wrote down the crystals she mentioned. She described their colors and qualities and gave me an address where to find them.

"Today the veil is thinnest. Magic is everywhere tonight. Go now."

I didn't argue. She clearly knew more than I did in this realm.

"Happy Halloween, Maverick. Say hi to Vanessa for me."

"I will. You're...well, you're awesome."

Her smile glimmered. "You're pretty awesome yourself."

I thanked her profusely and we hugged before I went off to find the wizard. Err, witch shop in Luna Falls, owned by one Georgia Rose.

She seemed as if she'd known I was coming and directed me to the right areas to select the stones. But she wanted me to pick the ones that called to me.

When I selected a Lepidolite crystal in a heart shape, I swore Georgia's expression melted. "She's a lucky woman, your Vanessa."

"Pretty sure I'm the lucky one."

I picked out Bloodstone for a healthy birth and rose quartz for bonding with the baby and just for love. Which wasn't a problem for us.

Vanessa loved me. I knew it. She knew it. But it just felt like a battle of wills which of us would say it first. I didn't mind losing that particular fight, because it wasn't one at all.

"And your babies," Georgia added as she bagged my purchases.

"Baby, you mean?" I assumed Luna had told her.

Georgia smiled and slid the bag of crystals across the counter. "There's magic oil in the bag. Happy Halloween, Maverick."

I was in my truck, about to head back to town when I realized the magic oil was lube. I laughed right out loud just as a text came in.

Van: It's almost sunset. I'm waiting.

Mav: You said eight?

Van: Okay, I'll just occupy myself until you're free.

Why did that sound salacious?

I'd just been given lube at a witchy shop. No wonder the Cove was full of babies. Everyone within driving distance was horny as hell.

Mav: If that means you're having a party I want to join, leave the best part for me.

Van: I always do.

I pulled up at home and found the place was entirely dark. Even the porch light Van always left on for me while I was working was out. Then while I sat there idling in the driveway, lights popped on one by one on the path along Van's gravel drive, leading to her bus.

I squinted. Were those tiki torches? It was a nice night, with a sliver of moon and a fairly warm breeze for the end of October. I'd toyed with handing out candy to the trick or treaters for my first year in my new house, but Van had devoured all the Snickers I'd bought, and I'd rather do it next year when the house was officially ours.

At least I hoped. She'd probably still have me waiting. But maybe with our peanut nudging her along, she'd weaken.

In the meantime, I'd ply her with sex.

I grabbed the bag of crystals and lube. Not like we needed that, but maybe we could use it for other activities.

Happy Halloween to me.

I grinned, imagining Van's shouted *pervert* in my head if she could hear my thoughts right now. Though she was the one who'd originally put the thought in my head that night in Tab's bathroom.

After climbing out of the truck, I frowned, staring at my house. Had she fed Francie?

A text came through at that exact moment.

Van: Your little girl is fed and watered.

Mav: Which little girl are we talking about?

Van: You getting kinky already, Daddy?

My eyebrows rose. Okay then.

Mav: You don't have to prove over and again that you're my dream woman.

Van: Good. Remember that. Now get over to my parlor.

It probably showed the depths of my depravity, but I couldn't have rushed over to her bus any faster if I'd had wheels. And if I did have wheels, they would always aim right for her.

And maybe, just maybe, I was beginning to believe the same was true for her.

I climbed up the steps to the bus, flung open the door and was blinded by light.

So many lights that all came on at once. Candles. Tons and tons of them. They were the flameless kind so no fire hazard here, which I appreciated.

In the center of them sat Van on her new bed, wearing something incredibly skimpy and red that showed off a heck of a lot of her alabaster skin. A glowing jack-o-lantern sat between her spread legs.

I dropped my bag. "Jesus."

Okay, so I wasn't terribly articulate when I was harder than the steel of the bus.

"I had a speech," she began.

"Talk later." I was already undoing my pants, about to say a fervent prayer of thanks that I could come inside her, condom-free. "Also, you better be glad I can't get you pregnant twice, because damn, woman, you are so hot."

She dragged her red nail along the cleavage revealed by her lacy getup. "My breasts are getting bigger."

"I believe it. Parts of me are getting bigger too right now."

"I'm manifesting it. Tab said I should."

"She said you should manifest bigger breasts?"

"No, she said I should manifest what I want, and I want—" She went silent as I stripped off my boxers, her eyes going wide at my current state. "Oh, come to mama, you needy boy."

I had to laugh as I knelt on the bed. "You're really selling this Daddy stuff, huh?"

She didn't laugh. "Will you marry me?" she blurted.

Good thing I was kneeling, because I would've fallen over. "What did you say?"

"I asked you to marry me, dammit. It's not a hard question. Yes—or yes." She lifted her stubborn chin. "You don't have an option to say no."

I didn't breathe. Or blink.

My gaze locked on her crystal blue eyes. She was frighteningly beautiful and smart and talented—and she was all mine.

All of these words spun in my head. But my mouth apparently had none of them available to say.

She'd completely sucked away my powers of speech.

Then the candlelight flickered and for a terrifying second, I thought I glimpsed a sheen of wetness in her eyes. The one and only thing I could never ever stand.

"I love you. So much. Do you get that?" I gripped her upper arms, shaking her harder than I intended. "Do you get that, Vanessa?"

Her lower lip dropped open. "Yes?"

"I was going to propose to you. Dammit. I hadn't found a ring yet. But I have the box. Well, sort of." My laughter verged on maniacal. This woman had pushed me to the edge of insanity, and I'd never been gladder for the trip. "Yes, I'll fucking marry you. Tonight. Let's go."

"Really? Are you serious?" She clambered up onto her knees to undo my buttons.

Evidently, I'd forgotten to undress my top half in my eagerness to remove my pants and boxers. Even now, my cock was fairly determined to fuck her right through her lingerie, since she kept writhing against me.

"Do I not seem serious to you?" I gripped her small hand and wrapped it around my length.

"That does make a pretty convincing case. I don't actually have a ring though. I thought I'd have time."

"We don't need rings."

"Speak for yourself, dude. I may live in a bus, but I want a ring."

"I don't mean forever, I mean right now. And you don't live in a bus anymore. You're going to be my wife. You're going to live with me in our house. But we can keep this bus." I kissed her hard, her lips curving against mine.

She eased back a fraction of an inch, kissing me between words. "Oh, sure, now he wants to keep my traveling porn bus."

I pulled back to breathe. "Of course I do. Is it up to date mechanically?"

"I'll pretend you didn't ask that question," she said with an indignant sniff before attacking my mouth again.

Admittedly, I didn't put up much of a fight.

"We're only, what, 3000 miles give or take from Vegas? It worked for Oliver and Sage."

She reared back to snap her fingers. "I knew someone had done it. Kinleigh was encouraging me to elope today."

"You told Kinleigh?"

"Yeah, I was looking at wedding dresses. Though not white, for obvious reasons. I mean, it worked for Tab, but I'm not a white gown girl—" She yelped as I picked her up in my arms, nearly knocking her head into the ceiling of the bus as I struggled to my feet.

"You have gained weight, I can tell," I teased, grunting when she yanked on my hair.

"Put me down. Where are you going?"

"To get my dog. We're getting married."

"You don't have pants on!" she screeched before she looked down at her lingerie. "I do look pretty hot in this. Not sure it fits the dress code, even for an Elvis chapel. Maybe I can whip up a quick train for the back though." She scrunched up her nose. "It's just butt floss."

I didn't even have an answer for that one, so I just kissed her. "Guess the lube really was magic."

"I do not even know what you're talking about, and I don't have time to find out right now. Though I gotta say I'm intrigued." She gazed down at me, her hold on my hair gentling. "Put me down, Mav."

Noting her tone change, I did as she asked. And she immediately fell to her knees, making my heart lurch.

"Will you marry me?" she asked in the softest, sweetest voice I could've ever imagined.

I cupped her cheek before sliding my fingers down to stroke her defiant chin. I loved that chin. I loved every part of her, even the stubborn ones.

Especially the stubborn ones.

"Yes. I'd marry you one hundred times, and then I'd do it once more."

This time, the tears that formed in her eyes slipped free. "I love you. More than I've ever imagined I could love anyone." Then she smiled. "Well, you're tied with our baby and our dog."

I dropped to my knees in front of her. "So what are we waiting for? Let's get married, baby."

EPILOGUE

VANESSA

WE DIDN'T GO TO VEGAS.

We did, however, sneak off at dawn to go to the courthouse. Step one—collecting my sister and Mav's brother to stand as witnesses, along with a very sleepy Presley, who somehow didn't wail her head off while she waited for us to get the deed done. Step two—beg the judge and courthouse manager to come in early and let us do this crazy thing.

Mav officially owed quite a few favors. And he would be catching hell from his family, but we were being spontaneous, dammit. And okay, there might be one bonus favor from the Chief, but we'd worry about all that later.

Tabitha provided my something blue and my something borrowed, my nod to tradition, though I got married in a perfectly respectable off-the-shoulder hot pink dress.

I also carried with me the crystals Mav had gifted me after we'd had monkey sex on the bus. There may have been some post sex blubbering, but I was pregnant and emotional and was trying to give myself some grace.

Oh, and underneath my respectable dress, I wore a thong. That was just for Mav's benefit since they annoyed the crap out of me.

Butt floss would never be my preference. Granny panties were actually quite comfortable, thank you very much.

After our quick ceremony with traditional vows and not a tear between us, thank heavens—actually, we both laughed so much during the ceremony that I think the judge was tempted to ask if we were sober—we took our witnesses home.

We realized that a larger—gasp, a minivan—would need to be in our future with the way the McNeills were expanding. On the way, I told them about my graphic novel deal. Secrets were bad, and I was determined to start this new phase of my life with that in mind.

At least ones like this. As far as the Honey situation, I still wasn't sure what to do there. We couldn't get a hold of her to include her in the wedding. She was probably still mad at me for earlier, but that was a problem for another day that wasn't today.

Holy crow, I was now officially a married lady. Talk about respectable.

Though a *motherfucker* had slipped out at the courthouse. Hey, change didn't happen overnight.

Once we'd dropped off a shellshocked Tab, a weary Brady, and an unconscious Presley, Mav and I had monkey sex one more time in the bus before dragging ourselves into our actual bed in our actual house.

Where we did more of the same and even managed to eat in between sleeping off and on during our official wedding day. And maybe we ignored our phones in favor of a little us time before we had to return to the land of responsibilities.

I woke the next morning and smiled into my pillow, only to see that I was now alone in bed. Where the hell was my husband? Didn't he know that he was supposed to skip work to keep me sexually satisfied?

"Honeymoon," I muttered. "Where's my honeymoon?"

"You didn't say anything about a honeymoon."

I opened my eyes and threw up a hand to block the death rays streaming in the window. "Turn out the light!"

"It's the sun, beautiful. Unfortunately, I don't have that kind of power." Mav strolled across the room from the bathroom in just a

COP DADDY NEXT DOOR

towel and bent down to give me a properly thorough good morning with his lips. "My wife is gorgeous."

I arched up to meet his mouth, letting the covers dip beneath my bare breasts. "Hmm, I may forgive you."

"What did I do now?"

"Want a list?" His playful growl made me giggle. "I woke up alone. That isn't allowed. You have to spend the day in bed with me."

"Taskmaster." He tweaked my nipple, and I let out a sound that verged on a purr even to my own ears. "I didn't exactly give notice that I needed vacation time."

"Yeah, well, too bad. They can get by without you for one day. Besides—" Light poured into my eyes and I screamed, at least in my own head. "What the hell?"

"First time you didn't yell motherfucker. Look how motherly you're becoming already." He grinned at me as I opened my eyes to scowl at him. At least I hadn't been permanently blinded.

Then my gaze caught on the carved lamp beside me, its deep green shade done in a woodland pattern with trees and creatures and…

"Is that a penguin?" I asked, running my fingertip over the small figure.

"It is. I know it's a little weird but the lamp matches something else I'm making. I just started plans for it yesterday, so that will have to wait a bit for the reveal." His Adam's apple bobbed as he drew open a small compartment at the bottom of the artfully carved wood. "This is for you too."

A gleaming silver and turquoise hummingbird ring sat in the drawer, nestled on an emerald bed of fabric.

"Oh my God."

He laughed as he lifted it and gestured for me to hold out my hand. "I know it's not rubies or diamonds, but I was lucky to find it this morning."

The ring slid on my finger like butter. I stared at it wordlessly, so moved I couldn't speak. He always remembered the details.

"I'm having another one made, but I figured this was a good placeholder—"

I threw myself into his arms, nearly pitching both of us off the bed onto the floor. Frantic barking sounded from the opposite side of the bedroom door but Mav ignored it for a moment while I clung to him and tried not to cry.

For the fiftieth time since yesterday, but who was counting?

"You hate it. You hate the lamp. You hate green. Penguins and birds in general make you mad. As a Cove loyalist, you are strictly a duck enthusiast and will not use objects bearing other fowl." He cupped my chin. "Talk to me, wife."

I giggled through my sniffles. "You make me so happy. What did I ever do to deserve you, Maverick McNeill?"

"You showed up on my dock and knocked me out with your see-through top and your smart mouth." He kissed the top of my head. "Did I tell you I love you, Vanessa McNeill?"

"No. Not even one time. Please say it again until it sticks."

He tipped up my chin and stared right into my eyes. "I love you. I love our baby. I love our life, as new as it is." He tossed an annoyed glance over his shoulder as Francie howled. "I even love that hairy pain-in-the-rump in the hallway."

"And we love you all too." I reached over the grab my lamp, pulling it into bed with me. "We totally messed up tradition by getting married without rings."

His eyebrow lifted as I cuddled the lamp against me like a child. "You know that's not a stuffed animal, right?"

"Yeah, I just want to stroke it for a while." I traced my fingers over the intricate carving. "This is going to go into my craft room."

"Sure, I was thinking—wait, your craft room?"

"Yeah, here. You don't expect a pregnant lady to squat on a bus to draw and crochet, do you?" I cocked my head. "Besides, we can always add on here as we need to. I may have a little money."

"Oh, yes, you just may. Fine, fine, c'mon in and join the family." He rose, deliciously naked, to pad over to the door to let in Francie.

She scampered into the room, her pink bow tilting, and started barking frantically for Mav to lift her up onto the bed. She could climb if need be, but she liked taking advantage of her daddy.

For that matter, so did I.

She ran up to jump on top of me as she did most mornings, but Mav scolded her gently to be careful of my belly.

And miracle of all miracle, there were no more waterworks. At least for now.

Being blissfully happy was exhausting, but I'd deal with it somehow.

Mav shook his head as Francie settled against me and adoringly licked my face. "I see where I rank around here."

"I'll lick you if you want."

"Oh, I want." He stroked my hair. "By the way, we're keeping that bus."

"Is that so?"

"It's so. We'll need somewhere to escape from the kid to make another one."

At my sharp glance, he smiled innocently and crowded in beside me against the pillows, the lamp between us on one side and Francie already asleep on her back on my other side. "I mean, to have time for romance."

"Watch it, pal. One is enough for now."

He kissed my forehead. "We'll see."

We appreciate our readers so much!
If you loved the book please let your friends know. If you're extra awesome, we'd love a review on your favorite book site.

Next up is Christian & Honey's story!
My first mistake was taking a taste of her honey. Now I'm in deeper than I ever expected—lock, stock, and baby.
Coming Spring 2023!

If you missed Luna's story and you're curious

271

WRONG BED BABY
Is now available in ebook, print, and audio!

Or, how about more small town romance?
Try our KENSINGTON SQUARE or HAPPY ACRES series!

For character charts, reading order list across all of our series—including spoiler free versions—please visit our website at tarynquinn.com.

Turn the Page for a sneak peek of CEO DADDY.
Our standalone Crescent Cove book!

CEO DADDY

I might be single and alone on New Year's Eve. But I'm not woe is me. No, ma'am. I'm looking at this moment as an opportunity to cherish my solitude.

WITH A SIGH, I SET DOWN MY PEN AND PICKED UP MY WATER GLASS. I should be drinking alcohol at least. Maybe I still would. I wasn't much of a wine fan, but I could use tonight to broaden my horizons. A cocktail sounded nice. Very adult.

A drink I could enjoy happily on my own.

Okay, cut the crap. In my diary, I should be honest. The diary I was writing in while I ate my dinner of consommé—fancy soup essentially —and garlic breadsticks, because who was I going to kiss at midnight? No one.

Joyfully solo, that was me.

In reality, I was fresh off another broken Tinder date. Broken by *me*, no less. I could never quite close the deal. Probably because a date with me held more weight than the usual hookup.

I'd been adult about that too. Virginity was a burden, so I'd just rid myself of it quickly and quietly. No fuss. Until the time came to actually meet Joe Blow in the flesh—yes, that was his name on the site —and I'd balked. I'd made up an excuse about getting together with an ex and that had been that.

As if I had any exes. Just a few high school boyfriends who hadn't amounted to much.

Since then, I'd stuck close to home, the dutiful older sister who raised her younger siblings after our parents had died in a plane crash. Now that the twins, Emma and Rachel, had turned nineteen and gone off to college, that left me at loose ends.

Alone for real.

"Can I get you anything else? Maybe you'd like a look-see at the dessert menu? The lemon bars are my favorite. They're my mama's recipe."

I blinked up at the grinning blond waitress. At least I thought she was a waitress, though she had a more commanding air about her despite her small town friendliness. "Your mama works here too?"

"Not anymore. She used to own the joint. Then she retired and sold it out from under me with no warning, but I got it back because of my lovable pain-in-the-ass baby daddy. Well, husband too. So, lemon bars?"

I rubbed my temple. Whoa, information overload. "You have a husband? You look…youthful."

Luckily, I'd managed not to say she looked twelve, which was a misstatement in any case. She looked at least sixteen. But not old enough to be married, at least in New York.

She laughed and sat down opposite me at the table. "Sure do."

"And a baby."

"Yeah, she's not even a year old yet. Star's the light of my life. Want to see?" She was already tugging a folding wallet of pictures—many, many pictures—out of her apron pocket.

"Um, sure?"

She showed me an array of photos of a chubby baby with bright green eyes and a drooly smile.

"She's beautiful. Her hair is so dark."

"Like Oliver's. Unless it changes. I hope it doesn't. It's my ace in the hole I wasn't impregnated by the milkman."

Unsure if she was serious, I smiled faintly. "I think I'll try those lemon bars, please."

She nodded enthusiastically and bustled off to the kitchen. She seemed sweet.

Everyone in Crescent Cove was sweet. It was a picturesque village, nestled against the long curve of Crescent Lake. At the holidays, the place really shone.

The big formal banquet room I was seated in was jammed with guests. Most were families, along with a good amount of couples and solo businessmen passing through the area due to the proximity to Syracuse. I lived in between Crescent Cove and Syracuse, in a town so tiny you could miss it if you shut your eyes.

Which you shouldn't do while driving, especially in the fall and winter. We were in deer and wild turkey country.

Spending New Year's Eve in Crescent Cove was a luxury. I didn't have the funds to spare on such things, but I'd asked for money for Christmas from my sisters and my bestie just so I could splurge.

Now I was wondering if it was a huge mistake.

I'd thought I would feel less on my own in a crowd.

Wrong.

I'd had to wait a half hour for this table. There was holiday music playing, and cheerful lights twinkling, and every surface seemed to be decked out with candles and poinsettias and big satin red ribbons. People were laughing and enjoying time with their loved ones.

And I was scribbling lies in my diary about how I didn't mind that my sisters had chosen to return to campus early rather than hang out with their big sister. That I wasn't at all jealous my bestie had a date for New Year's with a guy she worked with.

Worst of all? The prospect of homemade lemon bars excited me more than the gorgeous fireplace suite I'd reserved to spend the evening—you guessed it—alone.

"Here you go. I gave you an extra one. On holidays, calories don't count." The blond proprietress smiled and set the plate in front of me. "Can I get you anything else?"

"Yes, actually, you can. I'd like some champagne, please."

"Oh, sure." She nodded as if it wasn't weird at all I was ordering champagne with lemon bars after drinking water since I'd sat down. "Flute or bottle for the table?"

Did she know something I didn't? Was it usual for women dining alone to drink a whole bottle of bubbly? Maybe on New Year's Eve, anything went.

"Bottle for the table, please." The deep voice barely registered. In fact, I didn't even look to see the owner. He couldn't be speaking for my table. I definitely didn't know anyone who sounded like *that*.

Hello, man, not a boy.

The blond shifted away from me and I dazedly followed her gaze to where one of the businessmen I'd noticed earlier stood beside the chair opposite me. I hadn't seen his face, just the tidy queue of dark hair on his neck as he was seated. A solo diner, just like me.

Unlike me, he hadn't been writing in a journal with flowers on the tattered cover. No, he'd been flipping through a thick sheaf of paperwork, and he'd barely looked up long enough to order.

I hadn't seen his face, but he'd seen mine. Or else he was in the habit of joining strangers once the alcohol was served. Judging by his well-cut pinstriped dark suit and fancy Italian leather briefcase, he wasn't hurting for money. I preferred looking at those things rather than his features. If his looks matched up with his voice—

Well, let's just say I wasn't in any shape to handle that level of disappointment once he rethought his decision. Because, seriously? Why did he want to sit with *me*?

"Oh." The blond smiled. "Are you joining her?" She glanced at me. "Dinner date?"

Normally, the blond's presumptuousness might have irritated me, but it felt as if she was on my side. Like she was making sure I wanted this guy to sit at my table. I must be giving off vibes that I did *not* know this dude. No matter how handsome he was and how important he seemed, a woman had to be careful.

"Two people eating alone on New Year's Eve should eat together." His deep voice caused a tingle low in my belly. "Sage, you know I'm harmless." His smile was anything but.

The blond—Sage—raised an eyebrow. "So said Ted Bundy." She smiled sweetly and shifted to glance at me. "Your call."

He switched his briefcase to the other hand, allowing me to see the bundle of winter tulips he also held, wrapped with a burlap bow and with pine greenery overflowing the colorful tissue paper. Tulips were a weakness of mine, and I'd never seen a winter bouquet of them before.

As if he'd noticed me staring at them, he held them out as additional incentive. "For you."

I borrowed a page from Sage's book and lifted an eyebrow, saying nothing. But I accepted the flowers. I was no dummy, and the tulips were gorgeous. I could already imagine them in the center of my table at home, cheering me up as I experimented in the kitchen. The pale reds, pinks, and yellows were perfect.

"He can sit."

Sage nodded. "Would you like anything else besides the bottle of champagne?"

"A cup of coffee for me, please." His smile was easy and self-assured, and he never looked away from me as he took the seat opposite me at the table.

Sage left us alone with a waggle of her brows.

"Friend of yours?" I set the bouquet of tulips in my lap and drew a nail through the powdered sugar beneath the lemon bars on my plate. I rued not redoing my nail polish for tonight. The silver was chipped at the edges. Surely, a man like him would notice.

"Oh, Sage? No, not exactly, although we've met a few times. I make it a point to eat here when I'm in town. Something I'll be doing a lot more soon."

He paused as Sage brought over the bottle of champagne and two glasses. She popped the cork and poured for us both, then left us alone again. A moment later, she brought his coffee, which he largely ignored.

I picked up my glass, clinked with my new dinner guest, and sipped. The bubbly went straight to my head as it always did, so I set the glass down.

He was still watching me, his lips curved ever so slightly. He hadn't taken a drink yet.

"I'm Asher," he said as the silence extended uncomfortably. Somehow our personal silence was much more noticeable because of all the excited chatter around us.

"Hannah."

"Nice to meet you. What brings you here tonight of all nights?"

"I didn't want to sit alone at home." *Nice one, Hannah. Can you sound any more pathetic?* "It's a night for parties and fun." I saluted him with my champagne and drank.

Heat flowed out from my belly through my limbs. I couldn't decide if I liked the sensation or not. Or maybe the heat was from Asher's gaze. His eyes weren't as dark as I'd originally believed. With the candle flickering between us, I'd guess now they were a warm hazel, perhaps varying depending on his clothing.

Apparently, his black pinstriped suit didn't offer any appreciable change to them. But whoa nelly, that suit was working wonders on me.

Maybe three-piece suits really were the equivalent to lingerie for a woman. His was definitely revving my motor.

Revving everything.

"So, do you have plans after this? A party perhaps, or some other kind of fun?" He ran his fingertip along the rim of his glass.

"How old are you?" I blurted.

His dark brows drew together. "Thirty-two in March."

"Hmm."

"Is that a good *hmm* or a bad *hmm*?"

"I'm twenty-three. I've never..." I took a deep breath. *Try not to embarrass yourself again.* "Well, this is just sharing some lemon bars and champagne, right?"

"That's up to you. Why don't we start with some conversation and go from there?" His slow smile only served to stir me up even more.

Relax in this gorgeous, commanding man's presence? Not likely.

"Sure. Let's begin with why you came over to my table." I picked up my dessert fork and cut off the corner of one of my lemon bars, belatedly remembering he didn't have one. Sage hadn't brought over another plate.

By accident or design? Even without knowing her well, I could easily see her as the matchmaking type.

"Sorry, it's rude of me to eat when you don't have anything. Here." I set down the fork and lifted the plate toward him, swallowing deeply as he pushed aside the vase and the flickering candle to make room for the plate between us.

"We can share." His fingers brushed mine as he broke off a corner and lifted it to his mouth.

His perfect mouth. His lips were neither too full or too sparse. Just right.

As everything he possessed seemed to be. And I hadn't even gotten a look at him beneath the waist.

Probably good. I didn't need to be any more intimidated, especially by pinstriped thirty-two-year-old cocks. I was already freaked out enough.

Hello, out of my league.

"No fork?" I asked a little breathlessly. He seemed the fork-and-knife-at-all-times type to me.

"Nah. Fingers are better. See?" He broke off another piece and lifted it across the table to me, not dropping so much as a crumb. "Lean forward."

I obliged him and his fingertips brushed my lips as he fed me the treat. His voice was entrancing. I was afraid to imagine all the things he could make me do with just one of those husky commands.

His eyes held me in his thrall so completely that I barely noticed the burst of lemon as I swallowed. The bars were a delicious mix of sweet and tart, but I probably wouldn't have noticed if the dessert had been undercooked and bland.

"Good?"

I nodded and he repeated the move several more times. He wasn't even eating himself, just feeding me. He had long, elegant fingers with a surprising bit of ink swirling down his hands. The bold Roman numerals and heavy, old typeface of a latin phrase were mixed with a bit of artistry.

So incongruous to the buttoned-up businessman. It somehow made him even hotter.

Once, out of the corner of my eye, I noticed Sage start to approach with the bill in hand. She took in what was occurring at our shadowy table, widened her eyes, and sped off in the opposite direction.

I would've laughed had I not been so turned on that I could barely think.

What was happening here? We weren't even talking. Was this what occurred when under the influence of a lonely holiday meant for couples and some expensive champagne? I'd had a couple more sips in between rounds of Asher feeding me. Big, bolstering sips. The kind that made a normally shy, awkward woman feel bold.

"No ring," I said casually—or so I hoped. I'd had plenty of time to see his hand as it came closer to my mouth. "You're single?"

"Very. The kind of single that means I'm alone on New Year's Eve, just as you are." He lifted his thumb to his lips and licked off a stray crumb from the piece he'd just fed me. The movement was far more sensual than it had any right to be. "You are alone tonight, aren't you, Hannah?"

Something about the question and his use of my name made my throat tighten to the point that if I hadn't gulped more champagne, I might've choked. This time, I didn't mind the floaty feeling that overtook my body, or the resulting wave of warmth.

"I'm alone far too much these days. But right now? No. Neither of us is alone."

He nodded, lowering his head for an instant while his jaw locked. He finally took a few sips of coffee before he met my gaze once again. "I have a room upstairs. Just for tonight."

Questions flitted through my mind.

Who are you, Asher?

Why did you pick me to talk to?

Was it just that I looked lonely, so I must be an easy target for sexual advances?

In the end, I didn't really care. We were both alone, and no one was waiting for me at home. What did it matter if I chose this handsome man to spend the evening with? No one would be hurt. And I would finally be able to cross one thing off my bucket list.

Sex with a gorgeous man, check.

Sex, period.

But that didn't mean I'd make it easy on him.

"Who were the flowers for?" I stroked the downy soft petals of the pink tulip on top of the bouquet in my lap.

"My grandmother." He smiled wryly. "She thinks I need to get out more, so she'll approve that I gave them to the most beautiful woman I've seen since..." He trailed off, looking uncharacteristically unsure. Even with only knowing him a very short while, I was quite certain Asher rarely faltered. "Ever."

"I believe you don't get out much after that statement." I rested my cheek on my fist. "My hair isn't really blond, by the way. I put in a rinse today. Truth in advertising and all that."

"It doesn't look blond. Not exactly. More like the color of honey." His voice deepened. "Rich and luxurious."

"Glorious Tones hair color thanks you for your appreciation of their product." I toyed with the stem of my now nearly empty champagne glass. "When is the last time you approached a woman with that line about having a room upstairs?"

"Never. I've never had a room upstairs here before." His lips twitched. "And to be honest, I don't have one now. I wasn't planning on staying until I saw you. Writing so furiously in that." He nodded to my abandoned journal. "What were you writing?"

"Where were you going after this?" I countered.

"To my grandmother's. She was going to be who I counted down to midnight with." He finally reached for his champagne and took a single sip. Easing back in his chair, he licked his lips, slowly and surely. "I'd much rather kiss you once the ball drops."

"Which balls are we referring to?"

I didn't know if he'd find me funny or crude. It was usually half and half, depending on my company. But his laughter was quick and appreciative. "You're different than I expected."

"Oh, really? What did you expect? A meek little mouse who'd trot after you and hop right into bed?" Okay, this had to be the champagne talking, because this was next level, even for me.

"No. I wasn't even thinking about bed when I came over here. I just wanted to hear your voice. To see if you ever smiled. You still haven't, you know. Not at me."

"Smiles are earned. Keep trying. You might get there."

"Luckily, I don't give up easily. Why are you alone tonight? No family?"

"No." The lie came easily, and sometimes seemed far too true when my sisters were busy with school and out of touch. My family was a fraction of what it had once been. "Let's just say I live an isolated existence."

It wasn't that far from reality. I was alone too often.

I couldn't stand another moment of it.

"No lover." The word dripped off his tongue, laced with a sensuality that was far beyond my realm of experience.

"No." I tilted my head. "So, what's your story?"

His lips lifted on one side. "I'm a man who works far too much and spends New Year's Eve with his grandmother. What more do you need to know?"

Indeed.

I nodded at the bottle of champagne. "Think we can get that to go?"

NOW AVAILABLE in all formats!

Have My Baby

Claim My Baby

Who's The Daddy

Pit Stop: Baby

Baby Daddy Wanted

Rockstar Baby

Daddy in Disguise

My Ex's Baby

Daddy Undercover

Wrong Bed Baby

Lucky Baby

Daddy on Duty

Cop Daddy Next Door

Protector Daddy

CRESCENT COVE STANDALONES & SHORTS

CEO Daddy

Fireman Daddy

Mistletoe Baby

MORE BY TARYN QUINN

OTHER SERIES

Happy Acres

Kensington Square

Afternoon Delight

Deuces Wild

Wilder Rock

Walk on the wilder side with these stories

After Dark

HOLIDAY BOOKS

Unwrapped

Holiday Sparks

Filthy Scrooge

Bad Kitty

Saving Kylie

ABOUT TARYN QUINN

USA Today bestselling author, *Taryn Quinn*, is the sexy and funny alter ego of bestselling authors Taryn Elliott & Cari Quinn. We've been writing together for years, but we have decided to pull the trigger on a combo name just for fun.

And so…Taryn Quinn was born!

Do you like ultra sexy small town romance full of shenanigans? Quirky office romances full of steam? Okay, look…we pretty much just love writing steamy stories. If you're all about that, we're your girls!

For more information about us…
tarynquinn.com
tq@tarynquinn.com

QUINN AND ELLIOTT

We also write more serious, longer, and sexier books as Cari Quinn & Taryn Elliott. Our topics include mostly rockstars, but mobsters, MMA, and a little suspense gets tossed in there too.

Rockers' Series Reading Order

Lost in Oblivion

Winchester Falls

Found in Oblivion

Hammered

Rock Revenge

Brooklyn Dawn

OTHER SERIES

Tapped Out

Love Required

Boys of Fall

If you'd like more information about us please visit

www.quinnandelliott.com

www.ingramcontent.com/pod-product-compliance
Lightning Source LLC
Chambersburg PA
CBHW061945170626
46813CB00006B/2540